IF I
PROMISE
YOU
WINGS

✧ ✧ ✧

ALSO BY A. K. SMALL

Bright Burning Stars

IF I
PROMISE
YOU
WINGS

A. K. SMALL

ALGONQUIN 2024

Algonquin Young Readers
Workman Publishing
Hachette Book Group, Inc.
1290 Avenue of the Americas
New York, NY 10104
workman.com

Algonquin Young Readers is an imprint of Workman Publishing,
a division of Hachette Book Group, Inc.
The Algonquin Young Readers name and logo
are registered trademarks of Hachette Book Group, Inc.

Design by Kerri Resnick

Poem from *Love Her Wild* by Atticus (published in 2017 by Atria Books)
is used with permission.

The publisher is not responsible for websites (or their content)
that are not owned by the publisher.

Workman books may be purchased in bulk for business, educational,
or promotional use. For information, please contact your local bookseller or
the Hachette Book Group Special Markets Department
at special.markets@hbgusa.com.

Library of Congress Cataloging-in-Publication Data is available.

ISBN 978-1-6437-5028-6

First Edition January 2024

Printed in the United States of America on responsibly sourced paper.

10 9 8 7 6 5 4 3 2 1

For A because of C.

For K because of them, and for K just because.

For E because of your tattoo.

And for anyone who has grieved a deep friendship.

*It's not the fear of losing them
that scares us,
it's that we have given them
so many of our pieces
that we fear losing
ourselves
when they are gone.*

—Atticus

IF I
PROMISE
YOU
WINGS

SUMMER

CHAPTER 1

Mille et Une Plume sits on rue D'Orchampt, a back street of Montmartre. The boutique has a bay window, and behind the glass hang two pairs of wings. With the sun shining bright, it's a sight to behold, almost as if angels were speaking to each other. One set shimmers metallic while the other is black with streaks of electric blues.

Today, I not only stare at the wings, but summon whatever courage I have and knock on the door. Three short raps. As I fret on the sidewalk, I hear Jeanne say, *Louder, Alix.* Her absence crushes me. I knock again and kick the cobblestones with the tips of my Converse. Jeanne hovers and to stop the sharp grief from rising in my chest, I repeat a line from our favorite poem, *Hope is the thing with feathers.* The door swings open. A tall, brown-skinned woman with an explosion of curls and the darkest eyes I have ever seen appears wearing cigarette pants and studded pumps, her shoulders wrapped in a ruby-red cape. The crimson material, silk or satin, catches the summer light, and like the wings in her bay window, she sparkles, too.

"Que voulez-vous?" she says.

My face warms, and my voice turns to powder because this woman is Mademoiselle Salomé, the most famous plumassière in Paris. Who else but a premier feather artist would shine this way? I stare at the ground, and in my jeans and tattered T-shirt, sweaty from walking here at the height of day, I feel as small as a gravel pea standing before her.

"I'm closed," Mademoiselle Salomé informs me.

I nod, something I'm exceptionally good at, and discern annoyance, perhaps even unease, in the way she keeps her cape shut tight, but then I hear Jeanne say, *If you don't rise to the occasion, Alix, I'll order the prince of darkness to haunt you forever*, and missing my best friend more than watching our bloodred sunsets over the Seine, I blurt, "I've come to be your apprentice."

Mademoiselle Salomé laughs.

I point to the black wings with streaks of blues and try to tell her I once counted 980 feathers on each wing, and that I have stood several times outside her boutique too shy to knock, that I am not joking about being her apprentice, but my courage slips away. After Mademoiselle Salomé catches her breath, she looks at me again, this time slowly. She appraises my slender build, my short haircut with choppy bangs, the freckles on my nose, and down to the smear of dirt on my Converse.

She says, "What do you know about Mille et Une Plume?"

Certain she will shut the door in my face, I say, "Rumor has it a raven works here. And you opened the boutique twenty-one years ago on a hot day like this one."

The feather artist studies me again. "How would you know? You weren't born then."

I nearly tell her my mother attended her grand opening, then gave me the newspaper clipping with pictures of it when I turned ten—the last memory I have of my mother giving me anything—but that would mean a conversation about something I'm not up for having.

So instead, pointing to the wings again, I say, "They must be hard to make."

"Teens." Mademoiselle Salomé sighs, but then, peering at the inside of my forearm, she catches sight of my starling feather tattoo and says, "What's this?"

"Oh," I say, certain I'm blushing. "Just a reminder of—" I pause. "Things."

"Entres," the feather artist says, urging me through a parlor, past a bright room full of extravagant costumes and brilliant plumes, to an area with sewing machines and man-nequin busts. "You do realize it's Sunday?"

"Yes," I reply, though I haven't cared much about the dates since the accident.

I wouldn't even know it was July if it wasn't for the heat and all the litter on the streets: the red, white, and blue tinsel; piles of empty bottles; and party hats left over from last night's Bastille Day celebrations.

"What's your name? And how old *are* you?"

"Alix Leclaire."

I tell her I'm seventeen, that my birthday just passed, and that I received my baccalauréat with honors. Mademoiselle Salomé leads us through a door to a study that opens onto a courtyard where the most majestic oak bends, its thick and gnarled trunk hundreds of years old, its leaves dark green and full of oxygen.

Looking at the oak, I almost feel like I can breathe better and say, "I also collect and draw feathers. I——"

But my chest constricts. I see a flurry of sketches sur-rounding my bed, Jeanne admiring them while croaking a song by Charlotte Gainsbourg, then Jeanne sitting shot-gun in her boyfriend du jour's beat-up Renault hours before she died, platform boots propped up on the dashboard, wisteria-colored hair falling on her shoulders, and I can't explain the most important part, that I swore to Jeanne I'd become Mademoiselle Salomé's apprentice the way Jeanne swore to me she would become a rock star.

"Sit," the feather artist says, pointing me to a leather chaise. "You look pale."

I focus on the room, the high ceilings, giant windows, and posters of the Moulin Rouge. Everywhere, ivory bins overflow with feathers in every color. I've never seen so many. On one wall, there is a sleek floor-to-ceiling cabinet with an abundance of drawers. Everything is orderly, clean, yet cozy. I recite more of the poem in my head, *And sweetest in the gale is heard; and sore must be the storm.*

"Look, a lot of people collect feathers," Mademoiselle Salomé says. "But why work with them all day?"

It's not only feathers but birds I'm drawn to, I don't say. How they take flight and how I wish I were one so I could lift off into the sky. Sometimes at night, I dream of little nubs piercing through my skin, of the beginning of wings sprouting from my body. I even feel the pain. But, Jesus, all that sounds wild I know, so I say, "I don't see myself working anywhere else. I've always been around artists, creatives."

"You mean your family?"

"I guess."

I study the gnarled oak. I think of forests where tree roots entangle with other neighboring roots for strength and wonder how this majestic tree has weathered these years alone.

Mademoiselle Salomé walks to one of the ivory bins and lovingly rustles the plumes. "Tell me more about that feather on your arm."

Again, I feel Jeanne's presence, how everything we dreamed of was entwined. I say, "I chose the starling for intuitiveness. A quality I hope to carry forever."

Mademoiselle Salomé scrutinizes me with her dark eyes. "Go ahead. Mingle. Let's see if my feathers introduce themselves to you. They can be haughty sometimes."

I get up, pausing at a bin filled with burnt orange plumes. I take the fattest one, run my fingers along the tendrils, smell it. The scent is musky, alive, and gives me such a jolt, I twirl, then throw Mademoiselle Salomé's feather into the air and catch it as it falls gently back toward me. I hear Jeanne singing, Papa and his saxophone, his trills and offbeat melodies, the way even yesterday he clutched his instrument as if the brass and buttons were akin to a lover, a life raft, or both, and under Mademoiselle Salomé's roof, clutching the rust-colored plume, I confirm the art of feathers is like music. Something one is called to do.

"C'est une plume de coq flammé, a burning pheasant feather," Mademoiselle Salomé says as if I hadn't just spun around like a child in front of her. "We find them in Hawaii in dense shrubs. At Mille et Une Plume, we believe in molted feathers. I've traveled the world to meet sources who acquire these natural treasures. Where I come from, birds are as precious as their plumage."

Mademoiselle Salomé shows me the quill, says the down-like pieces known as fluff are also called the after feather, and that in this very room there are hundreds of different plumes from countless types of birds in color ranging from brun d'os (bone brown) to bleu coquille (eggshell blue) to fanfare (pearl gray). She also tells me that the apprenticeship, a role that might lead to following in her footsteps, *is* in fact newly open, and everyone striving for it will be incredibly busy this fall—but that, come to think of it, she does have a petite main position available. Nothing glamorous. The internship pays minimum wage and the person's job will be to mainly run errands, clean the boutique, make coffee, take out the trash, answer phones when needed while everyone else will be in the midst of sketching, designing, selling, sewing, and embroidering costumes, décor, and garments made of plumes. But, if I could show my worth somehow, growth is always possible when there is passion.

Perhaps because I swear the plumes are glowing in their bins and maybe because I am lightheaded from my twirl, I whisper, "'Hope is the thing with feathers.'"

Mademoiselle Salomé fixes her gaze on me, then recites the poem until I join in and we say the last lines together,

"'I've heard it in the chillest land, and on the strangest sea; yet, never, in extremity, it asked a crumb of me.'"

Jeanne hovers. My chest feels heavy. I'd give anything to share this with her, to say, "Oh my god, Mademoiselle Salomé reeled off Emily." But a knot forms in my throat, and I know I'll never share this moment or any other with her again.

"You sew and embroider?" the feather artist asks.

"Oui," I lie.

"The internship is yours, if you want it."

I nod, then thank her politely when what I want to do is throw my arms around her and promise I will not disappoint.

Mademoiselle Salomé leads me out the front door.

"Be here tomorrow at seven a.m."

As the lock twists, I wonder when I will meet the raven and what errands a bird might ask me to run.

CHAPTER 2

I hurry down the street, past le Bateau-Lavoir on Place Émile Goudeau, up hilly streets where tourists bustle and where merchants wash the stoops of their shops and gossip before closing. I keep walking until I'm on the other side of the Sacré Cœur, way past la Maison Rose and the vineyards, where women walk with purpose and graffiti lines the buildings. I walk until I am in front of our apartment building on rue Jean Cocteau, where the sidewalks are made of concrete, not of cobblestones, and where I have lived ever since I was born. I climb to the third floor and take a deep breath. It's like the place has been hit by tragedy twice. Once when my mother left, and now Jeanne.

I slip the key inside the door, walk in, and say, "Papa?"

I yearn for his footsteps, the way he shuffles when he's been holding music sheets for hours and is struggling with new stanzas. I want to tell him about Mademoiselle Salomé, about the feathers. Yet as I walk down the hall, I'm afraid of how I will find him, either in a low where he doesn't speak or, worse, on a high where his band has signed a new deal, which means that, if not now, soon he will be gone again. I peek in the living room behind his hand-painted partition, and there he is asleep among crushed beer cans, a mouthpiece, and swaths of cleaning cloths scattered on the floor, Hawaiian shirt unbuttoned, chest hair poking out, shiny tenor sax lying beside him. For a second, I'm so grateful to see him I almost kneel to pat his unshaven cheek, but then remember how upset I am. I put my foot on the edge of his mattress and bounce my heel up and down as hard as I can until he opens his eyes and says, "Stop, Alix. Please."

"You promised to do better."

I pick up the beer cans, stomp to the kitchen, dump them in the garbage where more empty ones reside. I rummage through the cupboards until I find half a pack of peanuts, Petit Beurre biscuits, and an unopened Coca-Cola bottle—Jeanne's favorite snacks left behind.

"You're the parent, remember?" I yell.

I eat the cookies and take a sip of the soda.

"I'm sorry, canard."

Papa leans against the doorframe, running his hand through his hair. The dark circles under his eyes shock me.

"For what it's worth, I miss Jeanne, too. I think of her every goddamn day."

"Well," I say, "at least you still have Zanx. Aren't you lucky?" I make myself smile, but the rough edge to my voice betrays my sarcasm.

"Don't be like that," Papa says.

Adeline Zanx is Papa's manager, the lead singer in their jazz band, and his girlfriend. She is not a terrible person, but her job is to take him away from me. Zanx gets the band gigs, and she is very good at it. In the past three years, they've been to Barcelona (five weeks), Madrid (eight), Berlin (three months), Stockholm (started as three weeks and turned to two and a half months), and Vienna (all of spring two years ago). Her dream is to take them to New York where she is from, but Papa thinks that's a bridge, or perhaps an ocean, too far. He says he likes knowing he can train or bus back to me. What a saint.

Papa taps the counter. "God, I see Jeanne right here. Don't you? Ass never in a chair. Used to drive me crazy and now—" He can't finish the sentence.

Of course, I see her, sitting on top of the Formica, legs crossed, laughing and drinking Papa's beer, freshly dyed wisteria hair on top of her head, kohl lining her eyes, Bruised Plum staining her lips, charisma pouring from her like glitter. Jeanne was famous before being famous. She was always waiting for someone from Canal + or TF1 to barge in with a camera crew and discover her. "You have to play the part before you get the part," she used to say. I should kiss Papa on the cheek, or pat him on the shoulder, empathize, tell him Jeanne loved him, which is true, but exhausted and feeling beyond sorry for myself because Jeanne was *my* best friend, I push past him and lock myself in my room.

Another day draws to an end. I open the window and look up at the stars blinking in the still blue sky, then tell myself to go ahead already, not to be scared, that if Jeanne could climb onto the windowsill and dangle her feet in the air while proclaiming our dreams, so can I. Carefully, I place my right foot, followed by my left onto the ledge—which turns out to be a lot skinnier than I'd thought—and through gritted teeth, I say, "Can you believe I knocked on Salomé's door? That she not only invited me in but that the apprenticeship is open?" I almost laugh because Jeanne would think the whole thing was epic, but I look down and grow woozy. The world below blurs. I grip the windowpane so hard my knuckles turn white, then I lower myself ever so slowly until I'm sitting on the ledge, heart banging like a drum, feet dangling in the air, my whole body shaking.

Hear ye, hear ye, I hear Jeanne say.

"Cheers," I manage because when Jeanne perched herself up here, she always said, "Life is about taking big fucking risks." Back then, I was unwilling, or afraid, to sit beside her. If Jeanne was in a good mood, she would bellow a song in that throaty voice of hers, unfazed at the void beneath her, or say something dumb like, "Chin up. Put your crown on, Queen." Papa would either bang on the door and tell her to be quiet or blow in his sax if he liked the way Jeanne riffed on the melody.

Now, I stay seated to prove a point but to whom I'm not sure. In the apartment building across the street, a mother has pinned her baby's onesies on a clothesline. Her neighbor planted geraniums in a box but never watered them. The flowers are brown and wilted, which makes me wonder if other households are as broken as ours. A car honks, and still gripping the window frame, I swing one leg, then the other, into my room, plop onto my worn duvet, and whisper, "I know it wasn't your fault, but why did you have to leave me, too?"

CHAPTER 3

On Monday morning, Mademoiselle Salomé invites me into the sewing lab. Pointing to an older seamstress, head bent at her sewing machine, thumbs stretching fabric, the feather artist says, "Alix, meet Faiza. She has been with me forever and knows tous les recoins, every nook and cranny of this boutique." Then Salomé motions toward a girl, slight in stature, but pretty with a strawberry-blond bob, who is hand sewing azure-blue feathers at the bottom of a Victorian skirt, and says, "This is Manon, my hand stitcher. Une merveille."

"Bonjour." I pretend to look over everything with ease as if I'd seen it all before, but in my ripped jeans and T-shirt with only a sketchbook full of feather drawings I haven't shown anyone except Jeanne, I feel so out of place I nearly turn around and leave.

The fluttering of the feathers and my desire to become Salomé's apprentice are the only reasons I stay.

The feather artist must feel my resolve because she signals me toward her study and says, "Viens. There is one more person I'd like you to meet."

Like yesterday, sunshine spills inside the high-ceilinged room and through the window the gnarled oak's leaves flutter in the breeze, but this morning a young man stands behind Salomé's desk, removing feathers from a pouch. A shock of tight blond curls frames his face and his skin is golden brown. He wears a crisp white shirt, tailored khakis, fancy loafers, and seems about the same age as me and the hand stitcher, but more important than everyone else. He holds himself with confidence, chest out and shoulders back.

"Raven," Mademoiselle Salomé says. "Alix will be helping us Monday through Friday. Would you spend a moment with her?"

The young man runs a palm across the antique pink feather he's just placed on the table. He lifts a pair of scissors as if deciding where to begin his first incision. "What école does she come from?" His voice is as sharp as the scissors he holds.

Mademoiselle Salomé sighs. "No need to put her through the paces. Alix is only interning. Give her the list of incidentals for the Marché Saint-Pierre or have her familiarize herself with fabrics."

Raven sets the scissors down. "Why don't you ask Manon instead? I'm——"

"Please. Manon is swamped," Mademoiselle Salomé says. "Besides Alix likes poetry, sews, embroiders, and draws, too, I believe." The feather artist smiles in my direction, then, waving goodbye, adds, "Plus, there's *something* about her. She spun amidst the burning pheasant feathers yesterday."

Once the door shuts and Salomé is gone, something tells me to brace myself.

"Alors, Pixie?" Raven says, an inkling of a smirk blooming on his lips. "Will you pirouette for me, too? Or wait, do you hide fairy wings behind your back? Can you fly? Swing on a trapeze? Shall I take a step back for your metamorphosis?" He takes the antique pink feather by the quill, points it toward me, and says, "Abracadabra!"

He knows how stunning he is. I avert my gaze and wish I could flick him the finger, but instead I say, "I'm a hard worker. I swear."

Raven chuckles. "Out of curiosity, why did you come to Mille et Une Plume?"

"Easy," I answer. "I love the boutique."

Raven lifts an eyebrow in a perfect accent circonflexe, then shoots me a sly smile.

It's hard not to be blinded by his charm. I imagine how Jeanne would flirt with this Apollon-like boy to get what she wanted because there was something special about *her*, not me, but as Raven comes around the table, I stiffen, pray, and wish Salomé or the other women would come to my rescue. No one does.

"What do you know about this business anyway?" Raven says.

"Some feathers are more expensive than others?"

"True. Pigeons are cheap. Other plumes are as rare as silk. Pheasant, peacock, or wildfowl de Sonnerat, like this one." He runs his index finger on the pink feather. "The most expensive is a cross between an eagle and a raven. Their feathers possess spiritual powers. Something about freedom. Light and darkness. At least, that's what Mother likes to say. Napoleon used to stuff his duvets with eagle feathers."

I see it now. Raven is Mademoiselle Salomé's son. Their brown skin, not to mention exceptional looks. Their ease in the world. Even their curls. I grow even more uncomfortable. I hope Raven will soon tell me to go sort fabrics in another room, but he takes a step forward, closing the gap between us, and I think I might faint at his proximity.

"If you were a feather, what kind would you be?" he asks.

I can't tell if his tone is playful or serious. I look out at the oak, think of Jeanne, what she would say, but because I am close enough to Raven to breathe in his scent—something piney as if I were standing at the entrance of la forêt de Fontainebleau—I draw a blank, then decide I'd be a vieux plumeau, an old feather duster.

"Not sure," I murmur.

There is a long silence, and before I can say something else, something courageous like, "I bet I have collected and sketched way more feathers than you ever have," Raven wriggles the antique pink feather against the tip of my nose, and says, "Has anyone ever told you, Pixie, that you're a giant bowl of fun?"

Ticklish and stunned, I swat at the feather.

Raven catches my wrist, stills, then slowly traces the outline of my tattoo with his thumb, causing a zap of electricity to zing right through me.

"Je l'aime bien," he says, making my cheeks heat up a thousand degrees.

He places the pink feather back onto the table and digs through bins until he holds two feathers, one sleek and the other vaporous.

"Which do you think is better to use for something lavish like a gown, the swan or the ostrich?"

"May I touch them?" I ask, hoping to feel their softness

against my fingers and to also distract myself from the lingering electricity.

"Non," Raven replies.

One snow white, the other birch, both on the larger side. The feathers sway. I choose the swan's—stronger, knife-like, easier to manipulate, I imagine.

Raven's gaze warms.

He says, "Like a tulip, an ostrich feather bends. La plume de cygne, on the other hand, blooms like a rose, straight up. Know its meaning?"

I shake my head.

"Beauté," he says. "Where Mother comes from everything is alive. A molted feather carries the energy of the bird to another living being." He returns the feathers to their bins, slips his hands in his pockets, then pulls out and jams a piece of paper in my fingers. "Buy what's on the list," he says. "Hand the purchases to Faiza." Raven fishes money from his wallet. "Better bring back change, too."

As I step into the hallway, I say, "I know this might sound crazy, but I'm meant to work here."

"I hate to break it to you," Raven replies, "but most petite mains don't last long."

I want to tell him I am not most, that he doesn't know a damn thing about me, and remembering Jeanne and my pledge to each other—our vows of becoming a rock star and a feather artist, of supporting each other no matter what—I say, "Why is the apprenticeship open anyway? And how *does* one become Salomé's apprentice? Is it years of experience? Talent? Title? School? What?"

Raven saunters back behind his mother's desk. He picks up the scissors, and in an impressive flurry of snips, he cuts the antique pink feather until it has become a series of perfectly styled miniature plumes, a mound of them on the table.

He says, "The apprenticeship is vacant because I no longer want it. As for becoming the new apprentice, all of it matters, Pixie, but want to know a secret?"

I wait half-frightened.

"The plumes will decide your fate."

A few hours later, back at the boutique, I finger the crumpled paper in my pocket. *Six rolls of cotton (size 50) thread. Ten rolls of bobbin thread. Five meters of off-white broadcloth. Fifteen invisible zippers. A jar of one hundred black shank buttons. Five medium-size sketchbooks. A box of thirty-two graphite pencils.* No feathers, thank the universe. I hand Faiza the bag, the change, and the rolled-up broadcloth, praying I didn't screw up my first assignment.

The seamstress inspects the goods, then takes me from room to room, showing me where everything goes. As we open drawers, she says I'm to sweep the floors, pick up whatever anyone needs, help customers with orders, assist with the overflow of sewing demands, answer the phone, take down messages, sort through fabrics, and keep areas free of clutter. During quiet times, like now for example, I am to shadow her and Manon. Salomé likes to call it training.

Once we have put away the final jar of buttons, Faiza sits on her stool, slips the border of a sea-green velvet cape inside the plate, and begins sewing. For a moment, I think the seamstress has forgotten about me, but above the whir of the motor and North African music playing on an old radio, she says, "Before I forget, here are a few house rules: Customers get fitted in the parlor. If you are to use a sewing machine, use the secondhand Singer. The wingback chair belongs to Manon. Salomé's study, as well as the upstairs, are off limits unless you're invited."

As I sit between both women, hoping to vicariously learn how to sew through them, Manon says, "I heard you just graduated but already have experience?"

"Uh-huh," I reply, gaze low.

Manon waits for me to elaborate, but when I don't, she says, "Well, I have been in the business since I turned fifteen, and Faiza started sewing in Annaba more than thirty years ago."

The hand stitcher lifts a new azure-blue feather as if it were a wine glass.

"Tchin, Faiza," she says.

A clock chimes.

After asking Manon about the best ways of attaching feathers onto garments only to receive a lecture on E-6000 glue, resin, and acrylics, I flip through the pages of a book on the nuts and bolts of the feather industry and learn that petite mains are the lowest on the plume ladder. Next up are the machine sewers. Then, the hand stitchers, who are in charge of embroidery and delicate feather work. Premières are seasoned stitchers with sales and customer experience. The larger houses hire sketchers. There are also the doigts de fée, fairy fingers or pre-apprentices, and finally at the tippy top of the apex is the apprentice, the person who does it all, and will one day inherit the feather artist's house.

"Who sketches here?" I say, itching to whip out my drawings.

"Salomé and, until recently, Raven," Manon answers. "But Faiza has drawn a few designs, too, over the years. Salomé believes in flexibility. She refers to us as touche-à-tout, jack-of-all-trades." Manon groans. "If you ask me, drawing is for the birds. No pun intended."

I smile.

As morning turns to afternoon then evening, I follow orders and mainly clean, wiping down the counters and tables without disrupting unfinished projects. In the costume room, when no one is watching, I admire the posters of galas with collections from Coco Chanel and Givenchy, then dare to run my fingers on flowing pants, poet shirts, capes similar to the one Mademoiselle Salomé wore yesterday, and gowns with intricate beading, lace, and loads of feathers. I try not to think of going back to Papa's, whether he'll be there, or not. Eventually, Manon hands me a plastic bag. She tells me to pick up every loose needle and scrap of fabric off the floor. She says that if I notice stray feathers I must bunch them together, then place them onto the worktable in the costume room.

"All plumes here are precious," she reminds me.

At six p.m., Faiza turns off the machines and the radio. Manon stretches, then lays the Victorian dress onto a cutting table. I have found twenty-one needles, nine safety pins, various pieces of tissue like taffeta or tulle, and one slender jet-black feather, which I almost slip in my pocket to draw later but think better of it and place it on the table next to the bag with everything else as Manon requested. Faiza flicks off the lights and locks the boutique. We file out onto the street. I almost ask if one of them is walking in my direction, but Manon hurries away, barely saying goodbye.

Faiza waves. "Get some rest, poulette, and see you tomorrow."

CHAPTER 4

Inside Papa's apartment, the hall light is on, a good sign. I can't wait to tell him about my first day, but as I head toward the kitchen Zanx's voice rises from the living room, aka Papa's bedroom, her timbre as clear and airy as the stillest mountain lake. I know what this means. When Zanx shows up and sings without the rest of the band, there is almost always something to celebrate. Like a new deal. I tiptoe toward the sound. In a pair of skinny jeans and a silk ivory camisole that shows off her smooth ebony skin, Zanx reclines on the green couch, her glossy mouth in a perfect O, champagne flute in hand. Yeah, definitely a deal. My father sits on the armrest opposite her and sips from his flute while stroking her bare feet. It's worse than catching them kissing. I'd prefer that.

"Do we have food or just alcohol?" I say, bypassing hellos.

Zanx stops singing, and my father says, "There is Vietnamese takeout in the fridge, canard."

I hate when he calls me duck in front of people but especially her, and I can also tell Papa wants to ask me where I was, except he knows I won't say much with the girlfriend around. Jeanne and I had a steadfast rule. Keep quiet around Zanx. Jeanne didn't like her either. I head to the fridge, pull out the carry-out boxes, plunk them on the table ready to dig in when Papa and Zanx poke their heads in the kitchen.

Zanx gives me her best smile and says in her drawn-out American accent, "Nous avons eu un super boulot. A fantastic gig. Your father is about to play in Harlem among the greats."

I plop down on a chair, open the first boxful of rice, swallow four spoonfuls, then to my father say, "Tu t'en vas quand? When, and for how long?"

"This Friday. Not sure." He searches his pocket for a lighter, grabs his pack of cigarettes from the counter, takes one, murmurs something to Zanx, who returns to the living room.

After a long drag, he says, "You okay?"

"Will it be good money?"

"More than what we have, but seriously you all right?"

I want to say no, I'm not all right, and plead with him to stay—story of my life—except standing here exhausted in this stupid kitchen where ghosts live, I think of my other lousy parent, how one sunny morning she left us for no good reason, how Papa is just trying to make a living under shitty circumstances, how that's different, so I do what I do best. I nod.

Papa pats the top of my head, then goes back to his girl-friend. I open more carry-out boxes. My mouth waters at the smell of chopped beef, ginger, and cilantro, and once again, as I shove food in my mouth, I see my mother, this time showing me how to use chopsticks, the two of us seated at this very table, giggling while trying to keep steaming noodles from sliding off the little wooden wands, and I wonder how she went from once loving us to leaving us so easily. How she chose a new husband, who I heard did not want kids, and who gave her an ultimatum, him or me. I probably shouldn't finish all the leftovers—that wouldn't be gracious—but I don't care. I tell Jeanne how much I despise grown-ups, how selfish they are, then I eat every little morsel, drowning in memories of us and scraping the boxes empty, until not even a grain of rice is left.

Months after my mother disappeared, after I turned ten, a new girl entered my CM2 classroom. It was so early the teacher hadn't arrived yet. Along with a few other kids, I sat staring out the window at the rain because being in school, which I hated, was better than at home where Papa's and my sadness stuck to the walls like a thick layer of slime. The new girl smacked her gum. She had long sandy hair and wore denim overalls. I pretended not to notice her as she chose the desk next to mine, sank into it, then dug through her backpack decorated with lavender pompoms, the same color as her shirt. She brandished an eau de toilette sample, which she rubbed against the insides of her wrists.

"I'm Jeanne." She shot me a megawatt smile.

I got a whiff of something spicy, like what a grown woman might wear, and wondered how she got a hold of such a fancy thing, but I was too shy to ask, and besides with only Papa and his bandmates as my role models I wasn't sure how to speak to girls anymore.

Jeanne said, "Like it?"

She leaned toward me and looked like she was going to say something else when the charcutier's son, an obnoxious kid who'd been held back and sat in the last row, snickered.

"Don't talk to Leclaire," he said. "Her dad is a beggar. He rattles his hat, hoping you'll give him change. I know you've seen him hauling his big old saxophone around."

The kids in the room laughed.

I flinched because Papa did play on the sidewalk sometimes.

But Jeanne didn't join in the laughter. Instead, she asked me, "What about your mom?"

I blushed hard staring out the window again until the same kid said, "Her mother dumped them. My dad says she got into her car one day and left. Not just Paris but the country because Alix and her dad are losers."

More laughter.

My cheeks burned. I was wondering if I should hide in the bathroom, when Jeanne again leaned over, her spicy scent spellbinding me.

"I wish my mother left the country," she whispered. Then, "Watch this."

Jeanne shot up and strutted to where the kid was sitting. My mouth popped open. Jeanne already glowed then, bigger than life. She hopped on his desk, crossed her legs like a grown-up, and grinned like one, too. Flustered, the kid stuck his tongue out, made kissing sounds, and at the speed of light, Jeanne shoved her chewing gum in his hair.

"Don't *ever* bother us again. Got it?" she said.

The kid grabbed at the gooey bright green wad, cursing, but the more he pulled the worse it got, the more his hair got stuck. I chuckled. I loved how Jeanne used the word *us*. When she sat back down, she unhooked one of the pom-poms from her backpack and handed it to me.

"Want to be best friends?" she said.

I nodded, clutching her gift in my palm.

From then on, Jeanne and I became inseparable. As fall turned to winter, Jeanne began walking home with me after the final bell. We'd hide in my room, sit on my ivory duvet, make heaps of pompoms, draw, and sing incessantly. Papa was so relieved to see me smiling again he offered to meet Jeanne's mother, a politician, in front of our school one afternoon and extended Jeanne a permanent invitation to rue Jean Cocteau. For Papa that meant more time with his sax because, with Jeanne around, I no longer clung to him. I don't remember much of the meeting aside from Papa saying to Jeanne after her mother left, "Is Claire always this stiff?" and Jeanne dissolved into laughter.

By spring, Jeanne slept over every Friday and Saturday. But, when, one Thursday afternoon after my thirteenth birthday, Zanx showed up at the carousel by the Sacré Cœur (my favorite place growing up) wearing leopard heels and bright red lipstick and kissed my dad on the lips, Jeanne said, "You need a shield, Queen." We schemed. Jeanne started carrying an overnight bag and stayed with us from Wednesday through the weekend. Then, one afternoon at fourteen—after Jeanne and I had spent hours in the bathroom bleaching and dying her hair the color of wisteria—she announced she was going to be a rock star, that she didn't care what her mother thought. Papa, who was running out to practice, had said, "Why don't you live with us full-time?"

Jeanne threw herself into Papa's arms.

By then, my room had become ours anyway. Jeanne's cutouts of Charlotte Gainsbourg, Alice et Moi, Phoebe

Bridgers, and Billie Eilish were tacked around my vanity mirror. Jeanne kept her clothes piled up in a corner, her eye-liners and mascara strewn on my desk, and she'd plugged in her three alarm clocks. I loved everything about her—her bravado, her unadulterated affection, and her presence as a shield against Zanx—but what I loved most of all was that there were three of us again at rue Jean Cocteau.

That night, when I asked Jeanne about dying *my* hair, when I reminded her I was an artist, too, Jeanne flipped open my Emily Dickinson book of poems, and after we recited "Hope Is the Thing with Feathers"—which, right then and there, became our anthem—she said, "What you need is a bird or feather tattoo. Emily would approve."

"Papa would never let me," I whined. "Not until I can do it legally anyway."

"Do you have to tell Fabien everything?"

"Yes," I said. "I don't like secrets. Will you take me to get a tattoo when I turn sixteen?"

Jeanne's wisteria-colored hair shook as she laughed. "Who knows where I'll be by then, but if I'm still hanging around here, sure."

"Jeanne!" I yelled.

I didn't become jealous of Jeanne until I was fifteen, until she had a fight with her mother's newest boyfriend, a far right ministre of something, who told her she was dirty because he'd caught her flirting with an Italian boy who was visiting Paris on holiday. By then, the newness of our friendship had died, and when I asked Jeanne what was wrong because I could see something was bothering her by the way she kept twisting her silver rings, she said, "Rien." All day at school, Jeanne pretended everything was fine. But later, once we were home, she ran to my father and cried on his shoulder.

My father was drinking, and when she showed him a new song she had written, he not only listened but played a melody to accompany Jeanne's terrible lyrics and said there would always be space for her here, that when Jeanne became a rock star, her mother and throng of her ex-boyfriends would be sorry. Jeanne went from crying to laughing, then asked if Papa really thought she could be a star, and when my father said, "Absolutely," Jeanne asked if she could have a drink and a smoke, too. Before my father could answer, she snuck two cans of beer into my room and guzzled them.

"Il est génial ton père. He is so cool," she said.

A few hours later, they performed a duet of her song, Papa drunk and Jeanne buzzed. I could barely look at them. I couldn't forgive Jeanne for going to my father first, and I disliked the way they leaned against the microphone, heads bent toward each other, like father and daughter.

"Why don't you go to Zanx's and hang out with people your age?" I said to my father after they were done.

"I thought you didn't like her, canard," Papa said.

"He is not wrong," Jeanne chirped.

"Shut up," I told her.

They shot each other conspiring glances, and I stormed out of the room.

As Jeanne and I were getting into bed and she accidentally kicked my shin with her foot, I said, "Did you pick me as your friend because of my dad?"

Jeanne flopped her head on the pillow. "What's with you tonight?" she said. "And no. I chose you because your heart seemed broken and sad, even sadder than mine if that's possible, and I wanted to cheer you up."

You picked me out of pity? Seething with anger, I said, "Why was your heart broken? Your mother never left you. You left her."

Jeanne turned to face the wall. "Obviously, you're having a bad day. Night." And then, she started snoring.

The next evening, I tried to show Papa my drawings. I tried to talk to him about my feelings, about him liking Jeanne more than me, about how terrible her song was, yet as I watched him, hungover, putting one of his Hawaiian shirts on, hands shaking a little, I suddenly felt like the bad guy and couldn't find the words.

"Want broth?" I offered instead.

"I'm okay," Papa said. "But thanks."

On my way out the living room, he added, "I'm sorry about yesterday, canard. I shouldn't have been drinking when Jeanne needed help."

I looked at my shoes, afraid I might start to cry, and almost said, "What about me, Papa? Do you notice how much I need help?"

Back in my room, I waited for Jeanne, hoping to apologize because in the end she hadn't done anything wrong and unlike my father, *she* noticed my ups and downs, but that afternoon she'd left without telling me where she was going, a first, and didn't return until I was asleep.

CHAPTER 5

Tuesday at sunrise, I tiptoe out of the apartment. I walk to Jeanne's and my bench, the one we always sat on when we were in school, the one at the bus stop across the street from Rabelais, our old high school. I run my hand on our initials, the ones Jeanne carved with her Swiss Army knife smack-dab in the middle of the bench— AL for me, JAC for Jeanne Aimée Chinon.

I swear I smell Jeanne's spicy perfume and can almost hear her laughter. I'm a second away from wrapping my arm around her shoulder when the squeak of a bus's wheels brings me back to reality, that it's just me sitting here at the dumb bus stop.

I wave off the bus driver since I'm not actually going anywhere, and as it pulls away the conductor lifts his cap, and I salute him. Once he is gone, I kick at an old newspaper and wish I could rewind time. I watch commuters hurrying to work and wonder what normal people do for a living, then thinking of my father, I momentarily consider dropping the internship and getting a real job, even if it means doing something soul sucking, like working as an admin. Wouldn't that allow me a little more stability, a better paycheck? Sure. But at what cost? I'd erase my one and only dream, voiding what Jeanne called BFRs—Big Fucking Risks. I'd rather lose my home.

I pull my sketchbook out from my backpack and stare at the feathers I have drawn over the years. Thousands. The most recent is from last night. In bed, I'd drawn from memory the slender jet-black feather I picked up off the floor, and this morning the feather looks almost alive, as if a gust of wind could lift it off the page. I wish I'd borrowed the plume for just a few minutes, though, because the soot black I picked was not exactly right. As I'm about to get up and head somewhere to grab breakfast, Bus 42 halts by the lycée's main doors. Blaise de Something or Other, a tall, lanky kid with thick-rimmed frames I recognize from an old lit class, hops out.

"Leclaire?" he says.

His voice is ocean deep.

As he crosses the street, I study his boyish face drowning in the glasses and remember him making insightful comments about authors like Marguerite Duras, Colette, and Simone Weil. I wonder what he is doing up this early during summer but not enough to ask. I pick at a loose stitch on my jeans and hope he'll go away. Except Blaise plants his fluorescent sneakers not too far from my Converse.

He pulls out a croissant from a paper bag and says, "I didn't expect to see a familiar face at this witchy hour. Mind if I sit?"

I'm about to say yes I mind, but Blaise collapses next to me anyway, takes a huge bite of his croissant, then rubs flakes off his lips. The sweet smell of butter is intoxicating. He looks for a moment like he is about to speak but again plunges his hand in the bag and, pulling out another croissant, says, "Want it?"

"You sure?" I ask.

He nods, and I cram the pastry in my mouth, devouring it. Blaise laughs. "Oh là là, gourmande."

I stand, embarrassed.

"Wait. I was joking." Then awkwardly lifting his hand, he adds, "I'm sorry about Jeanne."

"I have to go." I start to walk away. "It's just that——" I pause. "I'm not great company. Thanks again for breakfast."

I turn onto a side street, hoping he will let me leave without any further conversation, but Blaise calls after me, "I know we don't really know each other, but I was hoping we could get coffee. I think Jeanne would have liked that."

I'm not sure how he could know what Jeanne would have liked, so I continue on the side street until I make it to the corner of rue du Faubourg Poissonnière. I lean against a trash can and catch my breath, remembering Jeanne and me on the night she first mentioned wings.

It was last summer. At the Fontaine du Luxembourg, Jeanne pulled out a box of Ladurée macarons from her giant purse and a flask of bourbon, both of which she handed me.

"Cheers, ma reine," she said, lowering herself into the water in her sundress.

Jeanne pretended to be a mermaid, egging me on to get in, too, calling me a Goody Two-shoes because I remained on the edge hardly sipping from her flask, eating the macarons. She told me about this new crush, how hot he was—something about his hands and mouth and how they worked together turning her bones to liquid.

I must have made a sad face because Jeanne said, "Don't worry. I'll never love a boy more than you. Jamais."

She cheered.

I moaned because I knew what was coming—a loud and public declaration of our dreams.

"Hear ye, hear ye," Jeanne pronounced, standing in the fountain, dripping wet and unrolling an imaginary parchment. "We, Alix Leclaire and Jeanne Chinon, will soar through life, best friends forever. I will become a rock star and Alix a feather artist. We swear these words on Emily Dickinson's head." She lowered herself into the water, then brought her knees to her chin.

She said, "Did you know a girl drowned in this fountain a long time ago?"

"Stop it," I replied, rolling my eyes.

"I was thinking," Jeanne said. "When you get that apprenticeship, will you build me wings like the ones in the window? Make me look badass." She smiled, but her voice cracked a little.

"The feather shop never has openings," I said.

"Who cares? Go knock anyway. Say, 'I want to be your apprentice.'" Jeanne stretched out and floated toward the middle of the fountain. "Dreams don't come to you. You have to go to them. You have to risk everything. Besides, I have the feeling they will love you beyond measure."

I stepped into the water, walked to where she was, and reached my arm out to help her up.

"I love *you*," I said. "Promise we'll always be there for each other?"

"Toujours," Jeanne replied.

I was about to tell her not to ever mention sad stories like that girl drowning again, when Jeanne grabbed my fingers and yanked me down until we were both drenched, screaming and laughing.

CHAPTER 6

For the rest of the week at Mille et Une Plume, I sew every moment I can. I hide in the restroom, poking my needle and thread through discarded materials hoping the result will look right, but my fingers squeeze the needle too hard and the results are disastrous. The stitches are either too tight and overlap or flap loose and lopsided, my knots an embarrassment.

On Monday morning, Faiza says, "Has anyone mentioned the news to you?"

I worry she has discovered my pathetic sewing attempts and is about to march me outside, but I am relieved when the seamstress informs me about something called Bid Day, an event coming up this fall, and the Dream Show, another scheduled for next summer. Both are apparently creating a frenzy in the feather world. Faiza shows me a stack of envelopes with invitations to the first event, along with a list of Mademoiselle Salomé's VIP clients. She instructs me to write their names and addresses using my best penmanship, to place the invitations inside the envelopes, stamp and seal them, and to also answer the phone, if no one else does.

Before the seamstress takes off to the sewing lab to rectify the waist on a pair of flowing, feathered pants meant for an Alvin Ailey soloist, I sit at the worktable and say, "What's the big deal about these events?"

The older seamstress explains the Moulin Rouge will have a one-of-a-kind performance next summer, and how four feather houses, including us, will compete for the bid to dress the dancers, that I should feel honored to be part of such special occasions.

"I am," I say, and throughout the morning, I finish the Bid Day invitations making certain to write in my best cursive.

After lunch, Faiza ushers me to the sewing lab and hands me burgundy thread along with a needle.

"I have good news, poulette," she says, then explains that it's time to show her what I've got, that a new order has come in, and that she and Manon could use my help, to please hand stitch the hem of these three velvet capes, dark red, mustard, and heather oatmeal, in that order, and to steam them after I am done.

I should be ecstatic, except I nearly start to cry as Faiza places her hands on her hips and looks at me, waiting. I sit with the garment on my lap and replicate my attempts from earlier. I do such a terrible job that the older seamstress snatches the burgundy cape from my hand, snips the thread, and yanks it out before Manon, who is fitting a customer from the 16th arrondissement, notices my mess.

"Don't you know how?" Faiza says.

I shake my head.

"Bon dieu." Faiza makes me sit beside her. She takes a piece of thick gray cotton, plain white thread, and tells me to watch. She stitches the fabric, fingers agile, practiced, then hands it to me. "Now you," she says.

I try and try, but no matter how much I focus my stitches are crooked and uneven.

"Go to the costume room," Faiza orders. "Sit at the worktable. Place the cape on your lap and hide the patch of cotton beneath it. Practice and pray no one enters the room. If anyone walks by, pretend to do one stitch or two using the cape and the burgundy thread."

By the time early evening comes, I have not taken a single break and have stitched thirty-two slanted rows on the gray cotton swath. My right hand is so sore I can barely move my thumb and index finger. But what's worse is the humiliation. While Manon gathers her belongings, then chats with Mademoiselle Salomé in the feather artist's study, Faiza inspects each one of my stitches, eyebrows furrowed. She points to my imperfections when the stitch is too long, too short, or uneven.

"May I ask you something?" the older seamstress says.

I nod.

"Didn't you suspect that as a petite main in a feather shop you would have to sew?"

I swallow so hard my eyes tear up.

But then, everything spills out. That my mother long ago was a maquilleuse, a makeup artist, for cabarets around Paris, and that one Saturday night I got to watch the Moulin Rouge performers get ready. I must have been eight or nine. I explain that I fell in love not with the eyeshadows and the berry-colored lipsticks my mother adored but with the off-white feather bralettes the dancers snapped onto their busts and the long red feathers shimmering from their hips. And that when one of the girls handed me her soft pink powder puff, told me it was made of marabou feathers, and that I could keep it forever, I held the treasure in my palm, turned to one of the mirrors, placed the puff on my head like a crown, and whispered, "I am the queen of plumes." My mother's face hovered nearby in the mirror. She said, "Look at you, p'tite reine d'amour." And that night surrounded by the dancers, with my mother close, I felt seen and loved.

The memory of Maman's and my faces pressed together, of our dark hair and identical freckles, reels back to me so acutely I blink a couple times.

"I've been collecting and drawing feathers ever since," I say, then scramble for my backpack and hand Faiza my drawings.

She flips through my sketchbook, returns it to me, and pats my knee.

"Your drawings are lovely, dear," she says. "But if you want to stay with Mille et Une Plume, you will have to practice everything else. Read every book Salomé owns. Observe. I'll teach you how to cross-stitch and backstitch, how to use a glue gun. Sewing and embroidering is our alphabet, and you won't succeed without them."

I wish I could disappear through the floorboards. "I'm sorry I lied," I say.

Faiza offers me one of her motherly looks. "Don't do it again. When you are struggling, come see me. Manon is a terrible teacher and Raven is, well, a hothead, and unreliable. Also——" Faiza hands me a needle and thread and a new square of cotton. "Bring this home and sit and sew until your fingers fall off and your stitches begin to look professional." The older seamstress takes my god-awful swath of gray cotton and throws it into the industrial trash can in the back of the boutique. "Practice, practice, practice."

"Merci, Faiza," I say, grateful not only for her guidance but for her grace and understanding.

That night, alone in the apartment, I take a handful of the feathers I've collected in the city from a mason jar on my dresser, touch each one—the sparrow, the wren, the song thrush—then sew until the tips of my fingers blister. Around midnight, I curl up on the green couch but can't sleep. The memory of the feather puff and my mother has taken hold of me, and I can't seem to shake it. The silence is deafening. I long for Papa's music and am so desperate for sound I'd even take Zanx singing. If Jeanne were here, she would put on the stereo. We'd dance or, like last December, decorate the wall.

That afternoon, snowflakes fell. Jeanne held a can of black spray paint, ready to write the word *arte* above my bed. I was glad for her company but looking at the snow-flakes, I wished Papa, my mother, and I were a normal family who went out and got a Christmas tree. Jeanne rum-maged through her bag, found a flask, took a long swallow of bourbon, then passed it to me.

"Isn't it a little early?" I said.

Jeanne cut me a look, said I was starting to sound like her mother, but added, "Sorry. I know you mean well. Je te pardonne." She grinned.

I grinned back but wasn't sure why I was to be forgiven.

Jeanne shook the paint can and got to work, and as she drew the final letter, I said, "Hear ye, hear ye." I unraveled an imaginary parchment and waited for Jeanne to join me, but she swallowed more bourbon.

The afternoon was bleak, darkness falling fast. I scooped my drawing papers, heart aching, and went to the living room to sketch new feathers. I left the door open, hoping Jeanne would come sit beside me, but she got on the phone instead. I heard her laughing.

The snowflakes turned to sleet. Jeanne slipped on her coat.

"Wait," I said, ashamed of the plea in my voice. "I've been thinking about my tattoo. Will you come with me when I have the money?"

Jeanne pulled out a hundred euros from her pocket and handed them to me. "Let me guess, bird or feather?" She chuckled, then twirled a new key chain, a big red heart.

"How did you get that?" I said, staring at the cash.

"None of your beeswax," she answered. "Want it or not?"

"Yeah," I said, then reached for my pad to show her the amethyst starling feather I'd sketched moments before, but, already onto something else, Jeanne said, "Let me show you my secret." She clicked open the heart. A bright blue pill fell in her palm. "It was a love-at-first-sight gift." I didn't know if she meant the pill or the key chain. Jeanne popped the pill.

"Come with me now," I said.

"Maybe tomorrow."

Jeanne went on to explain she was meeting Key Chain Guy near la Madeleine. A business connection. A fantastic kisser. I tried to be cool, understanding, yet all I could see was her stupid red heart.

"À plus, ma reine," she said.

She careened down the stairs, the heels of her micro-suede boots clonk, clonk, clonking until I could barely hear them at all. I swung the door shut and placed my forehead against the wall.

A week later, perhaps because Jeanne felt bad, she told me she dreamed of a feather on my forearm, that she'd hold my hand while I got my tattoo.

But, again, she got busy. I waited until one spring day when Papa was gone and I felt lost among the sad walls of the apartment. I decided to go on my own. I took Jeanne's money, which I'd kept hidden in one of Papa's old records, left Jeanne a note in the kitchen telling her where I was, and went to TinTin Tatouages, holding onto my amethyst feather drawing as if it would change my life, or save it.

The outline of my feather was nearly done when Jeanne burst into the parlor and said, "I told you I'd come." Jeanne's breath reeked of alcohol, and she twirled her heart key chain so fast the artist asked her to settle down or leave.

She plopped on a stool beside me, then gabbed about Key Chain Guy, never once mentioning the amethyst feather appearing on my forearm.

At 3:30 a.m., I'm still awake. I try to sew again, but shadows flicker on the walls. Every noise makes me jump. I check the door, make sure it's locked, then put my sewing away and go back to the green couch. It isn't until the first pale yellow light of morning filters through the living room window that I relax and my eyelids close.

CHAPTER 7

When I open the door to Mademoiselle Salomé's study, everyone is gone except for Raven, who reclines in his mother's chair. I haven't seen him since my first day, and with the gnarled oak presiding at his back, he is the most beguiling boy I have ever laid eyes on. I am petrified at what he will say, if he will notice my tardiness. I clear my throat, tell him I can't find Faiza or Manon.

Raven looks at me, curls as bright as sun rays, skin flawless, eyes, oh God, I notice for the first time, a startling sky blue. He is dressed in his crisp white shirt and dress pants, and a silver coin hooked to a black leather rope dangles beneath his Adam's apple. I think of the slew of boys Jeanne flirted with or dated and decide that if she were here, she would say something clever. She would inquire about the coin or flip her wisteria waves. But I remain Alix, stiff, with short hair mussed up from lying down, a crease from Papa's couch pillow probably imprinted on my cheek.

Before I can apologize for disturbing him, Raven says, "The girls are at a feather salon, beauté."

My cheeks burn at his choice of nickname, and I am suddenly dying to know what a feather salon is except Raven gestures for me to sit. As soon as I have lowered myself onto the edge of the chaise, he adds, "Do I need to gift you an alarm clock?"

I shake my head.

"You're forty-one minutes late, Pixie."

He watches me squirm.

Right when I think he will fire me, he says, "Lucky for you, I don't technically work here anymore. The feathers are telling me to keep you around anyway."

I exhale, and Raven grins, which lights up his face and makes him even more stunning. My stomach flips. I tell him I will never be late again, then stand and ask him if I should go ahead and sweep the floors or if he wants me to do anything else like brew a pot of coffee or check voicemail.

Raven says, "Why don't you use me wisely? Who knows how long I'll stick around?"

I'm not sure what he means.

I say, "Do petite mains ever have a chance to work with plumes?"

Raven walks past me and says, "Haven't you learned already? Titles mean nothing here."

Raven leaves Salomé's study and returns with a steaming mug and a leather-bound journal. He plops the latter onto my lap.

I must make some kind of face because Raven says, "It's a work notebook. Everyone here has one. Use it as you wish."

He adds that some draw in it while others catalogue feathers by their names and colors like bleu de coquelicot, their textures and measurements, what bird they come from—a grue cendré, a silver crane, or a *lophophorus impejanus*, the Himalayan monal. Raven places his mouth on the midnight lip of his mug and takes a sip.

I wish I could elbow Jeanne the way we always did when we saw someone wicked hot and say, "On a scale of one to ten, don't you think he is a thousand?" Jeanne would laugh and I'm 100 percent certain say something far more salacious. Except, it isn't lost on me that because of a wicked hot and highly rated boy Jeanne is not here to joke. I steel myself and look out the window at the gnarled oak.

Raven offers me the mug.

I hesitate.

"What?"

The coin he is wearing dangles where his shirt opens in a V, the silver flat against his skin, a black bird in flight— a raven—carved into the center. If that isn't sexy enough, he smells like the forest, pine or cedar, as if the scent were concocted by woodland fairies. His sky-blue eyes stay steady on mine. I probably turn as red as the parrot feathers spilling from the bin by the window.

"You were staring at my mug. I'm offering you a taste," he says.

I bring the mug to my lips. The tea has the rich fragrance of jasmine, and for a fraction of a second I imagine what it would be like to be kissed by someone like him.

When I look up, Raven says, "There *is* something about you, Pixie." He nods at my forearm, at the tattoo. "The graceful lines in your drawing, the way your feather bends. The artist in you. But can you transfer that lightness into three dimensions? Create beautiful clothes and objects? That is the question."

As he invites me to sit at the worktable, I clutch the journal and feel how smooth the dark brown leather is. I have the urge to tell Jeanne and the entire universe that someone as fancy as Raven called me une artiste. Yet as Raven gathers blue moon feathers and loads of tissue, I remember I don't even know how to sew. *Whatever*, I hear Jeanne say. *Manifest. Tell this boy you're amazing.*

I perch myself on the stool beside him, plead with the Jeanne in my mind to hush, but feeling more daring, I say, "I want to learn how to build wings. I want to be a feather artist."

"Shocker," Raven replies with that little maddening smirk dancing across his lips.

Pointing to various swaths of material spread out on the table, he adds, "I wasn't sure if it was your tattoo, or you, standing in the rain in front of the bay window several times last year that gave it away."

My cheeks grow scorching hot again.

"Listen, Pixie," Raven says, "there are three stages to this business, regardless of what the project is. First, draw the vision. Second, construct it to scale. Last, sew and embroider."

"But aren't sewing and embroidering the most important?" I say. "Like Faiza told me, your alphabet?"

"According to the seamstresses." Raven laughs. "I bet the sketcher believes otherwise."

It's my turn to grin.

"Right," I say, then touch silk, gauze, taffeta, tulle, crêpe, velvet, velour, cotton, chenille, chiffon, linen, flannel, damask, denim, gingham, jersey, muslin, and my favorite for its softness, cashmere wool.

Raven tells me some are meant to be accents while others are baseline fabrics. He hands me an Australian parakeet feather, the color of a tangerine. He teaches me where the quill is thickest—at the edges—and where it's softest—in the middle.

He says, "Mother believes the tip of a feather represents adulthood, the veins the choices we make. The fluff at the bottom is our childhood. The quill is our inner strength, the path we are on." But then, Raven gives me the sharp scissors I saw him with on my first day, and says, "Cut the plume in two alongside the rachis, or the stem."

"Oh, I don't know," I answer. "Manon told me I'm not even supposed to hold a feather."

"How will you ever make anything then?" Raven says. "And take whatever Manon says lightly. If she were a bird, she would be a canary. The females weave remarkable nests and protect the hell out of them."

I snip the tangerine plume in half and swear the baby filaments flicker beneath my fingertips.

Raven runs his thumb along the feather. "Pas mal," he says.

We walk back inside his mother's study. Raven heads to the sleek floor-to-wall cabinet, climbs on a step stool, pulls out a drawer, reaches inside, and lifts a metal box. He unlatches it. Engraved on top of a large book are Latin words. When he drops the book on Mademoiselle Salomé's desk, a puff of dust spurts up.

"This is the dusty encyclopedia. No matter how much we wipe and lock it in this box, the dust always returns."

Pluma quasi lumen est is written in the center and beneath is the drawing of a curvy crimson feather with a fluffy tip.

"As light as a feather," I murmur.

Raven flips through the book and shows me hundreds of plumes, what bird they come from, detailed descriptions, their meaning based on where they're located. Pennaceous feathers are also called contour or vaned, and their purpose is to insulate. Remiges are flight feathers and filoplumes are hair-like and decorative. I moon over a section sorted by color. There is also a list of where to find molted plumes. One page catalogues various abandoned barns in France.

"Where did you find this?" I say.

"Mother swears that once on a long journey she dug the encyclopedia up from deep inside the heart of the Amazon rainforest."

I look up at him and smile. He quirks up his mouth.

I'm about to ask him why he chose to spend time with me today, and tell him how appreciative I am that he did, but the door to the boutique flings opens and everyone returns. Raven bangs the encyclopedia shut, places it back into the metal box, then onto its shelf. As the women carry bags with bunches of new feathers, I should be happy, delighted even, at what turned out to be a plume-intensive morning, but the truth is, I am jealous of the way Raven called Manon a canary but also uneasy, as if by hanging out with the feather artist's son and not sweeping the floors, I did something wrong.

As if reading my mind, Manon juts her chin toward the empty coffee pot and the blinking voicemail full of messages and asks what on earth I got accomplished while they were away. I look to Raven for help, but he is already gone. I sweep the floors, and when I find what I think is a bright green flight feather underneath the secondhand Singer, I pick it up, run my fingers on the barbules, and know at once that this molted plume comes from a duck. I hear my father say, "Canard," and perhaps because I miss him and because I am still mad at Manon for chiding me, I don't place the feather on the worktable with other loose plumes the way I should. I slip it inside my journal.

CHAPTER 8

I continue to run errands at the boutique, read everything I can get my hands on——l'*Étude de Plume*, *Dessins et Sketchs de Mode et Costumes*, *La Broderie*, and *Les Bases de la Couture*——and practice sewing, but with my father gone I have trouble concentrating. One morning, I fall asleep in the sewing lab and that afternoon Manon asks if everything is okay. I cringe, then think of Papa's text from the night before, the one that bounced around in my head all night, saying, *Miss you, all good here.*

"Why wouldn't it be?" I say.

The hand stitcher glances nervously in Faiza's direction and quietly leaves the room. When she is gone, I take out my practice sewing and show Faiza twenty rows of smooth, straight stitches. I don't show her the bright green——viridine,

I learn—duck feather that I'd practiced sketching and sewing last night.

Faiza kisses my cheek, then says, "Bravo, poulette!"

On a windy Tuesday evening, as I begin my walk back to the 18th arrondissement, I collide into the feather artist, who tells me she's been hoping to speak to me privately. Salomé wears a linen cape and powder-blue dress pants. Her curls are pulled back into a high chignon. In the twilight, her cheekbones protrude and give her the look of someone with royal lineage. She carries a canvas bag with a baguette and a head of lettuce poking out from the top, other groceries buried inside.

She says, "Raven told me your conversation the other morning. My son admires your curiosity, Alix, and he's not easy to impress."

"Thank you," I mumble, drinking in her citrusy scent.

"Faiza is also happy with your work," she adds. "She says you are making great strides."

I should thank her again but say, "Must be luck. I should go."

Mademoiselle Salomé places a hand on my shoulder. "Where I come from there is no such thing as chance, and I hate to be nosy, but whom are you racing to?"

I look away.

"Listen," she says. "Manon tells me you are always tired, that she and Faiza found you asleep in the sewing lab. Is everything okay"—she pauses—"at home?"

Tears threaten to spill, so I glance up and take a deep breath. I never talk about Papa's absences because he always comes back. Mademoiselle Salomé waits for me to say something but when I don't, she looks up at the sky as if the infinite space above us could provide practical answers to this awkward sidewalk rencontre, then she says, "I have an idea."

She leads me back inside the boutique where I think Salomé might point me to her study and tell me to lie on the chaise like a therapist would, but the feather artist walks briskly through the parlor, into the costume room, past the sewing lab to the end of the hall. She opens the last door and signals for me to climb up a set of creaky stairs. I assume she will put me to work, ask me to organize a closet full of long strands of ribbon, or sweep the floors up here, too. But Salomé guides me into a small room, walls the color of mint, the space bare, except for a twin bed, a hardback chair, a desk, and a cottage window whose panes are flung wide open.

"I've been thinking of renting it," she declares.

A sultry breeze with the fragrant scent of rosemary blows in. I inhale, and for a moment feel the feathers, their energy pulsing below us. The thought of sleeping above them floods me with joy, but I whisper, "I don't have the money."

"This room is yours, Alix," Mademoiselle Salomé says. "In return for effort because the key to becoming skilled at something most of the time is as ma mère used to say, 'De l'huile de coude,' nothing but elbow grease. Well, that and, a smidgeon of talent and lots of curiosity."

Salomé adds that for a few years, after her divorce, she lived here, that this room was always a reprieve. She says I can use the hall bath downstairs as long as I clean up after myself, that towels are beneath the sink. She tells me I can come and go as I please, that Mille et Une Plume can be my new home going forward, at least for now. If I want it.

I don't know what to say. Why would she let a lowly intern like me stay in a place like this?

Salomé rummages through her bag and hands me my first check, the baguette, a hunk of blue cheese wrapped in paper, a knife, an apple, and an old-fashioned brass key. She says, "My intuition tells me if you live among the feathers, something special might happen."

I think of the viridine-green flight feather, how much joy one single Mille et Une Plume plume has brought me, and how living in the shop will be like a dream come true.

"Merci, Mademoiselle Salomé," I say, wringing my hands together to keep my composure.

"Also," the feather artist says, "our work in the coming weeks will explode. I'd like for you to be in charge of not only your usual responsibilities but also of preparing breakfast and lunch for all of us as a way of repayment for your lodging."

I vigorously nod.

"Good," Mademoiselle Salomé says. "Underneath the counter where the coffee pot sits are a mini fridge and dishwasher, and in one of the cabinets you will find electric burners and pots and pans. Silverware, too." Salomé fishes for her wallet, opens it, then hands me a credit card. "Use it for groceries and please, dear girl, *sleep*."

I clutch everything in my arms and before I can thank her, the feather artist swings her cape shut; says, "Bonne nuit"; and is gone. I don't know how long I hug her treasures, but eventually, I place everything on the table, walk to the opened window, and am surrounded by a sea of dark green. Way above the canopy of leaves, August dusk smears everything seashell pink. More wind blows. The gnarled oak swishes its branches, welcoming me. I drag the bed beneath the window to be as close to the leaf-sea as possible, then I sit and eat everything Salomé gave me. Once I have wiped the knife clean and slipped the key and card under the mattress, I recline on the pillow and decide Mademoiselle Salomé is an angel.

Beneath me, the boutique breathes. The feathers, I imagine, billow from the ivory bins, suspending in midair, their myriad of colors and textures merging. I wish I could tell Jeanne how this room feels like a nest, but tonight Jeanne does not hover. Her ghost is silent. Yet, here, in the thick of night, ensconced above the plumes I feel safe. Safer. And closer to Jeanne, to our goal. I climb underneath the blanket; whisper "Hear ye, hear ye"; think of the breakfast I will make in the morning; and then for the first time in months, I fall into a deep and peaceful sleep.

CHAPTER 9

The following day, I hurry to rue Jean Cocteau after work and stuff socks, undies, and T-shirts, as well as my mason jar of city feathers, in a duffel. I grab my garland of the ruddy shelduck feathers that were the first plumes I hunted for, along with my sketch paper and colored pencils, my Emily Dickinson book of poems, and a photo of Papa and me dancing. Before locking the apartment, I text Papa about my new lodging, then walk back to my new home.

A few days later, Raven shows up in the sewing lab and asks if I am enjoying my new quarters. I have plucked an indigo Asian fairy-bluebird feather and am practicing sewing it on a 1920s Charleston headband per Faiza's request. When I give Raven a shy yes, he grins, then asks me if later

I will wear the headband and perform the Charleston for everyone. Raven kicks his right foot forward, then back, while flapping his hands. His sky-blue eyes shine and perhaps because I'm rested and am finally, confidently, sewing a feather inside the boutique in front of everyone, I warm and say, "In your wildest dreams."

"You underestimate my imagination, Pixie," Raven says.

I blush and am not quite sure what to say when the director of costumes for the Paris Opera Ballet comes into the parlor to discuss *Swan Lake* tutus with Salomé and Faiza. Manon gestures for us to be quiet. I try to finish the headband, but when I ask Manon if she can aid me with serging, the tricky binding-off of an edge of cloth—a skill I don't tell her I have just discovered—she says she is busy.

Busy flirting with Raven, I think, watching them banter.

The hand stitcher pleads with Raven to come sit by her. They murmur things to each other while I try serging on my own, which is a complete failure. After lunch, Manon begins to work on a new brassière for a performance at le Crazy Horse, a near replica of the ones I admired as a little girl. Manon crosses her legs and dangles a nude flat from her toes as she glues soft rose-gold feathers of a dark-eyed junco on the bra cups. After completing the persnickety work, then gluing the Swarovski crystals in the cups' bull's-eye center, Manon takes the brassière and slides one arm through the straps, then the other.

With the feather bralette fastened at her back and eyes sparkling like the crystals themselves, Manon shimmies her shoulders and, looking at Raven, says, "Don't I look stunning?"

"Stunning indeed," Raven says, pretending to swoon, making them burst out laughing.

Feeling more than awkward, I get up to leave, when Raven stops me. "I thought you were going to do the Charleston for us, Pixie."

I think of Jeanne, how she wouldn't care about any of it and would throw the headband on and dance. Right as I am about to, Manon tugs the headband from my hands and says, "Après moi."

Manon dances, the bralette still fastened to her chest, the headband complimenting her strawberry-blond bob. Raven joins her. Faiza turns her old radio to a jazz channel and as saxes and clarinets blare, all three flap their hands and twist their feet around the sewing lab as if they were rehearsing for the stage. I think of Papa blowing into his sax, his body tipping backward. The room warms, then Mademoiselle Salomé walks in. I wait, wondering what she will say, if she will reprimand everyone, but the feather artist saddles up to Raven, kicks her feet forward and back, then shakes her hands.

"Wilder!" she yells, laughing. "Make Josephine proud!"

Josephine Baker, one of Papa's favorites, whom he reveres even more than the average Frenchman.

When Faiza pulls me by the fingers and says, "Allez poulette, aren't you part of the family?" I nod, smile, and jump in.

That night, I am still giddy from our dance party when the front door opens and a ravishing girl walks in. Almost as tall as Salomé, she wears a black jumpsuit and pointy-toe boots. Two platinum braids reach her hips, and entwined in the blond strands are tiny neon-aquamarine feathers, a color I have never seen inside this boutique.

"You must be Alix," she says, extending her hand. "Pauline."

I smile, taken aback that she knows my name, by her warmth and age. She is hardly older than me.

Pauline and Manon kiss on the cheeks, then Pauline punches something in her phone and says, "So, girls? What's new?"

Manon tells her about the bralettes, how the soft rose-gold feathers of the dark-eyed junco were a bane to handle. Then, after a pause, she says, "And Alix lives above the feathers."

"You're joking," Pauline replies.

My face must turn crimson because Pauline says, "Don't blush, Alix. It's an honor! Sorry if I offended you." She grins and grabs my hand. "Now you'll be in the middle of the apprentice drama. I'll be coming to you for news."

Her smile is so bright I decide she didn't mean anything by it. I laugh a little and ask if she might want to check out my minty room, but she says, "Maybe later," and steps into the study where the feather artist envelops her into a hug.

I turn to Manon and say, "Do you want a tour?"

The hand stitcher follows me up the creaky stairs. Tucking a strawberry-blond wisp of hair behind her ear, she points toward the window where my feather garland is hanging and asks if she can climb onto the bed to look at it more closely. When I nod, Manon runs her hand over it in that methodic way of hers.

She says, "Aren't the simplest concepts always the prettiest?" Then, "Don't let Pauline draw you in. Okay? She is totally full of herself. Honestly, she should have become an actor."

"I'm not even really sure who she is," I say.

Manon sighs, sits cross-legged on the bed, then explains Pauline Bellamy is the pre-apprentice, or doigt de fée, of la Maison Lesage. That she had also studied with Pauline's mentor and that Pauline always does what she wants. That the only reason she hangs around here is because Salomé is the only main d'or, hand of gold, in France.

Manon's eyes catch on my dresser. She climbs off the bed, picks up my mason jar, then, squinting at the city feathers, she says, "What are those?"

"Feathers," I say. "From around the city. There are so many beautiful ones."

Pointing to the viridine-green duck feather I found under Faiza's chair, then stuck in the jar when I was moving in order not to lose it, Manon says, "This looks like one of ours."

I should tell her I was about to return it, that I borrowed it to practice sewing its quill on various types of material, all of which is true, but I freeze.

Manon says, "If you didn't already know, Mademoiselle is a stickler with plumes. I'm sure she'd already know if you'd taken one."

"I . . ." I pause and look down.

Before I can say anything else, Manon heads out of the room, down the stairs, and wishes me good night. I count the seconds until she and everyone else leaves, until I can return the bright green feather to its rightful place.

CHAPTER 10

One Saturday night, late August, I slip the brass key to Mille et Une Plume in my pocket and walk to the carousel at the bottom of the Sacré Cœur. The sound of Édith Piaf crooning from the speakers and the twinkling lights wrapping around the scalloped dome welcome me, and I sit on the bench closest to the manège and let the music fill me. Tourists amble and locals sit at terraces. A papa and his little girl ride on the white horses, him waving, her swinging her legs, reminding me of Papa and me when he was between gigs. The sky is still light, but a thin crescent moon shines. I try to think of the last time Jeanne and I came here, but I can't remember. The feeling is painful, like a deep wound. "Let's gallop to the center of the earth," I hear her say.

For a while, I watch the riders, then the girl with a nose piercing at the ticket booth, who sits on a stool managing a long line of customers. When I think I should get up and go, that unlike everyone else, I have no one to be here with, Blaise, the boy from my old lit class who gave me his croissant at the bus stop, finishes at the counter, and before I can hide, turns in my direction.

"Alix?"

His voice booms ocean deep again and carries so far people flocking the cafés across the street turn around. Tonight, his thick-rimmed glasses are slightly crooked, which makes me pity him. *Please go away*, I pray, but Blaise approaches me like someone might an injured fox, then drops onto the opposite end of the bench. His T-shirt has a washed-out skull printed on the front. He wears faded jeans and those obnoxious fluorescent sneakers.

"I guess we must be neighbors," he says. "Want to ride?" He holds out a ticket.

"Why do you keep offering me things?" I ask.

The carousel starts another round. The music is loud. A group of teens have climbed on the horses. I rub the brass key in my pocket.

Blaise looks to the carousel, pushes his ash-brown hair to the side, and says, "Because I'm trying to have a conversation. Like, for starters, how are you holding up?"

He takes off his glasses, and there is that baby face again.

Perhaps because it's the first time someone has asked me how I'm doing in a long time, and because I'm *not* entirely losing it, I say, "Okay."

"Ah, bien," he answers. "Bien, bien."

He shakes his head as if embarrassed, and for some reason that makes me loosen up.

"How do you know Jeanne?" I say.

"We met at a party."

Blaise explains that a waitress spilled wine all over the front of his white shirt, that Jeanne ran into the kitchen and brought out a roll of paper towels, then yanked off her oversized T-shirt and that in a black dress that clung to her like a piece of lint stuck to a dryer, she told him to go on and change into the damn thing.

"Sounds like her," I say.

"Wait, it's not over."

Blaise says that after he came out of the bathroom wearing a vintage Madonna shirt, or more precisely from the Like a Virgin tour, Jeanne took *his* shirt and poured salt on the stain, and then dabbed and dabbed until the bright burgundy turned a pale pink.

"And then," Blaise adds, "Jeanne told me to throw my shirt in the wash, that it would come out as new, and to find her in sociology first thing Monday. Because she expected her lucky vintage tee back ASAP. As if I'd keep it."

"That's Jeanne all right," I say, wishing with all my heart she was standing beside me in her ultra-tight black dress.

"How did you meet her?" Blaise asks.

I tell him it would take far too long to explain, but the truth is I don't want to offer up my Jeanne to anyone. So, I share a random incident, how Jeanne and I once climbed the Sacré Cœur steps on the windiest day of the year.

"Jeanne hoisted herself on this stone wall and spread her arms out like a bird, then sang 'Scars to Your Beautiful' at the top of her lungs. And a Japanese tourist asked for her autograph."

Blaise shoots me a smile, revealing a surprise dimple, then sighs.

"It's been hard dealing with everything," he says, "and I feel like you're the only one who might relate."

He stands up, unfolding his long body. He pulls a pen from his pocket along with a scrap of paper, scrawls something on it, then hands it to me. A Chopi receipt for milk, eggs, melons, and prosciutto. I turn it over and see an address and a phone number on the back.

"In case you ever want to talk, drop by, or whatever, text."

Without the glasses, his eyes are amber with flecks of gold, and his lashes are extra-long. He looks down at me intently, in such an unfiltered way, I nearly tell him no one can relate to my Jeanne being gone, and that he can keep his ticket, that I'm not riding the carousel without her anyway.

But Blaise continues. "I met you once, here, last spring. I must have made an indelible impression on you." He grins, and there goes the dimple again. "It was the day you got your tattoo. You and Jeanne were goofing off."

I think I do remember him stretched out on the bench like earlier but maybe with a beanie on his head on that cold spring day. I think I introduced myself in passing.

Now, I want to ask more questions about him and Jeanne, but all I say is "Thanks for the invite." I stick the receipt and the carousel ticket in my pocket.

As I walk away, I can almost see Jeanne with a redhead making out against our school building. I see her holding hands with this really cute drummer with dirty blond hair from another school, then I see her in the passenger seat of the Renault twirling her red-heart key chain beside what would become her final boyfriend, the dark-haired guy with a five-o'clock shadow. All boys who turned her bones to liquid, I guess.

"I don't mean to be rude," I add as I turn back to him. "But you're far from the only boy Jeanne hung out with and I'm not going to comfort every guy she charmed. Okay?"

I assume Blaise will tell me Jeanne loved him the most because Jeanne had that effect on people, but instead, he says, "Don't worry. I can comfort myself."

Inside Mille et Une Plume, I shriek when Raven pokes his head in from the sewing lab. His lips curve into the beginning of a smile, the aggravatingly sexy kind. I fold my arms. I wonder what he is doing here so late on a Saturday night. His sky-blue gaze and forest scent make my heart summersault.

"What do you need?" I say.

Raven beckons me into Salomé's study where he takes a roll of paper tied with a lamé ribbon off her desk, then opens the door to the courtyard. The gnarled oak seems to be waiting for us. Raven sits beneath the tree, then taps the roll of paper on the ground beside him. I sit, and under the canopy of leaves, I let out a mortifying giggle because the place feels like une cachette, a beautiful nook for hiding, and because this is the most romantic thing that's ever happened to me.

Raven says, "I don't *need* anything. And I don't think I've ever heard you laugh before."

He bumps his shoulder against mine, then loosens the ribbon, ties it around my wrist in one lovely nœud papillon, and as his fingers brush against my skin, my stomach now, like my heart earlier, does a strange flip. Raven unrolls the parchment, hands it to me. I stare at a drawing titled *Balançoire*. The paper is rough between my hands, and the charcoal is smeared in various places. It's a sketch of a girl on a swing with a giant pair of wings. She holds onto the chains, head down, staring at her bare feet. Her ankles are crossed, and she seems as if she's carrying the weight of the world on her shoulders. In a nightshirt, she is slender, short haired, and reminds me of me.

I think of Jeanne and perhaps because our backs are pushed against the oak, or because I spoke about her with Blaise and survived, or because I trust the leaves above our heads, I say, "My friend was on the brink of becoming a famous singer. Her name was Jeanne. She died in June. You would have loved her. Everybody did."

"I'm sorry, Pixie," Raven says.

He tugs on the ribbon around my wrist. Heat creeps into my cheeks. Night has fallen and stars peer through the leaves. For a moment, I imagine having worked at the boutique for years, dating Raven, putting my head on his shoulder. Then telling him about things like how my mother left. How sometimes I feel as invisible as the night. How the feeling frightens me. Or how I long for wings to extend from behind my shoulders, how if I twirl fast enough with them, I might take off into the sky and combust. The relief in that.

"Have you always loved feathers?" Raven says.

"Yeah," I answer.

The plumes inside Salomé's study awaken, making me tingle, but Raven pulls out a joint from his pocket and lights it. Eyes closed, he sucks on the joint, then passes it to me, its tip dark and wet.

"I don't smoke," I say.

Raven takes another drag, blond curls brushing his jaw. "No?"

I think of Jeanne slurring her words this spring, popping blue pills, how stained her fingers always were from nicotine. The stench of marijuana. Then and now. Papa so drunk one night he couldn't open the door to the apartment, so he slept on the landing. I wave my hand in front of my nose.

"That bad?" Raven says, laughing. "Have you ever gotten drunk?"

If it wasn't for the night enveloping us, Raven would see my blotchy cheeks, the red spreading into my neck. I'm about to stand and bid him adieu when Raven leans in so close his silver coin dangles near my nose.

"Ever kiss someone, Pixie? Ever been in love?"

The ground is damp. Moss spreads at the root of the trunk and tickles my palms. I think of Jeanne coming back from mysterious places at night, lips swollen, telling me about the way a boy's hands could make her forget everything, and I hate my silly heart for tossing around inside my chest.

"I take it the answer is no," Raven says.

I get to my feet and head toward the door but freeze, when Raven calls out, "Alix!"

He's never said my name before.

Eyes red, he hands me the drawing. "Part of creating something worthy is learning to let go, trusting your instincts."

I stand still.

"Do you feel things deeply, Pixie? Because you seem so buttoned up, like you are trying to keep the world shut out." He walks over to me and says, "You obviously don't have to smoke or drink, but you're going to have to let at least a small sliver of something in or pour a few of your feelings out."

"Bonne nuit," I say.

"As you wish, ma chérie."

Raven ties the ribbon around his neck, does a little spin, and bends into a révérence. In the courtyard, he holds me under his spell, and I think, *He could turn my bones to liquid.* For a second, I will him to kiss me, but I come to, yank the door of the study open, and walk quickly to my room. The feathers have hushed. I jump on the bed and bury my face in my pillow, heart still banging, *chérie* echoing like the last word of a sappy love song.

CHAPTER II

Sunday evening, Mademoiselle Salomé drops by the boutique. I'm sitting in the costume room practicing blind, running, and chain stitches, and hot gluing fuchsia tanager feathers on an old evening blazer. When she sees me, I say hello, and then, after a pause, I ask her if it's true that a turkey feather represents wildness, something a person cannot control. Mademoiselle Salomé holds up a finger, walks to the parlor, then comes back with a cylindrical tube and opens it.

She says, "Yes. La plume d'une dinde is a message from beyond the grave."

Salomé unfolds three posters, all depicting wings. She grabs clothespins, climbs on a stool, then the table, and attaches the posters to a rope that hangs horizontally from the ceiling.

I stare at the wings and recognize Raven's strokes. Each pair is different. One set is a pair of thick, heart-shaped angel wings. Another is light and whimsical, something a fairy might wear. The last pair is in the shape of a monarch butterfly, like the ones in the swing drawing. I blush at the memory of last night, of Raven and me.

"What are these?" I ask.

"Blueprints for Bid Day," Salomé says. "My son had a sudden burst of inspiration. Who am I to stop him?"

Before I can decide if she is being facetious or not, she adds, "Very soon, we will be transforming these sketches into wings, as tall as the ones in the parlor." Salomé smiles. "I'd like you to start thinking about what feathers we might use for each set. Their meaning, their look, their colors."

"You want *me* to think about this?" I ask.

"Didn't you come here to prove yourself?"

I nearly get up to, I don't know, kiss her or bow at her feet, but the feather artist is already headed to her study. I watch her scribble down numbers on a pad of paper, and she tells me the plot of the Dream Show: Ten angels come to earth to seduce a king using their wit and beauty.

"We will need to create sharp contrast between each dancer," Mademoiselle Salomé says. "The director also wants a set of dark, ominous wings."

I head back to the sewing room, thoughts swirling. I want to make wings, dream of it, but it feels way out of my league. I spend the next two hours working on the jacket from before until the feather artist hands me feathers from a bird-of-paradise. She tells me to practice sewing them onto the blazer's lapel because they are bigger, more complex to handle than the tanager feathers.

"Think of how you might have to cut them, the shape and the placement that will flatter that type of blazer."

After a minute of watching me stare and run my hands against the adobe-and-sunset-gold flight feathers, Mademoiselle Salomé says, "Sometimes, Alix, you remind me of a young me."

I must gawk at her, because she adds, "It's the way you connect to the plumes, how easily you grow frustrated with the thread and needle." She chuckles. "I didn't love sewing either. For me, this job was always about rendering feelings, about honoring the birds and their feathers. Yet, every little sewing choice you make matters, too."

"Mademoiselle Salomé—"

I almost tell her about my dream of wings growing from my shoulder blades, about the need to fly, about my promise to Jeanne, the desire to make her wings, except my voice turns to powder.

The feather artist gathers her belongings, then wishing me une bonne soirée, says, "Some things are hard to speak of out loud. In due time, Alix."

After her departure, I curse under my breath, tugging

at the threads, ripping out the stitches and trying again, cutting and recutting plumes. I try to push away the hard stuff, but the words and images keep bubbling to the surface. I look at Raven's sketches. I think of what he said under the oak. "You are trying to keep the world out." Well, yes, because the world is nothing but dangerous and sad. As if to prove my point, the June night I have been burying deep down for weeks and weeks comes rushing back like a spigot that suddenly came unscrewed.

It was the Friday after Jeanne and I passed our baccalauréat, after we'd run through the street with other students celebrating our high school freedom, and after she'd promised me a night out. Just the two of us.

"I'll pick you up at nine," she said. "We'll climb the Eiffel Tower to the tippy top, then pour champagne on ourselves and dance in our lingerie."

I laughed, relieved at Jeanne coming back to me, at us looking for adventure. Papa was gone again. That evening, I counted the minutes until her arrival. I smeared lipstick on and applied mascara to my lashes. I thought about dying my hair a bold color because I wanted to impress her, show her the two of us still belonged together, even after months of her hanging out with musician friends on the brink of fame, performing at nightclubs where people like Stromae and Zaz's agents had been spotted.

Nine p.m. came and went. No Jeanne. I shook off my worry and told myself she always ran late. I looked forward to the climb to the top of the tower, to telling her that on Monday I would grow brave and knock at Mademoiselle Salomé's door.

"I'm going to build you those wings, Jeanne," I heard myself say.

I closed my eyes, saw us on top of the tower shouting out our dreams, dancing in the summer breeze, skin sticky from the champagne, Paris a giant net beneath us. Our futures entwined again, the way they were always meant to be.

But at 9:45, Jeanne still wasn't there.

Then it was ten.

Ten thirty.

I was about to wash my face, scrub off the lipstick and mascara, when I heard her yelling my name out of the window. I flew down the stairs to the sidewalk ready to scold her, then hug her. But as soon as I saw the beat-up Renault, the one with a Pink Floyd bumper sticker, squeezed in a parking spot, a different kind of resentment flared. Jeanne never drove. Cars meant chauffeurs, better known as wickedly hot boys. When Jeanne poked her head out the passenger window, wisteria hair freshly dyed, then grinned, swinging her red-heart key chain and saying she'd changed her mind, that we were going to a party near the Panthéon where top music agents were invited, to hop in already, that tonight she was going to become famous, she could feel it in her blood, I said, "You're late." I prayed she would catch the pain in my voice and tell the driver she'd see him later, that best friends came first the way she'd always said, but Jeanne propped her platform boots on the dashboard and told me not to be a crybaby, to come on, that the night was young and ours for the taking. That three was better than two.

"I'm not going," I said.

"Dépêche, Alix."

I stayed feet planted on the sidewalk. "What about the Eiffel Tower? You promised."

"How old are you? Ten?" Jeanne said.

She added that maybe, just maybe, a designer, one who specialized in feathers, would be at the party, too, making her and her boyfriend whoop with laughter.

I walked back into Papa's building.

"It's a joke!" Jeanne cried.

I turned around one final time, and to make sure she knew how hurt I was, I flicked her the finger.

Jeanne's boyfriend leaned into the passenger seat, kissed Jeanne on the mouth, then said, "Come and I might give you some of this, too." He pointed to himself.

Disgusted, I stood there, heart breaking, until he turned the ignition and pulled out of the parking spot so fast, he left skid marks on the road. Jeanne called after me one last time. I banged shut the apartment building door and trudged up the three flights of stairs. For the next several hours, I drew feathers after feathers. Wings. Birds in flight. Birds diving. Screeching. Over thirty blustery sketches lay around my room, some finished, others not, the strokes thick and furious. Around three a.m., in the kitchen, still angry, I turned on the TV. The next day's forecast droned, more sunshine and heat, then the anchor reported breaking news. A car earlier in the evening, he explained, collided into a guardrail at high speed off the Boulevard Périphérique, shutting down all eight lanes near la Porte-Dauphine. Traffic in that area was still slow.

At first, I barely listened. I looked around for Jeanne's peanuts and Coke and extra pack of cigarettes, hoping to piss her off by eating and drinking the former and flushing the latter down the toilet.

"I'll never forgive you," I said. "I hope you're having the shittiest night of your life. I hope no one signs you."

Even if I didn't play music or sing or even if I didn't stroll around full of talent and glitter or with a saxophone draped around my neck, even if I was just a regular girl with freckles who liked plumes and who didn't kiss just *any* handsome boy, I could still have a meaningful and worthy life.

Couldn't I? I could still be loved. Couldn't I? But then the newscaster disappeared. From the side of the road a fire-fighter came on the screen. A camera lens zoomed in on the beat-up Renault, the one that hours ago had sat in front of Papa's apartment, now not only totaled but compressed, like an accordion, reduced to less than half its original size. I forgot about being angry over music, talent, or snacks, and kept staring at the TV. Glass was shattered everywhere, and the metal was so dark and twisted, it was hard to think it once had been a car. The thing is, I might never have known it was the same Renault until the firefighter picked up debris and showed us the license plate, part of a Pink Floyd bumper sticker, and one thing that was spared, a red-heart key chain.

Too light-headed to make it up the creaky stairs to the minty room, I head to Salomé's study and lie down on her chaise. The feathers ripple in their bins, warm and nebu-lous, like the salty air of the ocean. I'm not supposed to be in her study, but the feathers' energy wraps around my shoulders and helps me breathe. *You are here*, they whisper. I catch my bearings, slowly stand, then walk around, touch-ing each plume—the peacock, the burning pheasant, the bird-of-paradise, the wild parakeet, the swan, the ostrich, the indigo fairy-bluebirds. My dizziness dissipates. *You are*

here. I wish with all my heart I hadn't turned my back on Jeanne that night so that she might still be alive.

When the clock strikes midnight, I am still in Mademoiselle Salomé's study, looking out at the gnarled oak, afraid to leave the feathers. A blood moon shines through the bay window and everything glistens. I move to the albino eagle bin, pluck a handful, and arrange them in a bouquet. The plumes are warm and look like a cross between the ostrich and swan. They represent strength. They smell of blue skies. In the moonlight, they're translucent. Winter white.

"Un bouquet de courage," I murmur.

Holding onto their pink quills, I feel braver, as if the eagle's power arrowed its way through my fingertips, up my arm, and into my heart.

An idea takes hold of me.

I find my journal. In the moonlight, I sketch bouquets of feathers. In one, I draw eucalyptus leaves, which have a healing aroma, next to raw-umber wren feathers, in another straw and dried roses with coral woodpecker plumes for the loss of a first love. I make the bouquets big, medium, and small. I imagine song lyrics, poems written on lined notebook paper scraps. Secret messages, which I know Jeanne would love. Joy sparks inside my chest. Feathers, I realize, are not to be kept but meant to be given. Without thinking, I place all but one of the eagle feathers back in their bin, then holding onto the smallest one, I exit the boutique.

Rue d'Orchampt is deserted. I hurry down to le Bateau-Lavoir, make a left on rue des Trois Frères, and stop at the number twelve, the address Blaise gave me. I press myself against the porte cochère, my heart pounding, then push it open. I climb up to apartment fifty-one thinking I'll leave the albino feather propped against his door, but inside some-one is playing guitar. The instrument is quiet, and I can't help but lean against the banister, homesickness flooding me. This cannot be Blaise, the sweet-faced boy in neon sneakers. No. This is un homme. Someone older, who has been plucking chords for decades, who knows sound the way Salomé knows feathers.

I listen to the whines and wails, the rhythm, the tap, tap, tapping of the box, and as chords jump around, rebound, and ring, something resembling the soft cry of a thousand birds, I come to and begin to descend the stairs. Halfway down the landing, the door of apartment fifty-one flings open. I look up. In the dim flickering light of the stairwell, Blaise appears in a gray T-shirt and faded jeans, cradling an apple-red electric guitar, unplugged. His cheeks are flushed and his hair sticks up.

Without his glasses, he squints leaning into the stair-case. "Hello?"

His deep voice once again astonishes me. I'm so embar-rassed for being here in the middle of the night I flatten myself against the wall, hoping Blaise will go back inside.

What was I thinking? I hear his footsteps, then he is standing in front of me.

"I thought I heard someone," he says as if this were lunchtime and we were best friends about to stroll to the market.

I hand him the near translucent plume, which he takes between his calloused fingers.

"Thank you," he says with the slightest eyebrow raise.

It takes me a moment to find my voice, but I tell him this feather is from a white eagle, that I might have been a bit of a brat the other night, that he looked like he needed support, and that I'm sorry for his loss, too.

"Want to come up? Betty and I could use company." Blaise touches his guitar. "Don't judge," he says. "Blaise and Betty. Jeanne used to make fun of me for it. No need for you to join."

Jeanne. They were "musical" friends. I see them laughing and sharing a private joke, something about a song lyric.

But then, Blaise turns to me and says, "Sometimes saying her name out loud is hard. Isn't it?"

"Yeah," I reply.

I follow him. His apartment is messy. Blaise points to various gear and names them while taking off his guitar, making his T-shirt lift, flashing a sliver of his flat stomach. He tells me he's been playing guitar since he was four, then shows me potted herbs overflowing on the windowsills, and says, "I've also started growing stuff. Basil, thyme, dill, oregano." He pulls off a tiny piece of basil, eats it, then hands me a piece.

The taste is fragrant, like summer. I take in his futon bed, an ancient sofa with old-fashioned flowers, and decide to sit at his kitchen table.

"How long did you date?" I say.

I imagine Jeanne lounging on the futon, begging him to play. I wonder if Jeanne danced in the middle of the room or popped her blue pills with him.

Blaise drops the feather into a small glass. "I never dated her," he says. "We made music."

I roll my eyes, wishing I had befriended her musical friends so I would know who was who. "Sure," I say.

Blaise fills the coffee maker with water, spills ground beans into the filter, and starts the machine. "You don't believe me?"

As coffee drips into the pot, filling the room with earthy smells, I glance at his forearms, think of the flash of abs earlier. Jeanne loved rock stars with washboards.

"Why would it be so hard to say her name if you didn't date her?"

"Did you?" Blaise asks, then pours coffee into two chipped mugs, which he places on the table.

"She was my best friend," I say. "Like sisters. Jeanne lived with us."

Blaise sits beside me. "I know," he says. "We formed a

band for a second, the Bad Boys. I swear on my great-aunt's head." He makes a sweeping motion around the room, says, "All this is hers, Tante Constance. My parents don't love the noise I make, and my aunt is way too generous. So if something were to happen to Tante Constance, I'd be screwed. I never swear on her head."

He looks so serious I smile.

"What type of guitar is Betty anyway?" I say.

"A Gibson SG."

Blaise keeps talking like a little kid describing his newest toy, which is probably why I grow more at ease. I tell him about working at Mille et Une Plume, then about Papa, jazz, that Jeanne was more of the pop and rock 'n' roll girl, but I know he already knows.

As we sip our coffee, he shares the last few times when he and Jeanne performed at a couple outdoor events, how they joked around way too much while practicing. He says, "Jeanne had the shortest attention span of any singer on the planet, and she thought we sounded amazing even when we didn't," which makes me laugh because I know that's true, too. "She loved being the life of the party."

I tell him about her spray-painting my wall, and how once we broke into the Sacré Cœur and hid beneath the pews eating meringues. How we lounged on fountains every summer and hunted for bloodred sunsets over the Seine. How she called me a Sainte Nitouche when I wouldn't get into the water or smoke. How the first time I met her, when I was ten, she protected me from a bully by sticking gum in his hair. It's nice, the company. By the time I start down the stairs my heart still aches for Jeanne, but I feel less alone.

"Meet me Friday at the carousel?" Blaise says. "Nine p.m.?"

"Maybe," I reply.

When I'm on the sidewalk heading up the street, Blaise steps out on his balcony. It's almost dawn and the sky is slowly lighting behind him.

Cradling Betty again, he leans down and yells, "Encore merci pour ma plume."

CHAPTER 12

The next afternoon, when Mademoiselle Salomé invites me into her study, I almost tell her about my idea, how carefully constructed bouquets of plumes might help people connect to their emotions, even or especially the difficult and buried ones, and could I please be in charge of making at least a dozen, but as I am about to open up and show her all my drawings, Faiza bursts into the room, claiming we are missing an albino eagle feather.

My heart stops.

I know I should tell them I am the one who took it, but unlike last night when I was in this strange fever-like dream state, in the harsh light of day I understand that the plumes do not belong to me but to Salomé. I look at my feet. *Tell her,*

Alix. I'm sure Blaise would understand if I took the feather back from him, but everything feels too hard to explain, and, somehow, I still believe Blaise should have it. The clock ticks, and I say nothing.

Manon peeks her head in the study, holding a choker. The feathers are mauve wood, attached to three circles of mother-of-pearl.

"I stayed up late to finish the clasps," she says.

Mademoiselle Salomé gestures for Manon to hand her the necklace.

"Magnifique," she says. "Place it on the windowsill. A client of ours will want to buy it." Then Salomé asks the hand stitcher if she has seen the missing feather.

Manon shakes her head.

After the two seamstresses let themselves out, Mademoiselle Salomé stands from her desk and making her way to me, says, "Don't fret. My feathers like to play hide-and-seek. I am sure we will find it."

"Mademoiselle—" I start.

But Salomé cuts me off, then running out of the study, she adds, "Forgive me. I've just remembered. I have a meeting at the Grand Palais in less than an hour."

I wait, and when I know she's gone, I look at the bin of albino eagle feathers and am sure I see an empty space where the one I took should be.

Early evening, Manon is in the sewing lab on deadline for a new black gown, and as I am cleaning the costume area and picking up swaths of cut up cloth from the floor, Raven walks in.

He takes the cloths from my hands, tosses them on the table, and says, "I've been thinking about you. Isn't it depressing living upstairs alone?"

"No," I reply. "I have the old oak watching over me. And the feathers."

"Ah, the feathers. No wonder Mother likes you," Raven says.

He tickles my side, then drapes one of Salomé's capes around his shoulders, struts into the sewing lab, and bothers Manon, who tells him to please leave her alone, that she is overwhelmed enough as is. Coming back to me, he tucks a curl behind his ear, mimicking the hand stitcher to a tee, then mouths, *Stressed out.* I laugh but wonder what Mademoiselle Salomé would say if I tried on one of her capes without asking.

I am about to head into the parlor to find Faiza when Raven says, "Hang on." He plucks a silk scarf from a bin, steps behind me, and wraps it around my eyes.

"What are you doing?" I say.

"Playing a game."

I feel him move, and soon his fingers grab mine. I startle at his touch, but then Raven turns my hands over and drops a tiny feather into each of my palms.

"Let's see how gifted you are, Pixie."

I stand stiff as cardboard, trying not to inhale his pine scent but fail, the smell dizzying me.

"The kingfisher's plumes are almost the same size as the hummingbird's, but they're slightly thicker in the vane. A hummingbird's feather represents intelligence, and they are called the stopper of time. Tell me, which is which?"

I imagine a hummingbird in front of a flower gorging itself on nectar, its delicate green-and-pink wings buzzing. I brush the feather in my left palm, painstakingly feeling the vane.

"This is the hummingbird," I say.

Raven removes the scarf and looks at me. "Excellent, beauté," he replies. The sky blue of his eyes shines so bright I blink, and before I can pull myself together, he whispers in my ear, "Can we please hang out again soon?"

I heat up from head to toe and turn away.

CHAPTER 13

F riday evening, before closing, Mademoiselle Salomé gathers us in the costume room.

She says, "The time has finally come to build three sets of wings for the Bid Day competition. If we are lucky enough to clinch the bid, our second task will be to construct the five remaining sets for the Dream Show, as two pairs already hang in the window." She pauses, then adds, "Ten dancers. Ten pairs of wings. The wings should reveal the creator's artistry and bring the show to life but also represent Mille et Une Plume's aesthetic. Tonight," she says, glancing around, "what I would like to know is who might want to submit designs and why you think you deserve the honor."

Manon's hand shoots up. "I have the skill set, mademoiselle," she says. "I keep proving myself every day with my embroidery and attention to detail. Plus, I already have a vision for one of Raven's sketches. Those." She points to the most whimsical wings.

The feather artist thanks her.

Faiza clears her throat, then says that she knows Salomé best, and that she will honor her vision no matter what she is asked to create, that her years of sewing, gluing, fitting, and watching others in action will come in handy.

"Alix?" Mademoiselle Salomé says.

The stool I'm sitting on is hard. I search for my words, then explain that what I think I have discovered since my first day here is l'amour des plumes. "The feathers keep me afloat. It's physical. Like a sixth sense."

I think I see Salomé smile, but Manon frowns.

Jeanne hovers. Then we hear a loud thump, and when we rush inside the study startled by the noise, the door to the courtyard is open, and the Faisan de Colchide maroon plumes known for their incredible length lie on the ground like sabers.

"It's the wind," Manon says, slamming the door shut.

I pick up the plumes, put them away, and decide the hand stitcher might be right, sure, but still a piece of me believes the plumes are alive.

That evening, at the carousel, Blaise straddles a white horse. He is so tall the soles of his sneakers touch the floor, and he holds not the handlebars but the horse's ears.

I wave.

He squints from behind his glasses; yells, "I thought you weren't coming"; then turns to the kid working the ticket booth and says, "Her ride is on me."

I stand for a minute not wanting to get onto the carousel without Jeanne, and as if he could hear my thoughts, Blaise says, "Jeanne wasn't one to hold back."

He has a point, but I scowl at him anyway, hop up onto the platform, and climb onto the horse beside him, the one with a pink ribbon and faded mane. Tonight, we are the only ones spinning.

Blaise glances at me, smiles, flashing that one dimple, then says, "Did you get hung up at that costume place?"

I puff out my chest. "You mean at Mademoiselle Salomé's, the most famous feather boutique in France?"

Blaise smiles more and now two surprise dimples crease, and I can't help but smile back at him.

"What do you do there again? Build angels, wings, and things?"

That makes us laugh.

"Kind of," I answer.

"Tante Constance told me once that the shop was one of the last mystical places in Montmartre. She said a friend of hers went inside to purchase an expensive cape and saw birds flying around the ceiling and a talking raven perched in the window."

I giggle and tell Blaise about going to Mille et Une Plume three weeks after Jeanne died, how Mademoiselle Salomé took pity on me.

"God, I was a mess that day," I say. "I didn't even know how to sew, the one thing I needed to know how to do, and I lied about it."

But then I describe the ivory bins, the dusty encyclopedia, how sometimes I swear the feathers are alive and that I am lucky to live above them.

Blaise takes off his glasses.

As the carousel creaks and starts to spin again, I say, "You are going to think I am strange, but the day after the accident I woke up in that carriage." I point to the gold carriage ahead of us, then add, "I have no recollection of getting into it."

"You must have been in shock," Blaise says. "I was."

I close my eyes and remember how cold and achy I felt when I came to. The door to sadness creaks open. I shake my head. This is the first time I consider the possibility of having been in shock, but I push all those thoughts away.

"Did you always want to work with plumes?" Blaise asks.

I nod.

"It's harder than it sounds, and I still suck at sewing and embroidering even though I practice all day long. Truth is, the more time I spend there the more I'm unsure if it's what I'm meant to do."

Blaise drums his fingers on the horse's ears.

"You're taking a risk. And if the feathers don't work out, you'll find something else to love."

"I don't think so," I say.

"Why not?"

I think about how being around feathers helps me breathe.

I say, "What if you loved Betty, yet weren't good at playing her or didn't have rhythm? Or someone else played better than you? What then?"

"I'd still play. I'd create my own band. Isn't that what life is about?"

Blaise looks at me and gives me that unapologetic, forth-right stare.

Sick of spinning, I hop off the carousel and almost twist my ankle. I shake off the pain, wait for Blaise, then ask if we can walk around. Grief is back like a blanket over my head. Soon it will be fall, more than two months since Jeanne has been gone. When we get to an intersection, I must wait a little too long to cross because Blaise says, "What's the matter?"

"Nothing," I answer.

We keep walking. We pass the post office on rue Yvonne le Tac.

Blaise says, "Have you spoken to Jeanne's family since she died?"

I shake my head.

Blaise wrings his hands, and I realize it's because he seems anxious and doesn't have his guitar to hold onto.

"Do you ever wonder how everything went down that night?" he asks.

"I already know," I say, but then add, "Want to know the craziest thing? I never even learned the name of the guy who killed her."

We cross la Place des Abbesses, then push the gate to Square Jehan-Rictus open and walk to Le mur des je t'aime. I close my eyes and feel Jeanne beside me. I remember us in class whispering, walking while holding each other's elbows on the street, dancing like maniacs in the living room, feeling like the world was ours for the taking. Everything she said always felt top secret. Jeanne shone her light on everyone. I look up at the sky and nearly scream, but my voice is nowhere to be found.

Blaise tucks his hands in his pockets and leans against the gate.

I say, "I need to remember Jeanne always for the badass she was, okay? If I think of her any other way, I might lose my shit."

I cross over to a mural and trace *te amo*, then *ich liebe dich* with my index finger. The mood has changed. Blaise looks far away. I tell him I'm getting a headache, and we are quiet the whole time we walk back to rue d'Orchampt.

Near the boutique, I say, "Thanks for walking with me, but I can take it from here."

"Alix," Blaise says pausing, but then he mumbles something like, "Never mind, good night," and jogs away.

Inside the parlor, I greet the wings, run my fingers along the silver, black, and blues, and decide that hanging out with Blaise might not be the best idea after all. I want to keep Jeanne, my Jeanne, intact. I'm about to head up for the night when I hear a noise coming from out back. I tiptoe into Salomé's study, peer out the window, and find Raven standing beside the oak. Lights have been strung among the branches, and when I join him in the courtyard and look more closely, sketches of wings, more than a dozen, hang from clothespins like Christmas cards dangling from a tree.

Raven runs a hand through his curls. "Please stay. I swear I'll behave."

A car honks in the distance. Someone plays Gershwin on the piano by an opened window. The outline of his shoulders ripples beneath his shirt, and it takes everything for me not to say, "Is this how you charm all the girls?" But instead, I ask him if this is more one-on-one training.

Raven catches my eye. "If you want it to be."

I look away and say, "What if your mother asks me to design a pair of wings? I wouldn't even know where to begin."

"The same way you drew this, Pixie," he answers, reaching for my arm and gently tracing his thumb against my starling feather, making the tattoo catch on fire.

I am so hot I think I might implode, and as if Raven could feel the heat swirling under my skin, he steps forward, brushes his lips against the bridge of my nose, on my patch of freckles, and when I don't pull away but lean into him, inhaling his scent—part pine, part boy—Raven cups my face with his palms and kisses me.

The world slows.

Every cell in the universe including every single one in my body lights up. Raven's lips are soft, and when we part, I feel dizzy, illuminated, as if I grabbed all the starlight from the sky and stuffed myself silly with its beauty, and I think I now know what Jeanne meant by her bones turning to liquid. I manage a laugh, and Raven laughs, too, until he pulls me to the ground, under the old oak, and we kiss again, then lie on our backs, looking up at the lights, wings, and leaves flickering above us.

FALL

CHAPTER 14

On a glorious September day, as Manon and Faiza sit on the floor of the costume room, beginning to construct their wings, Mademoiselle Salomé requests I work on the third pair.

Manon, who is fussing with a cornflower-blue plume stuck to a prickly wire, looks up with a frown. She shoots a worried glance at Faiza, and when she asks if Raven will be a part of the construction in any way, if he will have to guide me through the entire architecture because I am obviously far too green to build Bid Day wings on my own, Mademoiselle Salomé points to Manon's work and says, "You're lucky Raven drew the blueprints. Next time—if there is a next time—you'll have to sketch, design, *and* construct."

At that, Manon goes quiet.

Salomé adds, "I will guide Alix, but remember that any project here is both an individual and a team effort."

Manon gives the smallest of nods.

For a while, I'm so stunned I just watch Faiza sort red-shouldered hawk feathers, but when Salomé asks where my head is, I close my eyes, then, trying not to cry, say that I'm a little overwhelmed but will figure things out.

"C'est normal," the feather artist says.

She tells me that once I have chosen my feathers and blueprint, the wings will lie flat on the floor, that I can begin by using wires, or light wood, like bamboo, to shape their frames, depending on how supple or stiff I want them to be. The final part will be to hand sew and glue the feathers onto the frames.

"You should breathe these wings night and day," Mademoiselle Salomé says.

She discusses the math, how every millimeter counts, the intricacies of cutting, which feathers might impress the judges and why, and how to make each plume look alive as if attached to muscle, not wire. When Raven shows up in a soft blue sweater and sits on one of the stools, I try very hard not to look at him, at the little jagged scar on his bottom lip that most might not even see, or at the silver coin around his neck, which I clasped in my hands just last night when he came into the parlor to say good night after everyone left.

Raven stretches, leaning back on his stool, then bedazzles me with one of his devilish smirks.

I can nearly smell his pine scent and feel his hands slipping under my shirt. This jolts me fully back to earth, the immeasurable task at hand finally setting in, and I blurt, "Just confirming but you want *me* to build a set of wings?"

Mademoiselle Salomé replies loud enough for everyone to hear, "Does it look like I'm joking?"

That afternoon, Manon asks me to clean up the costume room to give us more space to spread out. She suggests I get boxes at the Marché Saint-Pierre and pack up everything that's not Bid Day related.

"We want the entire area to be our stage," she explains.

I look to Raven, who is sitting beside me, hoping he will offer to go with me, but he gets up and walks away.

I trudge to the market where I purchase six boxes, which I carry back collapsed on my head. The temperature has dropped and I am cold in my T-shirt. My arms grow tired of balancing the boxes, and I bump the edges of the cardboard against a stop sign. The boxes slip and almost fall into the street gutter.

By the time I get back to Mille et Une Plume, I can't stop shivering. Raven and Manon are kneeling on the floor of the costume room discussing the width of her wings, and Faiza is comparing her frame to Raven's sketch. Beside them, I pack rows of shoes, boas, knickknacks, and dresses.

Around seven p.m., Mademoiselle Salomé turns off the lights to her study. I still have not begun my wings. Faiza waves good night. Manon wraps a beige cashmere scarf around her neck and walks out. Raven waits for his mother to depart, then he gestures for me to head toward the sewing lab and tells me to sit at the used Singer.

"Faiza can teach me," I offer.

I am embarrassed at my lack of skills, at my clumsy fingers, except Raven has followed me in the dark lab and is waiting. I turn on a light and am about to grab a book on coudre à la machine when Raven slips behind my stool and rests his hands on my shoulders. I want to shrug him off and ask what is going on between us, but my body heats beneath his touch, my cells parched for his attention, and I stay where I am.

Raven explains the terms—*power switch*, *spool spin*, *bobbin winder*, *tension dial*, *thread take-up lever*—and tells me that knowing this skill is critical, that Salomé was the best machine sewer in Paris. Maybe in all of France and Guadeloupe combined. Even better than Faiza if I can imagine. I want to tell him that Mademoiselle Salomé also said she hated sewing, but Raven adds that being an artist means not being afraid of tackling everything, especially what we are terrible at.

When he is done clarifying each part, he hands me a Renaissance-style chemisier and orders me to hem the sleeve. I sit on the stool, back straight, foot on the nonslip pedal. I glide the wide silken sleeve onto the needle plate, careful not to snag the ruffles, and I sew a semi-straight line without tangling the thread once.

"Silk doesn't lie," Raven says.

With his foot, he wheels Faiza's stool over, sits on it, points to the places where my fingers weren't pulling the fabric tightly enough, where the stitch is looser, and adds, "Tug harder next time."

He says for me to move over and takes my place at the sewing machine, and in a matter of minutes embroiders two delicate birds on the sleeve ruffles.

"*You* can machine sew that?" I say.

"Who do you think did Mother's dirty work growing up?"

"Did Salomé ask you to give me a lesson?"

"No," Raven answers. "It was my idea."

I touch a fingertip to the small, embroidered birds. "Thank you."

Raven swivels my stool until I face him. He pushes my hair away from my face, and in the dim light I reach for his silver coin, brush the raven in flight. The edges of our stools touch. Raven threads his fingers in mine, pulls me to him, and kisses me. I burn from the inside out and forget about the past few months. It's divine, like the feathers, this deep need for him, as if Raven's touch singes all the pain to ash. Yet when we part, I shiver.

Raven takes off his sweater and hands it to me. "Pour toi, Pixie."

As I pull the blue, pine-scented wool over my body, Pixie etches itself into my heart. I look at my sewing attempt, then at his embroidery, and say, "Why did you step down, Raven?"

Raven places his palm flat against his heart. "I don't love it here anymore. Or maybe I never loved it in the first place."

My jaw must go slack because Raven laughs a little, walks into the parlor, then blows me a kiss and says, "The plumes and I have faith you."

After he leaves, I sit in the costume room, at the work-table, dizzy for several long moments, then tiptoe inside the study and run my hands along the ivory bins. It isn't until I am near the purple peacock plumes—the dusty lavender, smoky grape, and wisteria—that I whisper, "Those, right, Jeanne?"

Bold. Bright. Feminine. Bigger than life.

I am certain Jeanne would approve. I pluck a feather and touch the electric-blue-and-turquoise eyes, or ocelli as Mademoiselle Salomé would say, then I climb on the table, lift the plume to Raven's middle drawing, to the heart-shaped wings. I imagine the peacock feathers cascading upside down.

Yes, I think.

Satisfied with my choice, I again sit at the sewing machine to practice. I hem and hem and hem until all I know is the fabric beneath my fingers and the whir of the motor. Silk, cotton, jersey, long and short stitches, wide and narrow. Once, the thread gets caught and knots. I patiently thread and rethread. As hours tick by, my eyes burn. Still, I stitch. Perhaps because I am overly tired, or because I fall asleep at the machine, Jeanne appears. She kneels beside me, then bursts into song. I want to tell her about Raven, about Blaise, about the wings. I want to tell her I miss her more than all the bloodred sunsets in the world, but when I sit up straight, open my eyes, and say, "Look," then reach for the peacock feather and turn back around, she's gone. Alone, in the sewing lab, I hold my head in my hands, blink until the tears stop falling, then tug on the thread and start the machine again.

CHAPTER 15

Days later, on a blustery night, I go for a walk. The wind numbs my cheeks. I walk past le Bateau-Lavoir, down rue Lepic until I find myself in front of 12 rue des Trois Frères. I march up to apartment fifty-one, knock, and when Blaise opens the door, I say, "Hi."

"Hi," he replies.

Tonight, Blaise is in his faded jeans, barefoot. He wears a black hoodie and a red apron with the words *Grand Chef* on it, and whatever he is cooking smells delicious.

I say, "Will you come visit Jeanne? I'm afraid to go by myself."

"Now?" he says.

"Yes," I answer. I don't tell him I'm worried I ruined my

wings earlier, or how I missed Papa's phone call and grew homesick at his voicemail.

Blaise readjusts his glasses. "Sure, hang on."

I lean against the door and watch him walk back inside, turn off the stove, take off his apron, lace his sneakers, put on his beanie, and then turn around to meet me in the hallway.

"Merci, Grand Chef," I say, and because I'm beyond grateful for his *sure*, I rise on my tiptoes and kiss his cheek.

Blaise smells like fresh laundry, and when I pull away, one of his dimples makes an appearance.

"Anytime."

We don't speak as we make our way to the cemetery. Once in a while, when we pass someone, Blaise booms, "Bonsoir," making people smile. Leaves blow off the trees. A few mothers push strollers with blankets covering their toddlers, and when Blaise picks up a fallen pacifier and returns it to its owner, the mother says to me, "Lucky you. He is a hottie and nice."

Blaise laughs.

As we walk through the gates, I realize I have never visited a cemetery at night. The lights illuminate the tombstones, and the place feels more like a garden full of hills than a graveyard. We find Jeanne. As I'm about to sit beside her, Blaise reaches for my hand and says, "I can go and come back if you need time alone with her."

"I'm good," I say. "I mean stay."

Blaise squeezes my fingers, then looks at Jeanne's neighbor. "This guy was a film producer," he says, reading the epitaph. "At least Jeanne is in good company. Right, Jeanne?"

I kneel by her tombstone and shiver. Hearing Blaise say her name as if she were standing beside us feels tragic. I say, "I heard once that people who die young and painful deaths stick around for a while. Like their energies are trapped here or something." I look up at him. "You think that's true?"

A strong gust of wind nearly takes off Blaise's beanie and I wonder if it's Jeanne.

He grabs the hat just in time, pulls it back down low on his forehead, then looks me in the eyes. "I think all of us try to make sense of something we humans have no business understanding." He kneels on the other side of Jeanne's grave and says, "Can I ask . . . Did I scare you away the other night?"

I don't know if it's because the moonlight or the lamppost nearby bathes him in a warm glow, or because the dead are listening, but I tell him the truth. "Kind of." I try to explain about *my* Jeanne versus *his*, how I want to keep my memories intact, how I am afraid I'll lose pieces of her if I begin to understand his Jeanne. "Or worse," I say. "I'll lose pieces of myself. Because Jeanne defined me in so many ways."

"How?" he asks. "I don't know if I agree. Your Jeanne. My Jeanne. Our Jeanne. I mean in the end she was her own person. And so are you, no?"

He runs his hand on Jeanne's grave and looks so caught up in memories, I say, "Are you sure you aren't in love with her? Because I swear you look like you are. And it's okay. Everyone was."

Blaise's dimples crease, and his smile lights up the entire graveyard.

"In love!"

He stands up, then removing the beanie from his head, he says, "Once and for all, Alix Leclaire—I'm not in love with Jeanne."

"Okay," I say.

"Want to know why?" He leans over, sticks his beanie on my head, offers me a hand, then pulls me to standing.

"Why?"

"Because I have a crush on someone else."

"Who?" I say.

"Ask Jeanne. She'll tell you."

I poke his side.

"Seriously."

Blaise grabs my hand and squeezes it. "Talk to her."

I want to ask her if she hates me, but I don't. Instead, I say, "I'm struggling. At the boutique, I'm having trouble building my wings, and I think Manon wants me to leave.

I don't blame her. Papa and Zanx are gone. I know, surprise!" I blink back tears and say, "I miss you."

Blaise tells Jeanne about his latest song, how Tante Constance was asking about her.

A cold wind blows, and as we shiver, Blaise says, "Let's go have some soup."

We say goodbye to Jeanne and walk back to his apartment, Blaise sharing stories about his parents, how he couldn't stay still in school and was always getting grounded for being restless. I want to tell him about Jeanne, how I should have pulled her away from the car, how we were mad at each other that night so I did the opposite—flicked her off, thought good riddance when she and her boyfriend were gone—but the words stay locked inside the fortress of my chest because I am afraid Blaise will blame me just as much as I blame myself.

A half hour later, Blaise is simmering a pot of soup on the stovetop. Something with vegetables, ginger, and garlic. I look around his apartment. Clothes are draped everywhere; the cords to his guitar are plugged into an amp. As he sets the table, he hums a Bob Dylan song. I'm about to take the silverware from his hands to help him when I get a text from Papa: *Just checking in, canard.*

I say, "Sometimes half of me hates my dad, and half of me misses him."

"That must be hard," Blaise replies, sighing.

He ladles the soup into bowls.

As we sip the broth, Blaise's glasses keep fogging up. I laugh at him, then reach for them and take them off.

"Thanks," Blaise says, dimples creasing.

We devour our first bowls, then each get another, and Blaise tells me his parents, two very kind humans, sell pharmaceuticals and tragically don't give a damn about his guitar. I tell him about my mother leaving when I was small, to please not pity me, and also about the powder puff, my journal and bouquets, Raven's wing drawings, and Manon's choker.

"Raven?" Blaise repeats. "Jeanne would have had a field day."

I turn beet red. "Jeanne would have dated him."

Blaise says he is sorry about my mom, then tilts his bowl, swallowing the last drops of soup. He takes off his hoodie and throws it on the chair next to him, then adds, "That's true about Jeanne. But the real question is are *you* in love with Raven because your cheeks are on fire, Alix Leclaire."

"Of course not," I manage, so embarrassed I'm certain the flush has traveled from the tips of my ears to my toes.

Getting up, Blaise laughs. "I'd be in love with him, too," he says. "An accomplished artist. Son to feather royalty who, I hear, is *very* good-looking."

"Did you do research on him?" I say.

Blaise takes his bowl, then mine, and drops them in the sink, the clattering startling me.

"Non," he replies. "Tante Constance told me. She knows everything and everyone." Blaise stretches, fingers nearly reaching the ceiling, then points to Betty. "This was fun, but I better get back to playing."

Before I can thank him for the soup and for coming with me to see Jeanne, Blaise straps on his guitar and strums a couple chords. Plugged in, his instrument is loud, intense. For a second, I wonder if he is jealous, but then my thoughts are swallowed by sound. I am transfixed by the long cries of his guitar and by his sinewy frame bending protectively over Betty, by the way his fingers travel up and down her neck, fingerboards, and frets.

I don't know how long I watch him. When I finally come to, I feel beyond awkward. Quickly, I wash the bowls, the spoons, and the glasses. I lay them on a towel to dry. I take off his beanie and hook it on the chair next to his hoodie, then leave, Betty's sounds following me down the street.

CHAPTER 16

A few weeks go by. Manon's copper frame, impeccably crafted, lies beside me on the floor, her left wing three-quarters done and a handful of the agami heron plumes fanned out at the top, just so. It's something a human-size Tinker Bell would wear. Faiza's wings, too, are beautiful so far, the hawk feathers long and lean. I try to use the skills Salomé has taught me, but I still cannot get the structure and scale of these peacock wings perfect. Sometimes, I touch the blue sweater Raven gave me and hope he might appear and help, but he hasn't been by in days.

That evening, Salomé stays watching me after everyone else has left, and we look at my wings. She tells me what I have done right and helps shape the upper part of the wiring, her fingers dexterously bending the copper. As I inhale her citrusy scent, then try to mimic her movements, the feather artist says, "You must turn women into birds with those wings." Salomé spreads her arms wide before gracefully lowering them, then brushing her fingers against my shoulder blades, she adds, "Think of feathers sprouting from your back, Alix. What that might be like."

"I do; I have," I blurt, but grow hot and don't tell her that sometimes I even think I feel the pain of them breaking through my skin, that the wings expand with my inhales and retract with my exhales.

"I know this is difficult," Mademoiselle Salomé says. "But remember, no day is wasted inside the boutique. Infuse these wings with what lives inside you."

Salomé wishes me a good night and I wait for her to close the door, then pray the plumes will give me a sign, but tonight they are still. I go to the parlor and study the two pairs of wings that have been hanging in the bay window for as long as I remember, both as tall and thick as the ones I am trying to build, then I sit on the floor of the costume room again to examine Manon's work.

When dawn breaks and a warm autumn light washes over me, I wake, disoriented, snuggled up next to my mound of peacock feathers. *Infuse the wings with what lives inside you.* The clock in the parlor chimes. I make coffee, then cut, measure, twist, and fasten the wire until all I know is the feeling of copper beneath my fingers, the angel shape I am creating, my thoughts faraway clouds. Only Jeanne and her megawatt smile and thirst for life flood from my heart into my fingertips into the framework. After several hours, the spine of my wings appears, a medley—part wire and canvas—no longer crooked and fragile, but curved, symmetrical, and pliable but sturdy. I live inside the wings. I tweak, pinch, hot glue, and hand sew feathers. Once in a while, I hear the rustle of the plumes in the ivory bins, and it sounds like a gentle approval.

I work for days, immersed in the feathers, and one evening when I pull back, I can almost see a Moulin Rouge dancer zigzagging across the stage with the wisteria peacock wings attached to her back.

Faiza kneels beside me, glides her fingers on the newest feathers, on the turquoise ocelli that pepper the wings, and says, "I'm proud of you, poulette."

"Merci," I say, then look at her beautiful auburn wings, drying on the floor, and whisper, "We did it."

"We did," Faiza repeats.

On the Friday afternoon before Bid Day, Mademoiselle Salomé calls my name. I am in the parlor taking a break and hurry back into the costume room where the feather artist points to my wings still lying on the floor.

"Ready?" she says.

I look over and see Manon kneeling in the corner, tinkering with her cornflower-blue wings, and Raven reclining beside her, pointing to tiny flaws on her design, suggesting how to fix them. I force myself not to stare, but I find I am more depleted than jealous, emptied from days of nonstop building. My fingers are sore, bruised, and sticky from glue. I'm about to ask Mademoiselle what I should ready myself for when Manon asks, "What do you think Pauline is building? She hasn't come around in a while."

"Your guess is as good as mine," Mademoiselle Salomé replies.

I don't know why but I blurt out, "Do you think Pauline would approve of mine?"

Raven laughs. "That girl is not thinking about your work. Pauline is busy trying to outshine everyone, Pixie."

I glare at him and want to ask why the attitude and where he was the other night when I needed him, but Raven must feel my irritation because he apologizes, then says that my wings look pretty good actually. Raven adds that had he built a pair himself, he would have gone for charcoal raven wings flying midair in battle. I conjure them, their look wild, full of movement and power. Terrifying and inspiring. *Why didn't you make them?*

Mademoiselle Salomé answers for me.

"The problem with you, Raven, is that you have big ideas. If only you sat down and built them. If only you committed to something. Anything."

"Touché," Raven replies.

Mademoiselle Salomé rolls a mannequin close to my wings.

"Back to you, my dear," she says. "It's a strange feeling to watch what you have created awaken."

Clipping a harness onto their spine, Salomé pulls my wings up and hooks them onto the mannequin in one fell swoop.

The wings, abruptly vertical, pulse back and forth like a great mythical bird.

First, I think they might collapse, but when they don't, I discern a million flaws but also hard work and a nod to Jeanne. I imagine her dancing with them onstage, saying something like, "Those are badass, Alix," then I see my best friend, taking off into the night, a flash of wisteria in the sky, and my eyes fill.

"What do you think?" Mademoiselle Salomé says.

Overwhelmed by a wave of Jeanne-grief, I turn away, unable to answer.

CHAPTER 17

That weekend, when someone knocks on the door of the boutique late, I think it might be Raven having forgotten his keys, but as I look through the bay window, Pauline leans against a parked car. Her platinum hair is up in a messy twist, and she wears a pair of jeans, a sweatshirt, and beat-up Converse, like mine.

"What are you doing here?" I ask, stepping outside and locking the door behind me.

Pauline points to the boutique and says, "Why didn't you invite me in? Did everyone tell you to keep the shop like a fort?"

"You know, Bid Day secrets," I say.

Pauline laughs. "I was bored and thought you might want to go somewhere."

I raise my eyebrows. "Go somewhere with *me?*" I say. "Like where?" I conjure Jeanne and me sitting by a fountain, watching a sunset.

"You'll see."

Pauline signals for me to come along, and I grow so thrilled at the prospect of hanging out with her outside the boutique, of going somewhere new, that I'm nearly certain I'd follow her to the end of the earth if she asked.

Pauline says, "Salomé told me you've never been to a feather salon, which is very different from a feather shop."

I say, "I know. Faiza mentioned them once. Aren't salons where the feathers get traded and sold?"

"Yes," Pauline says. "And, well, I thought I should fix that."

I look up at the stars, at the night sky, and say, "It's open now?"

Pauline winks.

We hop onto a bus and make our way behind Place des Vosges. We stroll under arcades, then Pauline pushes against a wooden door with the name Coco inscribed in gold.

"Is this legal?" I say.

But as we climb a set of lacquered, circular stairs, then arrive at another door, which Pauline unlocks with a silver key, I don't really care if what we are doing is legal. I want to learn about feather salons. Pauline flicks on a light and the whole place comes to life, making me gasp.

"Welcome to Coco Chanel's salon de plumes," she says.

A crystal chandelier hangs from a vaulted ceiling. In the middle of the room is an oak table twice the size of Mademoiselle Salomé's with the two reversed *C*s etched in it, and on the table is a myriad of feathers. Some I recognize— ostrich, parrot, wild fowl—others are foreign and look like they have been dipped in glitter. Yet the ones that catch my eye resemble damselfly wings, translucent and paper-thin except they're the size of my hand, far bigger than a libellule. They lie in a haphazard pile.

"How do you even know about this place?" I ask.

Pauline says, "I know people." She grins. "Seriously. Long story, but the short of it is, I've hung around here for years. I have connections."

She lifts one of the transparent feathers, then drops it back onto the table and says, "The feathers are not categorized by type and color, but by geography, price, or by which house they will go to."

When I walk around and take it all in, the cream couches, the busts, and oodles of feathers, wondering why Pauline took me here, the pre-apprentice says, "Chanel trades plumes. This isn't the store's primary business, but still it's lucrative enough. Know how much these cost?" She points again to the oversized translucent feathers.

"No," I answer.

"Three hundred euros per plume." Pauline adds, "Salomé comes here often. She and Paul Lugubre fight for molted ones. Unless this one new, hot American designer shows, because then bets are off. He'll arrive wearing silk pajamas and raids the place like a drug deal gone bad." Pauline laughs, then says, "My boss at Lesage, thank heavens, is more flexible or maybe resourceful. She has multiple feather dealers as she is not afraid of a bloody quill."

I shiver, then run my fingertips along the damselfly feathers. "Did someone rip their wings off?"

Pauline shakes her head. "These come from a swamp in New South Wales and can get up to about ten inches in length. Men scan the water for their particular shimmer."

"Dragonflies?" I ask.

"Damselflies on steroids," Pauline corrects.

Pauline puts on music, rummages through a black-and-white hand-painted cabinet, takes out a bottle of red wine, then sits on the cream divan and says, "What shall we toast to?"

She uncorks the bottle, and when she passes it to me, I take a careful sip, then say, "What if we spill?"

"You mean the wine?"

"Duh," I reply.

"The house of Coco Chanel will buy a new divan."

I think of Papa's apartment, the old green couch, how we couldn't replace it even if we wanted to.

"Speaking of spilling," Pauline says, "did *you* make something for Bid Day?"

"Not telling," I reply.

"You did," Pauline says. "I can see it in your eyes. God, Salomé must be desperate." Catching herself, she adds, "No disrespect to you, darling, but a petite main in a renowned feather house does not usually build anything for something as significant as Bid Day." Pauline takes the bottle back and, after gulping a few more swallows, says, "Though please tell me you all didn't make Raven's medieval wings, the boring ones hanging from the clothespins?"

I try to stand, but Pauline grabs onto my sweater, Raven's sweater.

"Not telling," I say again.

"You're so transparent. Which ones did Manon make?" Pauline gives me her most wicked smile, then says, "Between you and me, you must have destabilized the hell out of her by wearing this, because you know Manon thinks winning Raven means winning the apprenticeship." Pauline tugs on the hem of my sweater again. "Are you sleeping with him?"

"Stop," I say.

Pauline hands me the bottle, but I tell her I don't want any more.

"Fine. How about we play two truths and a lie?" she says. "I'll go first. Coco Chanel was my father's great-aunt, which makes me her great-grandniece. I may or may not have a crush on you. My father's lover and I don't get along."

I don't know if it's the wine, the salon, that Pauline's charm is off the charts, or that I don't know whom I should be loyal to, but I laugh and say, "Sounds more like four things and you don't have a crush on me."

Pauline takes the bottle from my hands, drinks, then says, "I suck at this game. You're right, I don't have a crush on you. But I could, maybe. Under that shy appearance, there is something captivating." She flutters her eyelashes.

"My turn," I say. "My best friend is a Charlotte Gainsbourg wannabe. My mother abandoned me when I was ten. And my father is in Harlem right now playing jazz for a living."

Pauline looks up at the ceiling. "I'm going to say that your mother did not abandon you. Tell me that's the lie."

For some reason the way she is looking at me, suddenly worried, face free of makeup, flusters me.

"Wrong," I manage. "My best friend *was* a Charlotte Gainsbourg wannabe. She died in June in a car accident."

"For fuck's sake," Pauline says. "How old was she?"

"Eighteen," I reply.

The doigt de fée grabs my hand, pulls us from the couch, and as we walk by the desk, Pauline picks up two glittery feathers. She opens french doors onto a balcony and tells me to hold one of the plumes out in front of me. Before I can ask how expensive they are and what bird they come from,

Pauline slips a lighter from her pocket, flicks it on, swipes the flame against the tip of my feather, then hers.

"Are you nuts?" I say.

There is a crackle. Flames grow, burning the feathers side by side, and I can't help but think of Raven telling me that Salomé believes the tip of a feather represents adulthood, and that the veins are the days of our lives and the choices we make, the quill, our inner strength. I watch the life I haven't even begun burn, but then I inhale the smell of something synthetic and realize the plumes we are holding are fake, and I am beyond thankful.

"Close your eyes and make a wish," Pauline says.

I can hear another song start playing from inside the salon and whisper, "I will become Mademoiselle's apprentice."

Pauline waves her feather, which crackles like a New Year's Eve sparkler, and when the flames reach the quills, she says, "Let go."

We watch the feathers on fire swirl toward the quiet boulevard below, then extinguish.

Pauline shuts the french doors, cutting off the music.

She says, "It's a good exercise. Lighting feathers means releasing the past. Seems like you need that more than the average person."

"Sure," I reply, not believing her, knowing deep down that the past is an appendage, something heavy like a weighted blanket you must pull along with you until you die.

We turn out the lights, and on our way out, Pauline says, "I heard your wish. That's bold for someone like you."

Again, I grow hot with embarrassment. "You mean someone so new?"

"That too."

"What did you wish for?" I ask, wondering if what she means is that I'm not connected enough to become Salomé's apprentice, the way Manon is, for example, because her parents are well-known jewelers.

Pauline throws an arm around my shoulders, and says, "I can't tell you, ma belle. Wishes don't come true if you say them out loud."

CHAPTER 18

After gathering us together for a final wing check, Mademoiselle Salomé says we should look forward to Bid Day tomorrow, that there will be something for each one of us to learn, that other plumassiers might go for more extravagance but that we, at Mille et Une Plume, always stick to molted, simple, and when possible practical.

She adds, "Take the rest of the afternoon off as we will have a very long day tomorrow, and make sure you dress nicely for the event. Several heads of haute couture houses and senior editors from *Paris Match* and *Vogue* will be attending. We must look the part."

We nod.

Manon asks Raven, who strolled in late looking for drawing paper, if he wants to grab a bite but he declines.

I retire to the minty room.

When I come back downstairs around dinnertime, Raven is still in the costume room, sketching.

"I thought you'd fallen asleep," he says.

I almost tell him I was drawing, too, feather bouquets in my journal, some for grief, others for regret, more for faith and compassion, but instead I look through the leftovers and try my damnedest to stay mad at him.

I say, "You disappeared."

He turns to me and says, "Honestly, I didn't know you noticed my whereabouts or that we were serious."

"We're not," I say.

When Raven slips his arms around my waist, sky-blue eyes roaming mine, then whispers, "Too bad." He pulls me closer. "I was hoping we were, and also will you forgive me?"

Raven hangs onto my waist and whispers that he was dying to come see me while I was building the wings but that he was trying to teach me a lesson, the one about teaching someone how to fish and not fishing for them.

I soften.

"Fine," I say. "But you'll have to make it up to me."

Raven slips his fingers through mine. "Let's go out back. I don't want the feathers to spy on us."

Under the gnarled oak, with the twinkling lights unplugged, it's cold and dark. Raven presses me against the bark, his body warm, familiar hands sliding under my shirt, breath sweet and spicy, like cloves.

I giggle but then say, "I didn't mean just this. I want you to come tomorrow."

"You're killing me, Pixie," Raven says.

He tugs on my sweater, pushes up my sleeve, then traces the blue-violet ink on my skin, making me tingle.

"God, everyone will be there. You're lucky I like you."

Raven presses his lips against mine, and I take that as a yes.

I'm not prepared for what comes next, for his intensity, nor for the way he tastes of bourbon beneath the cloves, or how he slides his fingers under my bra, then down my belly button and inside my jeans. At first, I freeze and almost tell him to stop, not because I don't want to. I do. It's just that this feels different, as if more of me is at stake somehow, but then he says, "Jesus, you're beautiful." He kisses me again, this time softly, and keeps touching me until something hot, like the sun, bursts deep inside my body. I tip my head back, lose track of time and space, forget about love and stakes, and when I breathe again, Raven chuckles, removing his hand from my jeans. He pecks the tip of my nose, then pulls a joint from his pocket.

CHAPTER 19

At eight a.m. sharp, Mademoiselle Salomé enters Mille et Une Plume wearing a fossil-gray suit with a feathered cape the color of sangria and bottines to match, Raven trailing her. At the sight of his sleepy face, or at the memory of us last night, I grow so jittery I nearly drop the platter of croissants I am holding. The feather artist urges everyone to ready the wings, to inspect the protective cases, and make sure they are zipped shut.

When we've packed up the wings, Manon slips out a pale pink knitted dress and pointy pumps from a flowery overnight bag. Raven heads to the restroom, and when he comes out, his curls are slicked back, and he is wearing a navy-blue suit, a white shirt, and suede loafers. I'm thinking of the obviously way-too-casual pants and top I planned to wear and am about to ask Faiza for help when Manon calls me over. The hand stitcher rummages through one of the boxes stacked up against the wall and pulls out a long-sleeved silk black dress with pewter feathers sewn around the collar.

She says, "Mademoiselle said this here should fit you."

Manon digs more, hands me a cropped black cape made of velour, then, voice just above a whisper, says, "Today will only be a success if we team up. Because of Raven bailing from the apprenticeship, the judges will be watching our dynamic. So will everyone, even people like Pauline. Okay?"

I nod, recalling last weekend, now a secret, the glittery feathers burning as they floated down from the balcony.

"Also—" Manon pauses, unable to finish her sentence. She gives me the world's longest sigh instead, then says, "I know I should have told you earlier, but your wings are fierce."

We stand awkwardly, as if our next words might make or break us, until Manon blurts, "Friends?"

"Friends," I say.

Minutes later, I bring her to the minty room, and we change. I slip the dress and cape on. The bottom of the dress hits me above the knee and the sleeves are a tiny bit long, but the shape is flattering. Manon buttons up the pink dress and steps into her pumps.

"Do I look decent?" she says.

I nod and decide that with her blunt bob, Manon looks distinguished, like someone important.

"I owe you." I point to my outfit.

Manon grins. "Your Converse add a modern twist. Very chic. Trop Parisienne."

We laugh, then Manon climbs onto my bed to touch my garland for luck. I kneel beside her and stroke the ruddy plumes, too, thinking of my parents, of the day we gathered the feathers, and just like that whatever tension Manon and I ever felt falls away.

Downstairs, Faiza takes hold of our hands and says, "You two come back with the bid. You hear me?"

We wheel the wings out the door. Salomé orders Raven, Manon, and me to drive the truck, that she will follow in her sedan.

Raven opens the passenger's side door. "After you, Pixie."

As we drive down the narrow streets of Montmartre toward l'Opéra, me squished between Raven and Manon, I can't stop thinking about how the exquisite hand stitcher called my wings fierce and about the beautiful boy sitting beside me. *Life isn't so bad*, I tell myself. But then we get stuck behind a Coca-Cola truck. I see Jeanne sitting on the counter of Papa's apartment, drinking from a bottle and scraping off the red-and-white sticker with her bitten-down nails, then wish more than anything she were here with me.

We pull up in front of a warehouse with huge windows close to the Galeries Lafayette, and when Raven kicks the door of the truck open, the nervousness I thought was mostly under control returns with a bang. I'm first to pull out my wings, then Raven and Manon grab theirs. We roll our projects into an art gallery with an opened loft-like area where others have already begun displaying their masterpieces. La Maison Février has built Icarus, a mannequin in flight bent like a horseshoe, chest tilted toward the sky with wings the color of chestnuts flying backward. A sun made of ostrich feathers hangs above Icarus. The work is so mesmerizing I can't peel my eyes from it.

"This way," Mademoiselle Salomé urges us.

The hustle bustle is intense. When we get to the place where we will build our installation and move the wings from their busts onto thick invisible threads, I catch sight of Pauline, whose platinum braids are twisted into romantic buns. She wears an off the shoulder sweater, slim-fit pants, and thigh-high boots and is running her fingers protectively against translucent wings, the size of a billboard, attached to the back wall. I have a sudden urge to run to her, say hello, look at her wings up close, and invite her to look at mine. Pauline's wings shimmer as if she's used hundreds and hundreds of the expensive damselfly feathers she showed me the other night, and she's spray-painted the wings' edges amethyst, the exact same color as my tattoo. The word *fly*, like a signature, sits at the bottom of the right wing.

After smoothing one last feather, Pauline turns toward us, and when she notices Salomé, her face lights up. She comes over and kisses us one by one on the cheek.

"My favorite competitors," she says.

"I am delighted to see that you chose molted plumes, Pauline," Mademoiselle Salomé says, then the feather artist turns to a man who is waiting to hook our wings onto a high beam running across the ceiling. Salomé tells him that she wants the bottom tips of the larger wings to hang no more than a meter off the ground.

The man nods, then climbs up a stepladder.

To Pauline, Mademoiselle Salomé adds, "Though I'm not a fan of the paint, you have such talent. A magician."

The man fusses with the threads, then begins his work in earnest, and as Salomé tells him the wings should hang close to each other, Manon turns to me and pretends to gag.

And then, as if calling someone from another house a magician isn't painful enough, Mademoiselle Salomé says, "Pauline, I've been meaning to speak with you about something. I wonder if you might consider joining us at Mille et Une Plume? I think you'd be a fantastic addition to our team, and if we win this bid, we'll certainly need an extra pair of hands." She gestures to Manon and me. "You could teach them something different about the art of feathers than I can, and we could decide once and for all if we are a good match. If you're interested, I will chat with your current boss to make sure she is aware of the situation." She smiles. "And I have a feeling your father will be pleased at our possible partnership."

Pauline gives Salomé a kiss and says it is awfully kind of the feather artist to offer her an opportunity inside Mille et Une Plume, that she is honored. She winks at Raven, then adds, "How could I not say yes? Working under the only main d'or in Paris? A dream!"

Manon looks pale.

Raven groans. "Thanks, Mother, for keeping me informed."

Mademoiselle Salomé throws her son a look that says he has already made his choices and that she will make hers, then excuses herself because someone from *Paris Match* is here to interview her.

As soon as Salomé is swallowed by the crowd, Pauline takes a long look at our trio of wings swaying from the hooks a few feet off the ground.

She waits for the contractor to remove the ladder, then says, "Let me guess? Those are yours, Manon." She points to the cornflower-blue wings. "Some intricate work, but I think you could have done more. You sold yourself short."

Pauline runs a finger on Faiza's hawk feathers, then says, "Pretty but stiff, no?"

I wait, scared of what she will say about my wings, except Pauline circles all three of our projects again, then says, "I wish you had constructed a pair, Raven. All this talent wasted. Dommage."

Raven points toward la Maison Lesage's installation and says, "The only reason your wings will matter is because they cost a fucking fortune."

Pauline crosses her arms. "Wrong, mon chéri. My wings will win because they are of today."

The doigt de fée wiggles her fingers and takes off into the crowd, while Raven heads in the opposite direction. Manon and I put the finishing touches on the display.

"Why didn't she say anything about mine?" I ask.

"Who cares what she says," Manon replies. "She's not God. All this art stuff is subjective anyway."

We smooth and fluff each set of wings, then we hide the extension cords under a gray cloth meant to represent water. When I pull back to look at our finished project, the red-shouldered hawk, wisteria peacock, and agami heron wings sway in a loose circle, and I feel a surge of pride when I watch my idea come to life: a high-tech fan blowing sparkles in an arc onto our wings. The wings look like dusted angels mid-conversation, as if they were hovering above water at the entrance of heaven's gate.

"I can't believe Pauline is coming to Mille et Une Plume," Manon says. "She has a way of making everyone insecure."

"Maybe we'll be less overwhelmed."

Manon looks around as if to make sure we are alone, then whispers, "I left my previous position hoping to get away from her. Pauline is nothing but an arrogant pain in the ass."

"That's not true," I say.

I'm about to share the night of the burning feathers with her, when Manon does her hair behind the ear tuck and says, "You know how I told you we needed to team up today, well, we'll need to, going forward, too. If not, Pauline will take over. And that will be our worst nightmare."

I only have a moment to consider Manon's words when a voice comes through a speaker explaining the floor is now open, that everyone may check out the installations. First, several invités mosey around and stare at the work. The three judges, from la Maison Dior and les Beaux-Arts, pace around each masterpiece, scribbling inside notebooks. When they get to our wings, they run their fingers lightly against them. One of the judges, a dark-haired woman nods at the cornflower-blue wings.

"Whose idea?" she says. "I like the slender tips, the whimsical feel."

"Mine," Manon nearly cries.

"And you are?" the same woman asks me.

"Pixie," I answer, pointing to the sparkles in the air and settling on the gray cloth like an iridescent puddle beneath the wings. "Pixie Dust."

The woman laughs.

Another judge wants to know the measurements of the purple peacock flight feather, how heavy they might be. I wait for him to ask whose idea those wings were. I imagine Mademoiselle Salomé pointing to me, everyone clapping, praising the liveliness of the work, but the three judges only chat among themselves. Before moving on to the next installation, after barely brushing her fingers against Faiza's wings, the dark-haired judge asks Mademoiselle Salomé how Raven is faring, and if she has found a new apprentice?

"Pas encore," Salomé replies. "It's a complicated task, but I have something up my sleeve." She looks at Manon and me, then at Pauline in the far back, and smiles.

Once the judges are gone, Mademoiselle Salomé scrutinizes the other projects from afar. She whispers that Paul Lugubre's multicolored bolero jackets will not win because they are too haute couture and not theatrical enough for the Dream Show, but that they are the most beautifully constructed pieces in the room. She says for me to study them, that their bright feathers must have shed from a young toucan. I try to listen, but I'm nervous and disappointed the judges didn't praise my wings and I cannot think straight. I ask if I can find a bathroom, and on my way to it, someone grabs my arm. When I turn around, I see Pauline grinning at me.

"What's the matter?" she says.

I mumble that my wings obviously suck as much as she sucks at two truths and a lie.

Pauline laughs. "Honestly," she says. "I didn't think you had this kind of imagination or any three-D movement experience. I mean look at Faiza's wings. They lack motion. Plus, the color you chose is gorgeous."

I half smile, feeling a little better, and tell her Jeanne used to dye her hair that color. "Wisteria."

"How romantic."

Pauline hooks her elbow through mine, then pulling me slowly back to her installation, she adds, "Well, my wings are a nod to you. I chose amethyst after looking at your tattoo. Seemed as good a color as any to add to the damselflies."

Pauline takes my wrist, then places it close to her wings. "I'm damn good," she says.

I should be flattered, I think, except I'm not. Something about her choice of words and maybe her tone doesn't sit quite right. *Seemed as good a color as any?* I'm about to ask her what she means when Stéphanie Orlevaire walks by us, a neon-pink boa wrapped around her neck.

She says, "Is that Salomé's latest petite main?"

Pauline introduces us.

I go to shake the woman's hand, but Stéphanie Orlevaire

looks at me or my outfit pointedly, then says, "I guess anything is possible with Salomé these days. No wonder she is trying to steal my pre-apprentice."

The owner of la Maison Lesage looks at our wings floating beneath the sparkles and adds, "I'm surprised the judges let you wheel those passé things inside."

After she leaves, Pauline whispers, "Don't worry about her. She is like a porcupine. So prickly."

I'm not sure what to say or do, but then the judges ring their bell, and a voice comes over the speaker again, asking les invités to pick their favorite project and stand by it. I rush back to Mademoiselle Salomé. A crowd gathers next to Pauline's translucent wings, and another grows near Icarus and another at our installation. The atmosphere vibrates with anticipation. Manon asks if I'm all right, and when I mouth, *Later*, she nods. I try to listen, but I am rattled by everything. I suddenly think of Blaise and wish he were here because he would be truthful and impartial.

The competitors stay close to their projects like ringmasters inside a circus as if the plumes could somehow come to life and take flight. With the smallest crowd beside him, Paul Lugubre keeps a hand on his bolero jackets, while Stéphanie Orlevaire gives everyone a pinched smile as she caresses the boa around her neck.

One of the judges turns on a microphone, opens her notebook, and says, "While we agree that every piece here should be shown to the public, we have decided the top individual prize, the Prix de la Plume, will go to Pauline Bellamy for her damselfly wings." The judge pauses while everyone claps. "And now for the big prize, the house who will create the Dream Show's costumes for the Moulin Rouge's June twenty-second performance: Mademoiselle Salomé and Mille et Une Plume."

People clap and holler.

The judge adds, "Mille et Une Plume's installation exemplifies imagination though their human-size wings are still quite functional. A perfect balance. Félicitations to Pauline Bellamy and to Mademoiselle Salomé et compagnie."

Pauline and Salomé wave. By the time the applause has lessened, I turn to Raven and Manon, feeling woozy. I should be overjoyed, yet all I can think about is June 22, the date of Jeanne's death, a coincidence surely. A photographer clicks photos of Pauline, Manon, and Salomé. In the midst of gleeful shouts, I look at everyone dressed up and feel like a fraud in my borrowed dress.

I want to erase what happened or turn back time, run after Jeanne and pull her from the car. I count the days since she's been gone: 116. There is so much noise. Cameras glare. I want to crouch down, lie on my side, and dissolve into the sparkles, but I stay standing. People yell for more time and more photographs. Then Mademoiselle Salomé calls my name. Seconds later, the feather artist pulls me toward her.

She suggests I keep my chin up.

She makes me shake hands with each judge, telling them that I am her newest petite main, one with a very bright future. Beside us, Manon is busy speaking to someone she knows, and when I look for Raven, he is slouched against a far back wall. He catches my eye and blows me a kiss.

CHAPTER 20

That evening, we sit inside Chartier, a brasserie on rue du Faubourg Montmartre, and eat des steaks frites, de la dorade, and de l'agneau rôti. A gift from the feather artist. Faiza and I flank Mademoiselle Salomé while Manon and Raven sit across from us. Wine flows. As the waiter pours more in my glass and says, "Un peu plus?" I smile, nod, and sip. Then, I think of earlier, of wanting to hide inside the trio of wings, and of Blaise, and how I stopped by his apartment before heading out to dinner, longing to tell him about everything, except when I rushed up the three flights of stairs and knocked on apartment fifty-one, he wasn't there. I waited, then plucked one of the smallest pewter feathers from my dress collar, slipped it under his door, and left.

After plates of profiteroles and countless stories, Salomé tells us she has a few more announcements.

"It's been such a tumultuous day, I thought I might as well surprise you with everything at once. Pauline has given her resignation to la Maison Lesage and will join us for a trial period in a few weeks. And," Mademoiselle says, raising her glass, "as of tomorrow morning, Faiza will become ma première. She will manage our highly lucrative clients, freeing up time for the rest of us to work on the Dream Show costumes."

Faiza thanks the feather artist and I realize that she did not want the apprenticeship, after all.

Standing up, Salomé says, "À la votre! To Faiza!"

We lift our glasses, but Manon quickly brings hers down, then frowns. Uneasy at what the hand stitcher might say and at the way Raven is bumping his foot against mine under the table, I drink what's left in my glass and accept another.

"Go ahead, Manon," the feather artist says. "We are family and with the show now in our line of vision, we must trust one another, be open, and work harder than ever."

Manon clears her throat. "As you know, I would like to become your apprentice, and mostly I worry that once Pauline arrives everything will change. And not for the better. I've worked with her in the past and—"

Mademoiselle Salomé fixes Manon with her dark eyes and says, "I know you mean well, Manon, but I shall decide who works in my shop. If I were you, I would continue collaborating with everyone, and everything will work out."

"I'll try, Mademoiselle." Manon drains her glass.

The feather artist tells us how proud she is of the way we handled the pressure throughout the day, that a long time ago she would have offered to take us on a boat ride to keep on celebrating this incredible night, but that she isn't getting any younger and is sadly ready for bed. Faiza laughs and agrees, and after the waiter collects the check, both women wish us young ones a good night and head home.

On the sidewalk, I push my hair away from my eyes and feel dizzy from the wine, thankful the restaurant is close to the boutique, but as I'm about to wish them good night, Raven says, "Where to, ladies?"

Manon shrugs.

"Don't be mad." Raven drapes an arm around her, and I watch the way his hand brushes her shoulder. "Not much will change inside the boutique even if Pauline comes. My mother is pretty hardheaded."

"Still," Manon replies. "That girl is your mother's favorite person in the world. And financially and politically plugged in. She'll become the apprentice in no time."

Raven smiles. "Don't be so sure. Your wings won the bid. Not hers."

"Let's do something," Manon says.

She and Raven debate going to a dance club or a house party at a friend of Manon's.

Perhaps because of the wine swirling inside me, the dizziness making me heedless, or because I despise parties, I say, "Want to climb the Eiffel Tower?"

"The Eiffel Tower?" Manon repeats.

"I haven't gone up there in years," Raven says. "Why not?"

We slip into the metro and ride to the Champs de Mars. The Eiffel Tower blinks gold, and as we step into the elevator, I think of how Jeanne and I were going to do this together. Raven sings "Sous le ciel de Paris" off-key. Manon tells him to stick to drawing. The operator gives us a dirty look. My ears pop as we rise. When the doors slide open, I leap from the elevator onto the narrow upper deck and wish I could fly. The view is staggering. Beams of aircraft warning lights crisscross the sky like a giant spider web. A full moon looks down on us and, beneath our feet, the tower is bathed in light. Raven and Manon trail behind me. Aside from a few tourists, we are nearly the only ones up here tonight. I open my arms and twirl until I am so dizzy, I collide into the protective net.

"How much wine did you drink, Pixie?" Raven says, catching up to me, his navy-blue jacket opened wide, curls no longer slicked back but unruly from the wind.

"Some," I say. "It's been a long day." I grin, peering down from the tower.

Paris is a dot beneath me. I tell him Jeanne and I were going to take off our clothes up here, pour champagne on our bodies, and dance in our underwear. "I should have brought a speaker. We could have listened to music." I twirl and twirl again, abruptly thinking of Papa, what he would say if he saw me tonight on top of this tower, then I think of Blaise, and, for just a second, I see him in his faded jeans, barefoot, bent over Betty. I get a pang in my stomach and wish he were here, too. I almost tell Raven about him, about his wicked guitar skills. I almost say, "I know this virtuoso," but giggling and giggling instead, I say, "Have you ever thought about being a bird, about wings sprouting from your back? Have you ever thought about soaring high, high up in the sky?" *It's the wine.* I spin again, and Raven grabs my hand, pulling me closer.

He presses his lips to my ear and says, "You are out of control."

I turn to him and whisper, "I wish you would kiss me already."

It's true. Half of me wishes he would, but Raven hesitates. We look back at Manon and notice how scared, afraid of heights she is, yet how, still, she said yes to coming and is making herself look down.

"Let's dance, Manon," I shout.

"Though you are very sexy tipsy, spinning hundreds of meters above ground, we should head down." Raven points his chin toward the sky.

I look up. Behind the beams of light, storm clouds drift above our heads covering the moon. Rain is approaching fast, but no one as beautiful as Raven has ever called me sexy before and who knows when I will come back to the tip-top of the Eiffel Tower? I take off my cape. Fat raindrops begin to fall.

"Is this a dare?" Raven asks.

The elevator doors open. The operator glowers at us, but then the doors shut again and as soon as he disappears, Raven slips off his jacket, unbuttons his shirt, then pulls down his dress pants until he is in nothing but a pair of briefs and suede loafers. I take off the 1940s dress. In a pair of black bikini bottoms and a matching bra, I sway.

"Who are you?" Raven says.

Manon shrieks. "Are you serious? It's about to pour."

She looks around, and when she sees us not going anywhere, she yanks off her clothes, too. She scans for the return of the elevators, and when they do not come, Manon does a wild dance in her pumps and lace thong. Raven whistles.

Under the lights with the tower shimmering beneath us, Manon, Raven, and I move, lifting our arms, shaking our hips, jumping around, spinning, surely making Jeanne, wherever she is, proud. But then there is a loud clap of thunder. Manon screams, grabs her dress, and runs to the elevators. The rain picks up and the deck grows slippery. Laughing, Raven scoops his clothes to his chest, then runs, too. I stay an extra minute, lifting my face to the rain, asking Jeanne if she can see me, if she still loves me. My eyes sting and more rain falls.

"Pixie," Raven yells.

He and Manon are inside the elevator. Lightning strikes. The doors begin to close, rain now battering the platform so hard I can barely see. I pluck my clothes, run as fast as I can, and slip inside in the nick of time.

"That was horrible," Manon says, but she is snorting with laughter.

"I could arrest you for indecent exposure," the operator warns.

In his uniform with the gold buttons on his jacket, the kid, because that's what he is, stands soldier straight as if he were guarding not a famous tower but a person, like Marie-Antoinette herself. A faint shadow of a mustache grows on his upper lip, and he seems bogged down by life.

I say, "I'm sorry. It was my fault."

The kid glares at me.

We wait, holding our breaths, but he eventually sighs, slips a hand in his uniform pocket, gets out a piece of gum, then pops it in his mouth.

"Vous êtes de vrais tarés," he says. "Lucky I'm in a good mood."

As we slip everything back on and squirm at the wet fabrics rubbing against our skin, at the puddles growing at our feet, Raven, Manon, and I glance at one another trying not to laugh. I place the wet cape back on my shoulders. Manon tugs her pink dress. Raven lifts his jacket on top of his head and says, "Man, my loafers are ruined." When the elevator doors open, we yell good night and run as fast as we can to catch a cab. Raven instructs the driver to take us to Mille et Une Plume and we laugh the whole way back. When he pulls up to the boutique, I hop out thinking here is where we say good night, but Raven pays the cab driver and pulls Manon out of the car.

"You didn't think we were going to part ways now, did you, Pixie?" he says, lifting his eyebrow in that perfect accent circonflexe.

As he opens the shop, Manon gives me a glance that seems to say, *Sure you're up for this?*

Inside, I run up to the minty room and throw on leggings, socks, and a sweatshirt. When I come back down, Manon is not in the clothes she wore earlier this morning but in a white chemise de nuit. She hops on top of the worktable.

"Where is Raven?" I ask.

"Behind you." In his arms, Raven holds an easel, drawing papers, and pencils. He is back in a pair of trousers and dry shirt, rolled up at the sleeves. "Can I sketch you, too?"

"I'd rather draw," I say.

Manon taps the worktable, but I shake my head. She laughs, pulls her nightie up on her thigh, reclines, showing off her neck, her strawberry-blond bob falling behind her, diamond earrings glittering in the semi-dark room.

"Give me huge wings, okay, Raven?" she says. "Like Pauline's damselflies."

For a moment, I think I'm dreaming. Too much has happened today, and while dancing at the top of the tower in our underwear was exhilarating, this posing inside Mille et Une Plume with the feathers close by feels funny. Wrong even.

Raven takes my hand and says, "Come on."

"Non merci," I say, then think of us, Raven and me, beneath the oak, the drawing he made of me on the swing, our kisses, where his hands traveled. I wonder how often he and Manon have late-night drawing sessions.

Before I can try to make sense of how I'm feeling, Raven comes close and says, "Please."

I smell his pine scent and if it were earlier, or yesterday, or the day before I might have longed to grab his silver coin in my hand, to feel his lips on mine in order to swallow all the starlight in the sky and forget about the pain, but Manon is still reclining on the worktable, and there is one thing I am certain of—I do not want to pose for anyone tonight. I smile at him and say, "This isn't for me."

"I bet Jeanne would," Raven says.

At her name, the wine feels long gone and everything comes rushing back, my grief and sadness, sharper than before. I escape upstairs, throw on my Converse, then walk back through the costume room without saying good night. I slam the boutique's front door shut and hurry down rue d'Orchampt, pass le Bateau-Lavoir, left on rue Lepic until I am at 12 rue des Trois Frères. I shove the porte-cochère open, take the stairs two at a time, and knock on Blaise's door. When he opens the door, bleary-eyed, in a pair of plaid pajamas, and looks down at me through his extra-long eyelashes, I catch my breath and say, "I'm sorry for waking you." And then, I start to cry.

Blaise gently pulls me to his futon. He grabs a pillow and a blanket from his bed, throws them on the sofa, then goes to an old wooden chest, and takes out a thick fur quilt, which he hands me.

"One hundred percent grizzly bear," he says.

I think I see one of his dimples crease, but it's hard to tell because it's dark, and I'm sniffling, hiccupping, and wiping my eyes with the back of my hands.

Blaise goes to the bathroom, returns with a box of Kleenex, and hands it to me. He lies down on the sofa, and once I settle down on the futon, he adds, "Bonne nuit, Alix," as if me coming here to sleep was the most natural thing in the world.

For a while, I watch the moon shine through his window. The pots of herbs are still lined up on the sill and overflowing. I smell rosemary and thyme and wonder how Blaise keeps summer in the fall. Betty is hung on the wall. A motorcycle backfires in the distance. I pull the soft furry quilt over myself and bury my head in his pillow. The sheets are warm and smell like laundry, like him. I feel so comforted I take the longest breath of the night, then say, "Thank you for letting me crash here." But the boy doesn't answer. He is fast asleep and all I hear is him breathing.

CHAPTER 21

When I wake, I think I'm on rue Jean Cocteau in my old bed because someone is tuning an instrument, and I want to tell Papa that I have a banging headache. Except when I open my eyes, Blaise is sitting at the kitchen table, plucking his guitar in his plaid pajamas. I'm so shocked to see him I sit straight up and hold the fur over myself as if I'm naked beneath it, though I am still in my hoodie, T-shirt, leggings, and socks.

Blaise plucks a couple strings, hitting high notes, then looks in my direction. "I tried not to wake you, but it's past lunch—"

"Oh god," I say, thinking about the boutique.

"Don't worry," Blaise replies, as if he read my thoughts. "I called them this morning. I was up at six and when you were still sleeping at quarter of nine, I thought it would be a good idea to cover for you." He plays a chord, then makes the exact same sound with his voice.

"Who did you talk to?"

"A woman named Faiza who said you're fine. Everyone got the day off."

"Did she ask who you were?"

"I said your brother because I'm not trying to make Raven jealous."

"My brother?"

Blaise raps his knuckles on the amp. "Je rigole. Faiza didn't ask."

I sigh, relieved.

"What's the problem with me being your brother?" Blaise asks. "I take offense. I'd be a great brother."

For a long time, I sit and say nothing, for so long in fact that Blaise gets up and brings me a cup of coffee.

"Hungover?"

I nod, then add, "No, I mean yes, I wouldn't want you to be my brother, I don't think, and I rarely drink."

"Of course," Blaise replies. He plays another few chords.

I look up at him and say, "It's true. I already have one unstable musician in my family. No disrespect but I don't need another one."

One of Blaise's dimples creases, but he also has this fervent look in his eyes, and his expression unravels me. I'm suddenly highly aware that I am sitting in this boy's bed.

"It's cool," he says. "I'm not one to judge. But just to clarify, I might be a musician, but I'm not unstable."

Blaise appraises me. I want him to know that I'm not unstable either, so as I drink his coffee, I blurt out every little detail from yesterday morning when I first woke up to when I banged on his door last night. I even tell him about Manon reclining in her nightie on the worktable, and Raven, high, wanting to draw us.

"A nightie? Oh là là." Blaise makes a sultry face, but then, serious again, he says, "Congrats on the bid. That's huge."

"Thanks," I say, then, "I'd better get going. I've already messed up your day." I put the coffee cup on his dresser, fold the blanket, and place it back inside his chest.

"Just so you know, not everyone gets the faux-fur treatment," Blaise says, fidgeting.

My eyes are drawn to Betty, dangling in front of his chest, to his pajama pants, hanging low on his hips like his jeans. The sun is filling up his apartment and shining on him, and I wonder if Blaise has a girlfriend, or even more than one. I suddenly realize Jeanne would have rated him a ten on the wicked-hot scale. *God.* I feel dumb and awkward, like I'm crossing the line or something by still being here, by having slept on someone's cute boyfriend's futon bed.

"Sorry I barged in," I mumble, hurrying toward the door.

Blaise follows me and pulls on the hem of my hoodie.

"Alix Leclaire," he says. "You didn't mess anything up. Stop apologizing."

I catch a whiff of his fresh laundry smell and the way he says both of my names somehow makes me feel seen. I shiver though it's warm in here.

"I can play guitar later," Blaise continues. "And for your information, I was surprised to see you last night but glad. Very glad."

He slips his free hand in the pocket of his pj's and pulls out the pewter feather. The one I plucked from the 1940s dress and left under his door.

"I wanted to thank you for this."

He grins, dimples blazing. The feather sits in his palm like an offering. His fingers are calloused, and I have the urge to run my fingertips over them, but instead I say, "You were glad?"

Blaise slips the feather back in his pocket, then tugs on my hoodie again.

"Really," he answers. "Drunk and all."

I play-punch his shoulder and tell him I wasn't drunk, just momentarily panicking, except Blaise laughs and says that dancing in my underwear with colleagues on top of the Eiffel Tower late at night is not normally something people do.

Blaise says, "What do you want to do?"

"As in you and me today?"

"You looked smart from afar. Yes, us."

I play-punch him again, but this time I do it because I want to get that whiff of fresh laundry.

"Anything but feathers," I say.

Blaise hangs Betty onto the wall, then turns around and suggests a visit to Tante Constance.

My eyes grow wide. "Sure," I say. "Though I have a question?"

"Shoot."

"Will one of your girlfriends be there? Perhaps a leggy singer with a top hat and a bold lipstick?"

Blaise's dimples crease and though I know it's purely accidental my heart melts a little.

"Girlfriends?" he says, emphasizing the s. "Would you mind if there was? Because I do love myself a girl with a top hat."

I laugh. "I wouldn't mind," I say. "Just want to be prepared."

Blaise goes back to the chest, takes out a towel, and flings it across his shoulder. "I think you're a liar, Alix Leclaire." He grabs another towel, then throws it to me. "Here is the plan," he says. "I'm going to shower, then you can, if you want to, then we'll go. But with one caveat."

"What?"

"Tante Constance loves to dress up, so we'll have to, too."

Without telling me more, Blaise walks into the bathroom and shuts the door behind him.

Seconds later, I hear the water running. For some reason, I can't stop smiling. I grab another cup of coffee and sit on the sofa, knees tucked under my chin, sun washing everything clean. Life seems better, less overwhelming, like I might be able to manage it after all, and as the water keeps running, I imagine Blaise shucking off his pajamas and getting into the shower. A hot flush invades me. *Stop it*, I think, except my mind has decided to go there, galloping despite my warning. I see not Raven and me, but Blaise and me under the old oak, Blaise pushing me against the bark, far taller than Raven, calloused fingers traveling from my rib cage down to my hips, losing track of place and time, which makes me want to get up and walk into the bathroom where he is still showering. Except the water stops running, and Blaise belts out "American Woman." I gulp the rest of the coffee and go to the windowsill, pick a small piece of thyme, place it on my tongue, hoping the bitter taste will chill me out, but when that doesn't work, not even a little bit, I go to the fridge, open it, and stick my head inside.

"What are you doing in there?" Blaise says.

When I turn around, he is in nothing but a towel. It's wrapped around his hips, and he is holding it up with one hand and looking at me, head cocked, a soupçon of a smile fluttering on his lips. I turn back into the fridge, snatch an apple from the fruit bin, show it to him, and say, "I'm starving."

Tante Constance resides on Avenue Frochot, a private paved street with tall wrought iron gates in the midst of Pigalle, Paris's red-light district. A concierge lives in a small house at the entrance of the street. You must punch a code to be let in, and when we do, the concierge recognizes Blaise and says, "Madame la duchesse de Vaugirard vous attend."

"Your aunt is a duchess?" I murmur.

Blaise winks from behind his glasses.

He pulls me up the windy street, and once in while looks at my outfit and chuckles, as I am still in my hoodie and leggings, but I am also wearing a faux ermine cape and crown. A dress-up crown with rubies that match the cape. Blaise is in a gray cloak and is also wearing a crown—his has sapphires—and he carries a scepter. Trees line the cobblestones. A few cats lounge in the sunshine along courtyard walls. An old man walks by and lifts his hat. It's a cool October day, and there is a feeling of festivities in the air. We walk about halfway up the street and on our right is a place that seems from another era, Victorian.

Blaise says, "The entrance used to be for horses and carriages. See?" He points to yet another wrought iron gate, smaller this time, where he shows me the remnants of what looks like stalls. "Tantine?"

"How long has she lived here?" I ask.

"Fifty years."

I hear what I think are chicken clucks, and a small gate creaks open.

"Come in," someone says.

We walk inside and I find myself in a garden with a table and chairs and a few chickens pecking at my feet. A fat tabby cat lies on the table sunning itself, and beside the feline is a woman with snow-white hair shorter than mine and a face full of laugh lines. She wears a crown, or more like a tiara, hers dainty and so glittery I wonder if her diamonds are real. She does not wear a cape or cloak. Tante Constance is in a pair of jeans and a satin shirt embroidered with lace. Manon, no doubt, would approve of the detailed stitching.

"You must be Alix," she says, taking my hands in hers as if I was a long-lost friend.

"Enchantée," I reply.

The duchess turns to Blaise, kisses his cheek, then gestures for us to follow her into the kitchen, which is full of fresh-cut flowers and heavy draperies.

"I hear you live in the world of Salomé's plumes," Tante Constance says. "It is an honor to make the acquaintance of a young feather artist."

I blush but I'm also elated by her use of the words *feather artist* in relation to me. We chat easily about where I'm from, or what I loved best in school, and who my parents are. The way she listens, Tante Constance actually seems interested in my life, and when Blaise tells her to stop being so nosy, she waves her hand at him, then she speaks of Mille et Une Plume again with a certain wonder. She mentions Salomé's signature capes and says she always wanted to acquire one. I ask her how she knows so much about the boutique, and she tells me that she was in theater, that she worked with la Comédie Française for nearly twenty-five years, which is not surprising now that she mentions it.

"Do you know Mademoiselle Salomé?" I ask.

"Vaguely," Tante Constance answers. "I was once introduced to her after a show, but long ago when I was still young and beautiful."

You still are beautiful, I think.

Tante Constance opens her pantry, then pulls out macarons from Ladurée, the ones Jeanne sometimes got for me. I am so unprepared at the sight of the chocolate-brown box with the gold ribbon that I think I gasp, except Tante Constance does not seem to notice, or pretends not to. Then suddenly, she says, "Jeanne was the only girl I knew who loved dipping macarons in vodka."

I chuckle, then say, "You knew Jeanne?"

The duchess nods. "She was a doll, charmante."

Blaise shakes his head, then she offers me the box and I choose my favorite, raspberry flavored.

When I bite into it, I swear I sense Jeanne. The sweet fruity taste bursts in my mouth, the kitchen is comfy and warm, and I hear Jeanne's scratchy voice, see us sitting in Papa's apartment, at our bus stop, and by countless fountains.

"Memories are a bittersweet gift, aren't they?" Tante Constance says, reading my mind.

She pulls a photo album from a grand hutch and shows me Blaise when he was little. There is a photo of him with a guitar at age four. Another of him playing outside at a venue at age eleven. One at thirteen, hair long in a bandana.

"I'm the one who gave him his first guitar. I knew he would be good." Tante Constance points to him as a preschooler. "But what I didn't know is how wonderful he would turn out to be. In here especially." She taps his heart. "A prince."

"Cheers, Tantine," Blaise says, lifting his scepter.

"No wonder you like coming here," I say, jiggling his crown. "All these compliments. Don't they make your head swell?"

Tante Constance says, "Oh, he wasn't always a prince, Alix. Ask his parents. If it weren't for me, who knows where this boy would be today. Aren't I right, Blaise?"

Blaise gets up. "I came to introduce you and to give you a kiss, Tantine. I'm not here to disclose my darkest secrets. Especially not in front of this one."

From behind his thick-rimmed glasses, he looks at me in such an earnest way that for a moment I forget about his aunt and picture him at home, on rue des Trois Frères, in his plaid pajamas, in his towel, and a hot flush returns with a vengeance, which makes me stand up, too.

"Young love," Tante Constance coos. "You two are darling."

"We're just friends, de bons amis," I reply.

"Please," the duchess says. "I know love when I see it."

Blaise points his scepter at her and glares from behind his glasses.

Tante Constance laughs, then says, "I almost forgot the eggs." She rummages through her fridge and pulls out a carton, which she hands over to Blaise. "Do you need anything else?"

When he answers no, the duchess whispers something in his ear and pecks his cheek. To me, she says, "Don't be a stranger. Come visit even without the prince if you want." She waves goodbye.

At the bottom of the avenue, Blaise salutes the concierge, and once we are back out on the street, I say, "That was epic."

"Yeah," Blaise answers, squeezing his scepter and the egg carton. "Constance is something."

As we stroll down rue Victor Massé, Blaise seems pre-occupied, even gloomy.

"What's wrong?" I ask, tempted to loop my arm around his elbow.

"Nothing," he replies.

For a while, we walk. There is not a cloud in the sky. I want to stretch the hours because this is my first weekday off since I've begun working. I ask Blaise where he wants to go next, that I haven't been to les Jardins du Luxembourg in forever, that perhaps we could go, that I need an adventure. A long bus ride. I start telling him about the time Jeanne yanked me into the fountain, and the afternoon when she took me up to the top of Beaubourg where we, or she, drank champagne and we people watched in that fancy café. All these memories come back. I share them easily, then think of the very first time I met Blaise, when he jumped out of the bus and asked about Jeanne. How I ran away. I smile because now the thought of sitting side by side on a bus with him, plastic crowns crooked on our heads and fake ermine capes around our shoulders, delights me.

I say, "You were right. Jeanne belonged to all of us. We *should* tell each other our stories." I ponder that, then add, "How often did you bring her to see your aunt anyway? Those two must have loved each other."

Blaise nods. "A few times."

He readjusts his glasses and wrings his hands. The playful Blaise from earlier is gone. As we keep strolling, I imagine Jeanne inside the duchess's kitchen sitting cross-legged in her wedges, cropped top, and faux-leather pants, long wisteria hair cascading down her shoulders, and I am jealous, not just of Jeanne enjoying the flowers, the chickens, and the fat tabby cat, but I suddenly hate that Blaise, Jeanne, and Tante Constance hung out without me, that Jeanne never told me about these incredible folks, who were my neighbors.

"Did you make her dress up, too?" I say, curious.

"Look, Alix, I don't want to talk about Jeanne today."

"Okay," I say. "Can I ask why?"

Blaise thinks for a bit. "I don't know," he replies. "My heart is heavy, I guess."

In that moment, I look into his face, into his eyes full of gold specks, and just like at the carousel on that first day when I met him, Blaise looks like he might cry, and I am nearly sure he loved Jeanne far more than as a friend. My breath catches a little, but I say, pulling myself together, "I'm here for you."

Blaise says, "Rain check?"

"Deal," I say, handing him my crown and cape.

That afternoon, Papa calls. I sit in the parlor, pressing my phone tight to my ear, and tell him about Bid Day, winning, the fact that our boutique will be creating costumes for the Dream Show, my dream of making feather bouquets.

"Félicitations," Papa says.

I also tell him I'm making friends. "And I met a duchess," I say.

Papa laughs. "What about boys?"

My freckles burn. "Didn't you hear me say how busy I am?"

"Sure," Papa answers.

But he gets quiet, and I suddenly wonder if he's been drinking too much.

"How are you and Zanx?"

"Ça va," he says, then he tells me that he is proud of me and loves the idea of feather bouquets but that he has to go, something about Janco waiting for him in the lobby.

Later that night, in the minty room, I say to Jeanne, "I can't believe you didn't tell me about Tante Constance. I could have used a duchess. We could have all been friends."

I recline on my pillow, open my journal, and begin to draw a bouquet but something happens. Like a tickling inside. I see the moment when Mademoiselle Salomé lifted my wings, how they pulsed like a mythical bird, what a difference it made to see them aloft. I can't only draw them; I need to construct them, too, like the albino eagle bouquet I made on the first night when I visited Blaise.

"How long did you two date?" I ask Jeanne.

The room is quiet. Outside my window, the gnarled oak sleeps.

"For what it's worth, he is a great guy," I say.

For the rest of the night, as I sit on my floor and make my first miniature bouquets from the feathers in my mason jar, one for longing, one for melancholy, one for love and joy, I think of Jeanne, and while my heart still twists, the pain remains sharp, and the darkness is real, I think of my new friendships, too. And of Blaise, of the two of us joking in his apartment this morning, of the unexpected music he brought me. As I place my small bouquets along the wall, I wonder if his gloominess is gone, if he played Betty and felt better afterward. I smile, but it's getting late and I grow sleepy, drop into my bed, and as my eyelids begin to close, the last thing I see is Blaise with his crown on saying, "Cheers, Tantine."

CHAPTER 22

The next morning, when Manon and Raven arrive, I have swept the floors, cleaned, and made breakfast and coffee. I am back in my ripped jeans, a long sleeve T-shirt, and Converse. Raven's sweater lies on the back of a chair because I am no longer sure I want to wear it, but as soon as Raven sees it, he grabs the sweater, drapes it around my shoulders, and whispers, "T'es fâchée?" He adds, "I feel like shit about what happened when we got back from the tower. We were maybe a little inebriated. Right, Manon? Seriously. I'm sorry. Especially if I mentioned Jeanne."

"I'm sorry, too," Manon says, walking over to the coffee machine.

"Forget about it," I reply.

"Where did you end up disappearing to anyway?" Manon asks, pouring herself a cup.

"A friend's."

"Who could be more important than us, Pixie?" Raven says.

"Yeah, who?" Manon echoes.

"No one." I chuckle.

Soon, we are all drinking coffee and recalling us dancing drenched at the top of the Eiffel Tower, how upset the elevator operator was with us, and we wheeze with laughter. When we catch our breath, Manon asks if I want to help her with hand sewing molted goldfinch feathers on shoulder pads, that after making my peacock wings, I should be able do some real work around here.

"Might be tricky," she says. "But I'll show you. It's a new order from Lanvin."

"I thought you'd never ask," I answer.

Minutes later, Faiza and Mademoiselle Salomé arrive. The feather artist asks how our day off was.

"Formidable," we tell her.

We sit, even Raven, at the worktable for a morning meeting. When the phone rings and a customer knocks at the same time, Mademoiselle Salomé asks me to answer the phone and asks Faiza to handle the client. I pick up the line in Mademoiselle Salomé's study, leave the door open, and discuss possible feather choices with the costume assistant from le Crazy Horse for one of their new shows, and by the time I get back to the costume room, afraid I didn't do it right or picked the wrong plumes, Salomé gives me a thumbs-up.

"You're doing well, Alix," she says. "I liked the idea for cormorant feathers, a nice contrast to the bralettes we created earlier."

My cheeks flush with pride, then Faiza returns and Mademoiselle Salomé says that she has noticed and is excited about our new friendships, about bonds forming inside the boutique.

"Only tightly woven teams create masterpieces," she says. "And the next set of wings you will be creating very soon will have to be as, or more, beautiful than the last."

I silently groan because the thought of building anything new is not only terrifying but exhausting. Salomé says we are to help one another and that we should keep working with our journals, that hopefully the dusty encyclopedia will continue to inspire us. She assigns Manon new pieces of embroidery, the shoulder pads Manon already mentioned, a few gowns, and a wedding train for the bride of a high-level official in Dubai who wants golden eagle feathers to trail behind her, though Mademoiselle Salomé says that Faiza will be in charge of delivering the train and fitting the bride. Salomé also tells us we will be sewing pearl-gray dove feathers on a series of jackets for an upcoming fundraiser at the

Petit Palais and that she hopes Raven will jump in at least until Pauline arrives and brings us some relief. That is if the boy is still unemployed and bumming around.

Turning to him, Mademoiselle says, "Please stop coming here to steal my graphite pencils and to flirt with my girls."

Manon is so taken aback by Salomé's comment that she drops the goldfinch feathers on the floor. Faiza laughs, then tells Raven to listen to his mother, and I try not to blush again.

Raven yawns, then bumps my shoulder as if to say he'll do what he wants.

When I pull away and ask about the timeframe for the new wings, Mademoiselle tells us she is waiting to get the green light from the Dream Show director, that she is meeting with the performers to get a feel for their personalities, for what wings they might like to wear, and that she is also still mulling over who might construct the set of malevolent wings, but that the more she thinks about it, the more she believes the wings will pick the artist and not the other way around.

"Malevolent?" I repeat.

Mademoiselle nods. "Don't you remember the story of the Dream Show? Out of the ten angels who visit the king, one dancer is a bit less kind-hearted but very powerful. She lures him in yet loses his love in the end."

"So, it's certain. One of us will be creating evil wings?" Manon asks.

"Oui, ma chère," Salomé answers.

Raven claps, and Manon says, "Well, I'm sure Pauline will know exactly what to do."

Mademoiselle Salomé raises her eyebrows, but then shakes her curls, laughs, and says, "Manon, give her a chance. Pauline hasn't even arrived yet."

This new Mille et Une Plume costume room morning gathering goes on for quite a few days. In the afternoons, we turn on lights and listen to Faiza's old radio. One day, while Algerian mandoles are playing, I gaze out the window, and a long-ago memory of my mother and me hand-in-hand walking rue des Martyrs rushes in. I am in a red hat and long coat, and I can smell fresh bread. When I look up, glittery eyeshadow adorns my mother's eyelids. She calls me sa p'tite reine, her little queen, and I smile. Though the memory now feels bittersweet, my spirits lift, and as I look around the boutique, I feel like I finally belong, like I am part of something, and have found a curious but wonderful family.

CHAPTER 23

The evening before Pauline's arrival, I knock on Blaise's door, but he doesn't open. I slip a bluebird feather—one I found wedged between the wall and the industrial garbage bin—through his floor opening, then walk to the carousel, hoping he might be there. This isn't the first time I've tried to visit him since I met Tante Constance. Last Saturday morning, I climbed the stairs of his apartment complex, stood at his door, and swore I could hear his unmistakable voice. I waited, knocked again, but still, he didn't open. Thursday night, I went, hoping he would be making dinner in his Grand Chef apron, but after I knocked there was silence. I almost can't believe how much I want to tell him I miss his music. I want news about his great-aunt and her chickens, and I hope we can head to the cemetery to visit Jeanne again. I want to tell him I have an itch to make big fat feather bouquets, that I was hoping for his counsel. I want to tell him I miss him.

The closer I get to the carousel the faster I walk until I'm finally standing by the spinning dome with the lights and the white horses. A handful of moms chat and watch their six-year-olds wave, and behind the ticket counter, I see Blaise perched on a stool, beanie on, grinning back at a couple of teens, his dimples bigger than moon craters. A little boy reaches for the counter, asking for a ticket, but Blaise and the others are so into their banter that they don't notice the customer.

The little boy gets up on the tips of his toes, pounds his fist on the counter, and yells, "Yo, pals," making them look up and burst out laughing.

And then Blaise sees me.

I stand foolishly, almost elated to catch his eye, but the girl with the nose ring snatches his beanie, and Blaise grabs her by the arm, trying to get it back. *Forget it.* I spin on my heels and walk briskly away. A moment later, I hear Blaise catch up behind me, then say, "Please don't run off."

I ignore him and speed toward the boutique, but when we get near rue d'Orchampt, in front of le Bateau-Lavoir, Blaise, who is now beside me, says, "Please, Alix."

I give up and lean against the back of a bench.

Blaise says, "Sit."

But I stay standing. "I bet your friends are looking for you," I offer.

"They can wait."

It's November. Leaves are falling and the air is crisp. Blaise steps forward and takes off his beanie.

"You're something else," he says, wiping sweat from his brow. "Good thing I wore sneakers."

This makes me laugh. I playfully smack his arm, then start to apologize for running away. I am about to tell him that I thought he didn't want to see me, that I felt like I was bothering him and his friends, when Raven turns the corner. He is in a baby-blue scarf, dress pants, and woolen jacket, and he pauses, studying us, then walks over and drapes an arm around my shoulder, making me jump.

"Who's this?" he says.

Blaise plunges his hands in his pockets, then blowing nonexistent hair from his forehead, replies, "I'm Blaise. You must be Raven."

I'm so shocked to be near them both at the same time that I stand there still and quiet. There is a long, uncomfortable silence. Raven pulls me closer and asks if Blaise is a customer, if he was in the neighborhood, hoping to purchase something from the boutique.

A teasing expression dances from behind Blaise's lashes as he says, "Nah. I'm not one to wear wings much. Though I do love a good feather."

I stifle a giggle, then long to tell Raven that I will see him later, but he keeps his arm around me and says, "Want to get out of here, Pixie?"

Blaise looks at me with that frank gaze of his, and when I don't pull away, he says, "Got it. Good night," then walks off.

A knot as large as a fist lodges in my throat. I want to yell his name, go after him, but Raven urges me toward the boutique.

"How do you even know that guy?" he says.

I shrug, then feeling as small as an ant, I reply, "I think he and Jeanne dated."

Inside Mille et Une Plume, Raven locks the door and pulls me to him. I look at the silver coin resting at the base of his throat and at the tiny, jagged scar beneath his bottom lip, but all I want is to head upstairs and curl up on my bed.

"I'm exhausted," I say.

For a moment, Raven looks sad but then says, "Sweet dreams."

CHAPTER 24

The next morning, we are on pins and needles waiting for Pauline's arrival. Mademoiselle Salomé has brought pink dahlias, which she places in an ochre vase on the parlor table. She'd asked me to make a special breakfast and to clean not only the floors but the windows and to wipe the baseboards. Raven hauls in a desk, the color of ebony, for the costume room because Pauline, we hear, does not like to work at the common table. She prefers her own space, and with her experience Salomé thinks it's the least we can do. Manon pretends nothing is happening. She sits in the sewing lab, in her wingback chair, spine straight as an arrow, stitching glorious Neptune-green macaw feathers onto a new A-line evening dress. Once in a while, she tucks a wisp of strawberry-blond hair behind her ear. Faiza bustles around and keeps checking the front door as if Pauline was not another employee coming in to work but royalty in need of the red carpet.

I try not to fret. After I finish my morning work, I sit, open my journal, and think of Raven and me, of the feathers stirring, and I decide to recommit to my dream. I think of Jeanne, the promise of wings I once made her. How special I want my next pair to be.

Around noon, Salomé comes out of her study and tells us Pauline has been delayed. As soon as her back is turned, Manon pretends to wipe her forehead and I can't help but exhale because, just by looking at the extravagant dahlias, the ebony desk, and the lemon crêpes I made, I realize that when Pauline does come, Mademoiselle will favor her far more than I expected. Raven looks at Manon and me. Taking a huge bite of his crêpe, he says, "I wouldn't worry too much about Pauline. You know she'll have a probation period, right? To see if she is a good fit? Keep showing off your work."

"Easy for you to say," Manon answers. "You've given up. All you do of late is sleep and smoke your days away."

"Ouch. Someone's touchy."

Raven licks sugar off his fingers, and when Manon leaves the room, he walks over to me. My journal is open on my lap with all my bouquet sketches, and I slap it shut.

"What are you hiding? Do you have grand new visions of wings?"

"I wish," I say, cheeks burning.

Raven bends down, and before I can add anything, he kisses my lips, his sky-blue eyes engulfing me, leaving the taste of sugar on my tongue.

"I'll tell you a secret if you tell me one," he says.

My head is spinning from the kiss, with the rest of Mille et Une Plume so close by, and I wonder if Raven wants to let the world know about us. The thought makes me giddy and a little frightened. I almost grab his hand to pull him up the creaky stairs to the minty room to show him my biggest secret: my miniature feather bouquets bunched together with twine and tiny song lyrics, all of them lying in a row on my bed. All of them made from the city plumes inside my mason jar. I almost tell him I'm dying to make them larger, that I know my bouquets will brighten people's lives, that I need bigger plumes, yet something makes me stay put and keep my journal shut.

I say, "I miss Jeanne every day."

Raven musses my hair. "That's not a secret, chérie." He adds, "Here's mine: I want to get a job at a hotel's front desk, or maybe work for Nike, or travel and do odd jobs. The pressure to be like my mother, outstanding, sans pareil, suffocates the shit out of me. Out of everyone really. Doesn't it?"

187

Sans pareil rings in my ears.

I want to say no, that all I want is to be like his mother, except on my own terms, with my own artistic voice, but Manon returns, and when she sees Raven with his hand on my shoulder, she asks if she should come back later.

"Non," Raven says. He blows us each a kiss goodbye and leaves.

As soon as it's the two of us in the sewing lab, Manon looks me straight in the eyes and says, "Doesn't he sometimes remind you of a Greek god, like he'll break each and every one of us with those ridiculous eyes?"

"Ha," I reply.

After the boutique closes, I go to Mademoiselle Salomé's study. I turn on a light and move among the ivory bins, and as the feathers stir beneath my touch, something inside me unleashes. I peruse the dusty encyclopedia again and again. Unlike Raven, it's not the pressure that scares me—I don't have those same expectations wearing me down—it's time ticking away, and humans I love disappearing. I tell myself that I will only borrow Mademoiselle's feathers to see what they look like, if they hold any value. Just an exercise. First, I make un bouquet de force. I use redwood and brush hawk flight feathers with dark branches. I move onto un bouquet de fertilité with bright green, deep blue, and yellow peacock feathers, which I wrap with a thick satiny ribbon. I spot the dark gray ostrich plumes and bind them with pink chiffon

peonies and voilà! Un bouquet de dignité. I add song lyrics
to each one. After I've assembled them, on another whim,
I bring each bouquet to the bay window and display them
below the wings by the spotlights, along with the miniature
ones from my room.

I walk outside and stand in the early evening light, in the
cold, and examine my work until a woman walks up to me
and asks the price of the fertility bouquet.

"Forty-five euros," I blurt.

The woman's face lights up. "I must have it. My daughter
had a few miscarriages. I'll do anything to help."

I know I shouldn't, but I look at the woman's face, at the
worried lines across her forehead, and make a split-second
decision. I fetch, then hand her the bouquet and suggest she
place it near a window in her daughter's home so the soft
light of dawn will illuminate the feathers.

The woman presses money into my palm and thanks me.

"What's your name?" she says.

"Pixie."

Pixie Dust, I think. From that moment on, I know it will
be my nom de plume.

Minutes later, another woman wants the bouquet of
strength for her sister who is battling breast cancer. A young
man asks about the bouquet of grace for himself as he is writing a memoir on his partner's addiction. Suddenly, I think of
Mademoiselle Salomé, and as if waking from a fever dream,

I come back to, shiver, then explain that unfortunately, the bouquets are not for sale. The young man offers me two hundred fifty euros.

"Désolé, monsieur," I answer, my heart breaking.

By the time evening is over, I have run out of the boutique several times to sell all my mini bouquets. My mason jar is nearly empty. I make over a hundred euros and the unexpected bills thrill me. I prop myself on the parlor desk and sit stunned, thinking about the possibilities for the future, that Salomé might even encourage me once she sees how well they sell, and I swear the wings in the parlor sway.

Later, in bed, I conjure Papa's music notes, Jeanne singing, and Blaise playing Betty. Blaise. I wish I could tell him about these bouquets, but I remember the look on his face when Raven put his arm around me, and I remember the pledge I made to myself: plumes, plumes, and only plumes.

Pauline doesn't show for the rest of the week, and probably because the boutique is overrun by new orders and the printer breaks, no one notices the missing peacock feathers. The following weekend, I wake with another idea. I make un bouquet de joie, but this time only with scraps of fluffy mandarin duck and golden pheasant feathers, the damaged ones Salomé cannot use. I dig them straight from the garbage bin. I cut and cut until the scraps look like oak leaves and heads of dandelions. I wrap these earth-tone beauties and some baby's breath with a sleek silver ribbon. I think of the Florence + the Machine song "Sky Full of Song," write it on a piece of notebook paper, fasten it to the ribbon, and then I go visit Tante Constance.

"What a surprise," the duchess says when she sees me knocking at her gate.

Today, Blaise's great-aunt wears a black sweater dress, a wig with loads of ringlets, her tiara, and an enormous ruby on her finger.

"For you," I reply, handing her the bouquet.

She dips her face toward the feathers and says, "Is it me or are they alive?"

I grin.

Once Tante Constance has placed the bouquet in a vase, we head to her living room where we perch ourselves on armchairs she calls Napoleon fauteuils, and I tell her I'm sorry for not dressing up today, that I forgot until I was at the bottom of the wrought iron gate.

"The bouquet is its own magnificent costume."

The duchess smiles and I wonder whose sister she is. What side of Blaise's family she comes from.

"Darling," she says, "how is everything?"

I tell her all is well, but as we look out onto her garden where the chickens cluck, I grow nervous. I know the bouquet was meant for her and that my visit is about Blaise and Jeanne, but I'm not sure where to start. I run my hand on the thick upholstery and hear a clock ticking in the background.

Constance looks at me with interest.

I say, "I know Blaise and Jeanne were close."

I clear my throat, and the words come pouring out of me. I tell her that, sometimes, it becomes hard to breathe. And when I think about Jeanne in her final seconds, I get so sad, anxious, and angry I feel untethered, like I might fly away. I say I wish we all knew one another back when she was alive, that perhaps together we could have prevented her from picking the wrong friends, getting in the car with them, and dying.

Constance nods. "I think of her often. I know Blaise does, too."

"Did they ever—" *Date.* I pause.

"Visit often?"

"Yes," I say.

"She did. Blaise took Jeanne under his wing, you know, how he is."

"No. What do you mean?" I say.

"The prince always helps damsels in distress. He cannot help it. Cet amour de garçon. He has always been like that. Well, except for that one year when he, for a few months, showed terrible bouts of anger, but dieu merci for the electric guitar, the conservatory, and for rue des Trois Frères. His safe haven."

I have a million questions, but Tante Constance says, "Enough about the prince. Tell me about you."

Perhaps because Constance is holding my gaze with something that feels like compassion, I open up about Papa, and even about Zanx, how they have been gone a long while, then I tell her about my mother, how she left us when I was ten. How Laurence was a makeup artist who adored Mille et Une Plume. How she called me sa p'tite reine d'amour, which seems oddly fitting here. Tiara and all.

"You must live angry," Tante Constance says, placing her cool hand on mine. "I'd be enraged if I were you."

"Can't stay mad forever," I say with a small laugh, surprising myself.

"Right," the duchess replies, but then she sighs and pulling herself to her feet, says, "I bet you have plenty to do. Go on, dear."

I pet her tabby cat, who is lying in a patch of sun on the rug, then as we walk through the kitchen and out the door, the duchess adds, "Sometimes I think of Jeanne at the final moment, too, darling. I think of Blaise, how he might have been one, or even the last one, to see her alive, and I weep for her, for him, and for all of you, jeunes gens, who must confront death far too early."

"The last?" I repeat.

But Tante Constance has already turned away. She waves, her chickens by her feet, and closes her gate. I wave back, and as I begin my walk toward Mille et Une Plume, I have what feels like a rock in the pit of my stomach. I think back on Jeanne's accident, the news on TV, the car hitting the guardrail, and I wonder where Blaise was that night.

WINTER

CHAPTER 25

Pauline arrives in late November on a frosty day when Faiza is traveling with a caribou-feather gown to Belgium and Mademoiselle Salomé is traveling to Cannes for a feather festival. It's only Manon, Raven, and me inside the boutique. I'm finishing sewing goldfinch feathers on a set of shoulder pads, and then I have a new list of groceries to pick up, and, of course, the new wings to think about. Manon is head-down working on the Dubai wedding gown, and Raven, who should be done with the outline of the five remaining wings for the Dream Show—his mother's last big ask—is nose-deep inside his sketchbook, drawing, but what, I'm not sure.

When the front door swings open, Raven has just handed me a sketch of a girl with ruby-red wings, flared jeans, and a shaggy overgrown haircut. The angel crosses her arms so that we cannot see her bare chest, just an amethyst starling on her forearm.

"Like it?" He grins. "What about this one?"

He hands me another drawing of a girl dressed in his blue sweater with frayed wings, barefoot, the shape of my legs outlined perfectly. I'm about to tell him never to show those to anyone and to stop messing around, that we need his wing sketches, ASAP please, when Pauline breezes into the costume room, unwraps a black pashmina from her shoulders, then slaps a cardboard box onto her ebony desk.

"If it isn't the Mille et Une Plume baby crew," she says, winking, then, flashing us her most radiant smile, she tosses the pashmina over Salomé's capes, then adds, "Where are the old dames?"

"Gone for a few days," Manon answers. "And outerwear goes into the parlor closet."

I haven't seen or spoken to Pauline since Bid Day, and the truth is half of me is relieved to see her because we are working around the clock, and Pauline will help us no doubt. All that talent. Red carpet, and special treatment. But Manon did say she was an arrogant pain in the ass. And as I watch Pauline march to and from the parlor, then slam the closet door shut, I also think of the fragile balance among Manon, me, and even Raven, how one new person might upset our dynamic. The way Pauline takes up space would make you think she already owned the boutique. Raven stows away his drawings, then gets up and greets her. Manon does not.

I give Pauline a wave, finish hand sewing a final gold-finch feather on the left shoulder of a jacket, then walk over to the stores of plumes, hoping a few might inspire a new set of wings, but I've had zero inspiration of late. As the pre-apprentice strolls around looking at and touching everything, I close my eyes, breathe slowly and deeply, and remind myself that Pauline is human just like the rest of us.

"So," Pauline says. "How does it feel to be Bid Day winners, working on the wings for the Dream Show? Carrying all that magic?"

"Stressful," Manon replies.

Pauline laughs, then says, "It's so damn quiet in here." She turns on Faiza's radio, asks if we live in the fourteenth century as she fusses with the knob, and when Middle Eastern music flows from the speaker, Pauline changes the station.

"It's Faiza's radio. Her station," Manon says.

Pauline pretends to shed a little tear. "Who cares? She is not here now." She settles on a classic rock station and turns the volume up.

Electric guitars scream, and I think I see the feathers recoil in their bins. I'm transported back to Blaise's apartment, his hair sticking straight up, bent protectively over Betty. My chest tightens, but Pauline brings me back to the present. She goes between the sewing lab and costume room and caresses the feathers and the dresses, then she slips on a taffeta cream pearl cape—Mademoiselle's favorite—shaking the cape to the music until the song ends. It's a commercial, and Pauline loses interest. Dropping the cape on the back of a chair, she saunters into the study, where she takes out the dusty encyclopedia from its box and presses it to her chest. Raven trails her, and Manon turns the radio down.

Raven says, "Don't you know you're not supposed to go in there uninvited? Do you need a reminder of the house rules?"

Pauline grins, then hops on top of Salomé's desk and crosses her legs. "Love the view," she says.

It isn't until Manon yells, "Why don't you put yourself to good use and handle this other urgent gown please," that Pauline slides off the feather artist's desk, heads to the sewing lab, snags the elegant silver silk column-shaped dress from Manon's hands, eyes the neckline, and drapes the gown on her workspace. She sprinkles a handful of dove feathers on the décolleté.

With agility and speed but also playfulness, Pauline cuts the quills and hand sews the plumes. She doesn't sit. She stands and sometimes touches the feather, closes her eyes, listening, and adjusts the next feather. She snips bits of plumes here and there and exclaims, "Trop beau," when she is happy with something. By the time she lifts her head and takes a break, half the décolleté is done. She has placed one single bright red cardinal plume among the light gray. The gown, I must admit, looks stunning. Unlike Manon, whose feathers almost always look deeply etched into her gowns, Pauline's plumes are légères, barely attached, as if only hanging on silk by a thread.

I am awed at her work.

Pauline gestures toward the hem and says, "I wish I could spray-paint the shit out of the bottom or cut a slit right there." Her eyes light up. She takes a pair of scissors, slices the gown from bottom to mid-thigh and hand sews dove feathers along the opening, almost in a garland shape, like the ruddy one in my window.

Manon, who has just placed the wedding dress on a hanger, cries, "Pauline! This gown is for an older woman. I think she is in her seventies."

Pauline runs a palm on the slit and says, "She'll look divine in it. Should I keep the dress silver or spray-paint it rainbow at the bottom?"

Manon crosses her arms and inhales as if she were about to scream.

Pauline says, "Okay! Okay. Don't freak. I'll change this place one feather at a time."

Even I giggle at that, but Manon exhales loudly, then leaves the room.

Raven, who had disappeared, returns and says the vibe feels hostile. I shrug, handpick blue guinea fowl flight feathers from Kenya and baby ostrich semiplumes, then think of Jeanne and try to imagine what these feathers might look like behind a Moulin Rouge dancer but nothing clicks. I put the feathers back in the bin, and then, as I look out the window, a sliver of something begins to appear. I think of a million tiny candy-red cardinal feathers, how gorgeous they might look sewn on big Lucifer-style wings, but even I know Pauline will point out how challenging that would be to execute, how impossible male cardinal plumes are to acquire.

"Don't put so much pressure on yourself, Pixie," Raven says.

After everyone leaves the costume room, I put the radio back on Faiza's station, then pick up Mademoiselle Salomé's cream pearl cape off the back of the chair. I dust it off and hang it.

The next day, before seven a.m., Manon hurries inside the boutique.

She takes off her coat and hugging it to her chest, says, "I couldn't sleep. I'm afraid that as soon as Mademoiselle returns, she will ask us to create the next wings from scratch since Raven isn't helping."

"Isn't that what we did last time?" I ask.

Manon shakes her head. "I bet Salomé will request that we draw the wings." She emphasizes the word *draw* and looks beaten, then murmurs, "Unlike you, I can't draw. Not even a stick figure. I don't think I could dream up wings from thin air, much less put them to paper. I must have an outline. Or a design. At least a pattern."

I smile.

"It's not funny," Manon says, glaring at me.

Still clutching her coat, the hand stitcher for the first time ever seems like a regular person who is scared of failing, and it dawns on me that even with all of Manon's prior experience, her insecurities might be the reason why she sometimes snaps, that she, too, yearns to matter, and that if she doesn't become Mademoiselle Salomé's apprentice, a part of her might legitimately shatter.

"Can I tell you something?" I ask.

"Only if it's helpful," Manon answers.

I take her coat and hang it in the parlor closet. "I'll help you draw your wings."

"Vraiment?" Manon says.

"What are friends for?"

Manon tucks that wisp of strawberry-blond hair behind her ear, then folds me into the longest hug I've ever gotten.

"I love you, Pixie," she says.

I smile and almost tell her about my night burning the feathers with Pauline and my feather bouquets, but at the thought of the green, yellow, and blue peacock one I sold when I shouldn't have, at least without permission, I shrivel, and my voice shoots up somewhere high above me.

That evening, Mademoiselle Salomé and Faiza return from their trips.

And as Manon anticipated, with her purse still clutched in her hands and her luggage at her feet, the feather artist says, "Well, since I have everyone gathered here, I'd like to share that it is once again time to plunge back into building more wings." The feather artist sighs, then says, gesturing to the ceiling, "Since I do not see Raven's new sketches hanging, it will be up to you, girls, to draw them, too. Better get on it, as I'd like at least one or preferably two pairs built before Christmas."

I think I see Manon forcibly pale.

Pauline squeals with delight, and then Salomé and Faiza kiss Pauline and welcome her with such warmth, I'd think she already was the new apprentice.

On Monday, Manon, Pauline, and I open our journals and sharpen our pencils. Soon, Pauline is biting on her eraser, then furiously drawing. Once in a while, she stands up and walks around the ivory bins. She yanks out a feather, holds it to the light, inspects it, then drops it onto the floor if she doesn't like it. Eventually, she plucks a spoonbill plume, slowly runs her fingers over its long quill, then takes it back to her desk.

"Parfait," the pre-apprentice exclaims, placing the hot-pink feather on her partially drawn sketch.

I should be working, too, but I'm stuck, unable to think of any shape for my new pair of wings. I sigh, get up, walk around, pick up Pauline's discarded feathers off Mademoiselle's floor, then return them to their bins. Back at my seat, I stare at the Bid Day wings hooked on busts in the corner of the costume room, at my purple peacock feathers, and wonder if I'll ever construct another pair. Then Manon asks for help. She tries to explain what she is interested in making, what her vision is, and as she speaks, I draw a pair of playful cherub wings. By the end of the afternoon, while I have accomplished nothing of my own, Manon shows me a handful of snowy owl plumes, how small the black-and-white feathers are yet how dense and delicate they will look attached to a dancer's back.

"Do you like them?" she asks. "I mean, for the drawing you made."

I nod.

"Then, these will be *our* cherub wings," Manon whispers.

Later, just before closing, Pauline gets up from the floor, stretches, studies the frame she has already begun assembling, then, pointing to the blank papers on my lap and smirking, she says, "What kind of wings are you making, Alix? Invisible ones?"

"Don't know yet," I reply, scowling at her.

CHAPTER 26

A few days before Christmas, Raven tells me about his mother shutting down the boutique for break. We are in the costume room and perhaps because Raven hasn't been doing anything but lounging around, and I have been struggling with ideas and designs while staring at Pauline and Manon's freshly finished spoonbill and snowy owl wings, I cross my arms, huff, and say, "What are you talking about?"

Raven explains that every year Mille et Une Plume closes between Christmas Eve and New Year's Day, that everyone goes on vacation, and that his mother likes to save money on heat and water. He says, "Mother turns everything off and when we get back, we freeze for an entire morning until the heat is running again. I keep telling her the plumes don't love it, but she advises me to mind my business. Who am I to argue with her these days anyway?"

The thought of returning to rue Jean Cocteau even for just a single night makes me crumble inside. I swallow hard, then say to Raven that surely Mademoiselle Salomé will allow me to stay, right? That I don't need heat or water.

Raven laughs. "Have you been outside, Pixie? It's snowing."

Embarrassed by how desperate I am, I look away.

Raven says, "You do have a place to go back to? Right?"

"Yeah," I reluctantly reply.

"Hey." Raven pulls me into his arms and goes to kiss me, but I break our embrace, which makes him lift an eyebrow. "What's the matter? Talk to me."

I tell him it's been a long day.

"I have an idea. Let's go on a date before closing. You've only been hanging around with Manon, and I miss you."

"A date?" I repeat.

He tells me that he and Salomé will be flying to Guadeloupe on Christmas Day, that he wishes I could come with, that tomorrow after work he will take me somewhere special, like the Christmas market by the Sacré Cœur. I nod and even smile because I'm a sucker for Christmas markets, then Raven bumps his shoulder against mine, and says, "À demain alors."

"See you tomorrow," I reply.

The next morning, it's cold and gray. I try not to think of the boutique closing and dress a little fancier than usual for my date with Raven. The Christmas market does sound lovely. I put on lipstick and tuck one of Jeanne's old silk blouses into my jeans, but as I make breakfast, then lunch, and sew more of the fundraiser dove jackets in the afternoon because I still have no inspiration for wings, Raven never shows.

CHAPTER 27

On the eve of Christmas Eve, Faiza bustles into the costume room, grumbles about how she despises end of the year Sunday cleanup, then says, "At least Countdown is on. Salomé says twenty minutes to closing."

Everyone cheers.

I clear my throat and growing more anxious by the minute, I pull Faiza to the side, then say, "I wanted to celebrate Christmas with the plumes. Is there any way I can stay?"

Faiza gives me a sad smile. "No, poulette. I'm afraid not."

Pauline pokes my shoulder and laughs. "Alix, the feathers aren't pets," she says. "Don't you want to go on vacation? It's only a little more than a week."

Raven tells her to cut it out and mind her business.

I want to say that a week can feel like a miserable lifetime and that not everyone goes on vacation, but my voice again has left me and when everyone throws on their coats and Mademoiselle Salomé comes out of her study, a velour cape wrapped around her shoulders, then says she will be gathering new and rare molted plumes while she is away, I go to her. I think of Raven, how he said he wished I could come to Guadeloupe with them, and say barely above a whisper, "Can you take me with you? I'll make myself very small, nearly invisible."

The worst part is I mean it.

The feather artist gazes at me and seems to be considering my request. She says, "Never make yourself small and maybe someday, Alix."

Manon comes over, takes my hand, says that she would love to bring me home, but that she and her parents go to Bordeaux every year to care for her grandmother. Pauline doesn't acknowledge or notice my distress.

Inside, I scream that I have no one. My mother doesn't exist. My father is cavorting in New York City. My best friend is dead, but I pretend everything is fine. In my most casual tone, I say, "Joyeux Noël." I run upstairs, grab my toothbrush, and slip it in my coat. As I head out Raven comes after me in the parlor and apologizes about skipping our date.

"I got caught up with stuff," he says, wrapping his arms around my waist. "Let's do it after the holidays. Okay, Pixie?"

I extricate myself from his grasp. "The market will be closed by then, but yeah, sure, whatever."

Raven tries to catch my hand.

But I leave so quickly I slam the front door, and the wings in the bay window swing. I walk to the Christmas market alone because I cannot fathom going back to rue Jean Cocteau right away. As I hurry on rue d'Orchampt, I even think to sneak into the boutique later. No one will ever know I was there. I'm not worried about the lack of heat or water. What I do not want is to break Salomé's rules or disappoint her and Faiza. I have already caused enough trouble as is. The street by the Sacré Cœur is packed with families. I wander around the wooden huts and smell roasted chestnuts and the sweet scent of nougat. I peer at nativity cards and at delicate glass ornaments. One vendor sells wooden trains and another elf-like hooded sweaters. The spirit of Christmas floats around me. I think about having *my* stall someday with feather bouquets decorated with bright red or green ribbons. I see the name Pixie Dust hanging above the gable, and my mood momentarily lifts.

But an icy wind picks up and soon the market clears out. I grow cold, blow into my hands. When a middle-aged man approaches me and says, "Salut, ma belle," I take off and make my way first toward the boutique, a reflex, and when I peer over my shoulder and see the man following me, the words *damsel in distress* appear in front of my eyelids, and I decide that perhaps I am one, that the only friends I have, besides everyone at Mille et Une Plume, are Blaise and Tante Constance. Ten minutes later, I swallow my pride, knock on Blaise's door, and tell myself that if he doesn't answer I will head to rue Jean Cocteau once I am sure the creep is gone, but the door to apartment fifty-one flings open. In his Grand Chef apron, Blaise takes up the doorframe. He looks festive. Everything behind him smells sweet. I am so thankful to see him that I look down at my Converse, hoping he won't notice the flush and relief on my face.

"Entre," he says. "The more the merrier."

Silver tinsel and red garland hang from the ceiling. I look for his friends from the carousel, certain they'll be sitting on his sofa chatting about people and things I don't know or care about. I have already prepared a speech, that I just came to say Merry Christmas, when Tante Constance emerges from the bathroom in a Santa hat.

"Darling," she says, rushing over to me. "You look half-frozen."

The duchess's warm gaze makes me blink a few times too many. I start to say something but afraid I will lose it I stand silent and take in the fact that Blaise is making a bûche de Noël. Tante Constance bustles around, then brings me a grenadine and tells me to make myself at home.

"I didn't know you baked," I say to Blaise.

Not sure where to sit, I lean against the arm of the sofa, remember him sleeping there, and my heart flutters.

"Ça fait longtemps. It's been a while, Alix Leclaire." Blaise peers at me from across the kitchen table, one dimple creasing.

He holds a spatula covered in chocolate. I gulp my grenadine, then realize he called me by both names, which makes me think he is not mad at me anymore for walking away that night at the carousel. I smile back and relax a little. Constance tells me to come over, that Blaise is making his famous log for her supper tomorrow night, and as I make my way behind Blaise at the sink, his great-aunt offers me the bowl with melted chocolate and orders me to lick it clean.

I turn to Blaise and say, "Are you okay with this?"

Blaise is concentrating on placing a marzipan fawn at the edge of the log, but he turns toward me and replies, "Whatever the duchess says always goes."

I crack a smile, notice his new haircut, and lick every morsel of chocolate. By the time I have wiped the bowl clean, Blaise has placed the log under a dome in the refrigerator. He urges me to sit on the sofa, and when we are seated, he brings us each a cup of onion soup.

"Mon amour de garçon," Tante Constance says.

Blaise lifts his cup.

We eat. I go slow because I know that after this is over, I will have to leave. I must turn inward because when I look up from my soup, Blaise and Tante Constance are waiting for me to answer them, but I have no clue what they asked.

"I'm sorry," I say. "Holidays are hard."

"Spill." Blaise's eyebrows are knitted, and he seems to be warning me that if I don't open up, he might get mad.

I say, "The boutique closed for the week and I have to head back to rue Jean Cocteau and I know it's silly, but Papa's apartment without Jeanne gives me the creeps."

"Rue Jean Cocteau?" Tante Constance says. "Oh là là. Stay in my guest quarters. Your father should be ashamed to have you stay there alone."

I shake my head. "I couldn't, but you are too kind. Thank you. And Papa is just on tour trying to make a living."

Blaise removes the bowl from my hands, then takes the one from Constance. He brings them to the sink and says, "Tantine, don't sweat it. Alix can stay on the futon for a few days."

I sit statue-like, as if one movement might make him change his mind. When Blaise asks me to help wash dishes, I return to the sink and scrub everything until the whole kitchen is spick and span. Even the floors. Afterward, Blaise puts on music. We talk about everything, from politics, to art and theater, to women like Eleanor of Aquitaine and Joan of Arc, to what Blaise will do next year—play and teach guitar—and when my father might come home. I learn that Blaise's parents live outside of Paris and rarely visit, and that Tante Constance is Blaise's paternal grandmother's sister, that she was once very much in love. Little by little, the duchess begins to yawn. Near midnight, she has fallen asleep on the sofa and snores, Santa hat crooked on her head.

"Do you want me to walk her home?" I offer.

"Have you lost your mind?" Blaise replies. "Never wake her. She is a terror when woken. Remember the grizzly bear?"

He opens the trunk, pulls the cover out, drapes his aunt with the fur. He unfolds the futon bed and says, "She sleeps here sometimes. She gets lonely and aside from the snoring, she is pretty great." I must look at him perplexed because he adds, "What? Doesn't everyone have a great-aunt who snores on the couch, wearing a Santa hat?"

I grin. "You got a haircut."

His dimples crease, making my face warm.

"How will you play Betty?" I say.

Blaise whispers to follow him, that he might have a spare toothbrush, except I remember mine, go to my coat, and brandish it. As I walk into the bathroom, Blaise shuts the door behind us and steals it.

"Was this visit premeditated, Alix Leclaire?" he asks.

He waves my toothbrush so high above his head I have to jump up and down and swat at it, but then he laughs, returns it, and explains he won't play guitar until his great-aunt leaves, and that I don't have to answer about the visit being premeditated, that I can always crash here if I need to. We wash our faces, brush our teeth, then Blaise walks around the apartment, turns off the lights, and says, "On the count of three, I'll turn around if you want to slip off your clothes. Take the right side. I always sleep on the left."

For a second, I'm confused but realize that because of Tante Constance, Blaise and I will share the futon, and before I can ask if he is okay with that or if I'm okay with that, Blaise is already counting to three. I hear him rustle out of his clothes, then plunk his glasses onto the floor. Quickly, I pull off my jeans and get under the covers in my undies, T-shirt, socks, and hoodie. My heart slams against my chest and I make sure to turn away from him.

"Comfy?" he whispers.

"Yeah," I say.

Though I'm not sure it's true. Constance snores louder than a train whistle, and I wonder if I'll ever sleep, but Blaise turns on his back, and I get a whiff of his laundry detergent and breathe easier.

"I'm sorry about the other day," he says.

His voice is deep. I'm not sure which day he is referring to, the one after we visited the duchess for the first time or the one when he met Raven. The thought makes me squirm.

I say, "I'm sorry I keep running away."

217

"'S okay."

Blaise lays a hand on my shoulder. His palm is warm and the gesture is gentle, caring, and suddenly this studio apartment with a sleeping duchess, a guitar named Betty, silver tinsel, red garland, and this boy feels like the coziest place I've ever spent the night.

Blaise says, "I know it's none of my business, but you did look pretty close with Raven. Are you guys a thing?"

My cheeks burn so bad I think they'll make his pillowcase catch on fire. "It's complicated," I mumble.

"I bet," Blaise replies, but he squeezes my shoulder, and I swear I hear him chuckle.

"Are your dimples creasing?" I say.

"How the hell would I know?" Blaise laughs, and I'm afraid he'll wake his great-aunt.

I sit up, look at him, lit up by the moonlight.

"They are," I tell him.

Blaise presses his index fingers inside his cheeks. "Truly my best features, don't you think?" he says, making me laugh.

"Hush," he adds. "Tomorrow, we'll go to Tante Constance's for Christmas Eve. It's always a big bash."

"Are you okay with me staying here?"

Blaise sits up, too. He sighs so loudly it's like a shudder. Our feet bump and I wonder if he is wearing his plaid pajama bottoms under the covers.

"I wouldn't have offered if I wasn't," he answers.

We sit side by side for a long time, then his great-aunt makes another fierce whistling sound, nearly waking herself, and we collapse onto the futon in a giant fit of giggles. Minutes later, we catch our breath, then fall asleep.

CHAPTER 28

The next morning, with her white hair sticking up just like Blaise's, Tante Constance drinks an espresso, then waves goodbye.

"Be there on the dot," she says about her party. "À tout à l'heure, darlings."

Then, it's just Blaise and me, and I suddenly feel shy. I look at the herbs lining the windowsill. Blaise tells me that cooking and baking have been a refuge. As I make the bed and fold the fur back into the trunk, I ask him about the conservatory, and wonder what he means by refuge.

"How do you know about that place?" he says.

I blush. "I went by your aunt's the other day and dropped off a joy feather bouquet. Long story."

"Go ahead. We got nothing but time."

I say, "I felt like the bouquet belonged to her. I also sold another one made with Salomé's feathers." I pause. "I probably shouldn't have." I look up and before Blaise can say anything, I continue. "Are you mad at me for visiting Constance without you?"

I wait for Blaise to say yes, but when he shakes his head, I add, "Tante Constance is the one who told me about the conservatory." I think about what else she said and almost bring up the night of the accident, but remind myself that none of it will bring Jeanne back, that the logistics, the who, when, and where, don't really matter—do they?

Blaise wrings his hands, giving me that earnest look. "Want to be my sous-chef?"

"I can try," I reply.

"What's with second-guessing yourself?"

I shrug.

"You know who was a terrible cook?" Blaise asks.

"No."

"Jeanne. She burned everything."

"That's true," I say, except annoyed, I snort, then can't help but add, "Your aunt also told me you rescue damsels in distress. Is that what Jeanne was to you? Is that what I am, too?"

Blaise takes off his glasses, pulls his apron over his head, and asks me to tie it. For an iota of a second, I wonder if this is a ploy to kiss me, but after I'm done making a bow with the strings, Blaise doesn't even turn around. He goes back to the kitchen, and I feel dumb. *Why are you always thinking about kissing boys?* I admonish myself. He yanks open a cabinet, pulls out potatoes, carrots, turnips, and leeks, which he dumps on the counter, then he grabs two knives from the drawer.

He says, "I am going to share a few things with you, Alix Leclaire, and hope this puts a stop to your inquiries."

His tone catches me off guard. I sit on the sofa and say, "I didn't mean to—"

Blaise holds a palm up, then speaks as he peels the potatoes. "Remember Madame Foucault's lit class?"

I nod.

"I first noticed you there. You were like a blotch of color in a sea of gray. You always sat in the front row, and every time she called on you, I perked up and stopped slouching in the back because I was curious to hear your answers."

I must scrunch my nose, pout, or something because Blaise says, "It's true. Just listen and learn to take a compliment. I liked your wit, the sketch pad you doodled in nonstop, how you held your breath before discussing Colette or George Sand, and how you'd blush as red as a fire hydrant if you thought you didn't answer something correctly."

I'm pretty sure I'm blushing now, but Blaise keeps going.

"That year, I kept trying to figure out a way to ask you out, but I never found the courage."

He throws the newly peeled potatoes in a bowl, rinses the carrots, then begins dicing them.

I walk to the kitchen counter and, standing beside him, say, "I'll help."

Blaise glances at me, hands me a turnip, then tells me to cut it in cubes.

He adds, "The conservatory is a little like you. A colorful place. It makes me perk up and not want to slouch or throw fists around. When I'm there, I focus and feel a sense of worth, of belonging, of discovery." He grins, one dimple creasing. "Like I said, music saved me, and I owe everything to Tante Constance and to Betty."

We dice the turnips, then the leeks. As Blaise concentrates on the task at hand, again I notice his baby face.

"What about you and Jeanne?" I say.

"This again? What about us?"

I frown at him. "I mean, you two were close."

"Sure. I saw some of me in her, the anger mainly, then one time at a rehearsal between songs, she brought up your name, said she was besties with Alix Leclaire, that she lived with you, loved your father like her own."

"She said that?"

"Yes. For a second, I thought I'd hit the lottery, that I'd finally get to meet you and maybe even dazzle you with my ridiculous charm, but when we did meet at the carousel that day, you, for the most part, ignored me."

I'm not sure how long we stand at the counter without making eye contact, but by the time I look at him, Blaise has placed a pot on the fire and is simmering a chunk of meat.

"What on earth are we making?" I ask.

Blaise laughs. "A pot roast."

He rinses the chopped vegetables, then says, "I don't know about you, but I feel much better having that secret off my chest."

I give him a small smile.

Blaise dries his hands with a cloth, and I have the urge to grab onto one of his belt loops, but all I do is fidget because I'm not sure if his crush on me is a thing of the present or the past. Plus, there is Raven and Mille et Une Plume, and I'm not the kind of girl who kisses several boys at once, I don't think, without at least clarifying things for me and for them first.

I say, "Well, look at us now. A grand chef and a petite main cooking side by side."

As if to confuse me or my heart even more, Blaise's dimples appear and he says, "Also, you're not a damsel in distress. Neither was Jeanne. She was more like a bomb, and you are kind of like a flower, a peony in bud. But don't tell Raven. He'll get jealous."

"Whatever," I say, flustered, then add, "Can we please be friends then?"

"Maybe," Blaise replies.

"Maybe?"

Blaise plucks two pieces of mint from the windowsill. He eats one, then handing me the other, says, "Okay, deal."

I swallow my mint, giggle. "Know something?"

"What?"

I twirl, then say, "Being a splash of color in a sea of gray or a peony in bud are the prettiest compliments I've ever gotten, but oh wait, did you steal that from Anaïs Nin?"

"Don't insult me," Blaise says.

He then recites Anaïs, the quote about the risk to remain tight in a bud being more painful than the risk of blossoming.

I stare at him.

"Told you I was charming," Blaise says with a grin.

That evening, Blaise and I stroll from rue des Trois Frères to Avenue Frochot. He carries his guitar and the pot roast and I carry the yule log, and every few minutes, because most of the streets are downhill, he makes sure the dessert is flat under the dome.

"If you ruin it, I'll kill you," he says.

"Have a little faith," I reply.

We should be embarrassed or perhaps awkward after our earlier conversation, but if anything, there is a new sense of ease between us.

At the tall, wrought iron gate, I stop and say, "I feel like I owe you rent money."

Blaise nods to the concierge, and as we walk up the cobblestone street, he says, "I don't need your money." He chuckles. "I'm covered."

I scowl. "Fine. Tomorrow can we visit Jeanne?"

"Sure, we can visit Jeanne if you swear not to mention how shitty today's practice was. I thought Betty might quit on me."

"I swear," I say.

Soon, we are welcomed inside Tante Constance's quarters. We drop off the roast and the dessert in the kitchen, then head to the living room. A massive Christmas tree wrapped in lights resides by the window near the fancy chairs, Napoleon fauteuils, I think they're called. Men in tuxedos and top hats shake hands while women in theatrical gowns with tiaras greet one another, except for Blaise and me who are in jeans and hoodies. When we sneak into the dining room to admire the crystal chandelier from the eighteenth century, I stare at the enormous table, something from a fairy tale, and my feather bouquet is the centerpiece.

"Darlings," Tante Constance says. "Why are you two still dressed like peasants?"

The duchess, wearing a ruby princess dress, signals for us to follow her up the back stairs until we are standing in a vast bedroom full of gowns, hats, tuxedoes, and wigs.

Constance points and says, "Please change into something presentable. Dinner will be served shortly."

"This place is crazier than Mille et Une Plume," I say once the duchess is gone, running my hand on the gowns. I find a wig I like, the color of wheat, with 1930s finger waves, and place it on my head.

Blaise grins. "Constance was one of the most well-known actresses of our grandparents' time. After she left the Comédie Française, and her husband died, the only thing that made her happy was pretending to be onstage off-stage. The theater still gives her old costumes, and during the holidays, we pretend with her."

Blaise finds a tuxedo on a hanger and lifts it up to him-self. "This will fit, right?"

I find a copper gown with a high neck and before I can look for a place to change, Blaise sheds his clothes. In nothing but boxers, he grins and says, "Don't tell me you're scared to undress in front of a friend, especially when you danced nearly naked with colleagues on top of the Eiffel Tower. And last night we slept next to each other in our underwear."

"And T-shirt, hoodie, and don't forget, socks," I reply.

Blaise chuckles.

The room has a dusty, old-fashioned lamp with tassels. It's dark but not so dark that he won't see me. But I *did* sleep nestled against him last night. And I'm wearing a wig, which makes me feel like a different person, someone daring. A bell rings from somewhere downstairs, so I pull off my jeans, hoodie, and T-shirt. In my wig and undies, I unzip the gown and when I look at Blaise, he is across the room, half-dressed, facing away from me as he buttons his shirt.

I step into the gown, and nearly as soon as I've slipped the straps over my shoulders, Blaise pulls on his jacket and turns around.

"I barely recognize you with that wig," he says, looking carefully at my face, then lowering his gaze to my arm. "Thank god for your tattoo. Jeanne always said it was your signature, and I couldn't agree more, especially now."

His words make my skin tingle. Jeanne never called my amethyst feather a signature to my face. It's like I'm receiving a compliment from the grave, as well as from Blaise. I also remember Raven running his thumb on it, how powerful his touch and his words made me feel then, but now I would prefer Raven didn't touch it anymore.

The door to the bedroom opens, and Tante Constance comes in and says, "Come on, lovebirds."

She orders me to turn around, zips me up in a flash, then fixes Blaise's shirt and nœud papillon, and whisks us downstairs where I am seated at the far end of the long wooden table between two women. A tanned blonde on my right, Anne Cazel, an established coiffeuse. She says she would love a centerpiece like this for her salon. I take her in—her sharp features, the beauty mark on her neck, the rose-gold ring on her finger——and conjure a bouquet of glamor, traditional swan feathers mixed with sweet alyssum and dried sea holly. As les entrées arrive, Blaise, who sits beside an attractive neighbor, makes her laugh. I glance at them and wish he'd look in my direction, but as I slice my smoked salmon, I remind myself that *I* am the one who is taken. Aren't I?

Champagne, Sancerre, and Grand Bordeaux flow. There is a gift exchange. Blaise's dessert along with meringues, tartes aux amandes, and caramel flans are tasted. For the most part, I observe the scene from one of the chairs where I am joined by the tabby cat that comes and curls onto my lap. Around midnight, one of the ushers lifts the needle off the record player, stopping the classical music, and asks everyone to congregate by the tree.

A crowd of merrily drunken guests forms around me, and the sound of Blaise's electric guitar bursts from the back stairs he and I climbed earlier. Blaise appears cradling Betty. His eyes are closed, and his fingers work the frets so fast they are almost a blur. He plays a Christmas tune, which makes people laugh and sing along, then morphs into something else, something quick and alive with an intensity that sounds more like a plea. Everyone stares at him entranced. The cat hops off my lap, disappearing beneath the seat. Tante Constance watches Blaise with the proudest look in her eyes, and yells, "Allez, mon garçon!" The strangest thing is that I feel the same immense sense of pride for him. As I sit on the chair, notes wailing, a mix of nostalgia, longing, and pain floods me. I want to lose myself in my art in the exact same way Blaise is losing himself in his. I know without a shadow of a doubt the guitar has saved him, and believe the feathers will save me as well, if I am lucky enough to remain in their company.

By the time Blaise strums his final note, lifting the guitar against his chest, I think he is the most beautiful human I have ever seen.

CHAPTER 29

Around 2:30 a.m., the guests scatter on the cobbled street, calls of "Merry Christmas" echoing, church bells ringing in the distance.

Back in street clothes, Blaise carries Betty on his back.

"So? What did you think?" he says.

I'm about to tell him when someone walking past us yells, "Et le prince, that was insane."

The attractive woman who sat beside Blaise at dinner comes over and kisses his cheek, says good night, and maybe because I'm exhausted, maybe because I'm jealous, I stay silent and watch her walk away.

It isn't until we are halfway back to his place that I finally say, "I'm not sure how to explain what I felt."

"Not sure? Okay."

When we finally get upstairs and Blaise offers me the futon, I shake my head and point to the sofa. The vibe between us is off. Blaise hands me the grizzly-bear fur and a pillow, but when we head to the bathroom to wash our faces and brush our teeth, he says he needs a minute alone, asks me to go after he's done, then shuts the door. I hear him turn on the sink. I slip under the cover and feel like an ass.

Before we fall asleep, I say, "About earlier."

"Which part? The crush or the performance, the one you don't know how to feel about?"

I think of hawks, the muscles beneath their plumage, their soaring strength. How once on a trip in the Pyrénées I spotted one, sunshine illuminating its plumage high in the sky. I think of wings growing from my shoulder blades, the pain of skin breaking, and I say, "You and Betty turned into a bird. That's what the sound felt like. You became a hawk or made *me* turn into one. It was beautiful. Thank you."

Blaise stays quiet for a long time, then says, "Joyeux Noël, Alix Leclaire."

Sometime after we fall asleep, I wake up thirsty. For a moment, I forget where I am until I see the red garlands and the sleeping boy spread out on the futon. Quietly, I get up and go to the bathroom where I drink from the tap. When I come back to the couch, Blaise has turned on his stomach and kicked off his covers. He makes a fist with his right hand and his left knee is bent, foot falling off the edge of the futon. There is something so vulnerable about him that carefully, hoping not to step on any electrical cords, I make my way to him, pick up his blankets, and cover him.

CHAPTER 30

Hours later, when I open my eyes, Blaise is in the kitchen wearing the Santa hat. He slips a hand in his pajama pocket, brandishes two tickets, and says, "Are you up for a train ride?"

I hesitate, thinking it might be best if I leave because, well, because last night my feelings for Blaise's music were intense and kind of startled me, and there is Raven, but it's Christmas morning, and Blaise does a little hip shimmy, making me laugh.

"Okay," I say, and decide I will leave his place after, perhaps tonight or tomorrow—what's a couple more hours?—that until then I might as well enjoy it.

After getting dressed, we hit the sidewalk, Blaise in his

beanie, unzipped parka, glasses, and an olive hoodie that reads, *I'm unstoppable.*

He says, "I thought we could ride first, then visit Jeanne to wish her a merry Christmas."

As we walk, I remember one year on rue Jean Cocteau at Christmas. It was just Jeanne and me, and I broke down and cried because Papa was gone again and because there was no tree. Jeanne wrapped an arm around my shoulder and said, "We have each other and that's something." Jeanne turned on music, told me stories, sang, then drank bourbon. She didn't mind the loneliness, the lack of family, the way I did. God, it's been more than six months since the accident. I have been so consumed by my struggles that it feels as if I haven't mourned her enough because in the end, out of everyone, Jeanne was always my North Star, my true family. When we get to a light, I stand beside Blaise and in her honor, recite "Hope Is the Thing with Feathers."

Blaise claps.

I tell him how after the accident I used to say the lines of the poem over and over to soothe myself, how Jeanne and I discovered Emily one night inside Shakespeare and Company and fell in love with the way she wrote about beauty and pain. How I have been a neglectful friend in life and in death.

"I don't think so," Blaise says. "Isn't that what's supposed to happen? With time, wounds heal, and we learn to accept the grief."

I shake my head. "How will we ever keep her alive if we begin to forget her?"

"I'm not saying forget. I think we should celebrate her while moving on with our lives. Jeanne would want that."

"I guess," I say, then add, "There is something I have been meaning to ask you about the night of the accident. Something Constance brought up. Something about you being one of the last to see Jeanne alive. Is that true?"

Blaise loops a hand through my elbow. "You want to talk about this now?"

I shrug because his tone scares me, like perhaps it would be better if I didn't know.

Blaise says, "How about we enjoy the train ride, and I tell you when we visit her grave. We can sit by the tomb-stones, and I'll answer anything and everything then. Let the dead be our witness."

I almost press him to tell me now, but behind his bubbly demeanor and extra-long lashes, there is a look of pain that frightens me.

"Fine," I say. "Have it your way." I add, "Plus, it doesn't matter. I already know what happened. Dumb boy driving intoxicated. Life being random and unfair."

In front of the Moulin Rouge, the petit train de Montmartre idles, yellow and white with four cars. I can't remember the last time I rode it. Probably with Jeanne the year we first met. Blaise and I are the only ones who climb onto it, and we choose the very last seats, me on one end, Blaise on the other. The conductor smokes a cigar and turns on a guided tour. As we cruise up rue Blanche and get honked at by cars and food trucks, Blaise reclines on his elbows on the seat and whistles. Eventually, the train turns onto Place du Tertre, a tourist trap, but today there is no one except a few locals because everyone is opening gifts and preparing their repas de Noël. The square is quiet. The conductor chats with a painter who has set up his easel near the paved street. The recorded tour tells us about the importance of the square, how it was once the mecca of modern art and opened to the public in 1635.

"1635?" Blaise says.

He starts to sing "Depuis toujours," an old song by Francis Cabrel, and the driver turns toward him, then joins him, his voice as scruffy as the bottom of a barrel.

Close to the final stop, the red whistle blows and the train chugs, slowing down. We make our way to the back of the Sacré Cœur and on a ruelle, Blaise grabs my hand, and we jump off the train, yelling goodbye to the conductor.

"Where are you taking me?" I say, acutely aware of his fingers entwined through mine.

Minutes later, Blaise points to a salon de coiffure, and I recognize the name Anne Cazel from last night's party.

"Tante Constance is waiting for you inside," Blaise explains.

I raise my eyebrows.

Blaise says, "You'd mentioned wanting a real haircut——" He pauses, then releases my hand and gestures to my bangs, which are now so long they hide my eyes. "Consider it a Christmas gift."

An hour later, when Anne is done, my hair is pixie short again, wispy in all the right places. Tante Constance says I look famous, like Jean Seberg or Audrey Tautou, and I feel light and free. A few times, the hairdresser mentions my feather bouquet and says that if I ever decide to open my business, she'll be one of the first to request a few for her salon, and that her daughter, who is getting married next fall, would be interested in a feather-themed wedding. My heart sings at the words.

Outside, Tante Constance slips on her fur coat and says, "I should be your manager, Alix. Emotionally resonant feather bouquets are a fabulous idea. They will be a hit. Trust me."

I want to tell her how I shouldn't have given anyone any of the bouquets yet, that they are more like a big mistake, but Blaise says, "Tantine, Alix is smart. Besides, her feather art is between her and Mademoiselle Salomé."

Constance pouts. "Salomé has nothing on me aside from a little bird magic."

We laugh, and I think of all the colorful plumes waiting to be given out and decide that wings are incredible to create for the stage, but that bouquets can enter anyone's home. The two are like the difference between haute couture and prêt-à-porter. Upon Salomé's return, I will speak to her, tell her about my feather bouquets, and hope she will want to partner with me on it, that this new business could be lucrative not just for me but for her, too.

For us.

As we stroll through Place du Tertre, the duchess tires and Blaise hails her a cab. Then, he and I meander down cobblestone streets toward Place Clichy on our way to the cemetery. I am so deep in thought I take a wrong turn, and Blaise asks if I'm okay.

"You look light-years away," he says.

Though the day is cold, the sun shines. Blaise leans against an apartment building, takes off his beanie, and stuffs it into the front pocket of his hoodie. His hair sticks up, making me want to smooth it, and as I glance back at the hoodie, at his unzipped parka, I remember last night, Blaise sleeping, limbs spread like a starfish. When I look back at his face, into his eyes, my cheeks heating up a million degrees, his expression unhinges me. Because Blaise is studying *me* with such gentleness. The gold flecks in his eyes make me want to head back to rue des Trois Frères, on top of his futon more precisely, but I stand there fidgeting, unsure what to say, my voice hovering somewhere above me.

"You look a mess," Blaise says softly. "What am I going to do with you, Alix Leclaire?"

His dimples appear, and before I can stop myself, I step forward, rise on tiptoes, wrap my hands around his neck, and pull him to me until we are kissing. At first, Blaise is so still I think he will push me away, but he lifts me up until my feet are off the ground, and with my legs wrapped around his waist, I hold him so tightly I swear my heart might fuse with his. Which is the only thing I want. I think I say it out loud. "Our hearts are fusing." And I swear, new wings deploy from me, from us. We become one with the hawk, or no, the phoenix, yes, the phoenix, but then my brain shuts off, and it is all body, lips, tongues, dimples, fingers, hands, and his arms holding me up until our breaths become so shallow, and our skin so blazing hot, I think we will die right here in front of a random apartment building.

"Waouh," Blaise says once we have separated, still blocks away from the cemetery.

I can't look him in the eyes for fear I might assault him again or start to cry.

Blaise laughs and says, "Oh là là, ma timide, why so shy all a sudden?"

I lift a shoulder and am about to try and explain that I've never felt anything like this before, but then as we get to the rounded archway, the main entrance, Blaise stops and says, "I guess it's time for me to tell you about the night of the party."

That's when I crash back down to earth and remember that Blaise is about to share something presumably important about that night, but I'm feeling so discombobulated, I only shake my head, then, glancing at him, say, "Okay."

We keep on walking through a maze of pavers and sinuous paths. When we get to Jeanne's grave, Blaise slips his hands in his parka and shudders. I kneel and run my hand on the tombstone.

"Joyeux Noël," I say.

I wait for Blaise to begin, his voice deep and ocean-like, but he remains quiet, looking at me now with a frown, and I'm transported back into his arms and have to turn away.

"If I recall," he says, "you started it. Earlier, I mean."

When I say nothing, he wrings his hands, then adds, "For what it's worth, that was one hell of a kiss. I hope you feel the same way."

I study Jeanne's grave and want to tell him I could probably kiss him again right now surrounded by hundreds of dead people and lose myself in him, but somehow my stomach feels like a rock, and I keep thinking of Mille et Une

Plume, too, of Raven, and I don't know how to merge Blaise and my feelings for him with the rest of my life.

I say, "Can you please tell me about the party?"

Blaise runs a hand through his hair, making it stand up again.

"I went," Blaise begins, "because I was invited. Jeanne arrived with some up-and-coming musician. An addict. She saw me and waved. I waved back. Then a couple famous agents showed up and went straight to Jeanne's guy. The buzz around him was off the charts, and Jeanne was trying to hang onto his hand. She looked all smiles and bravado, but I could see a sort of desperation, oozing from her."

Blaise stops, clears his throat.

"For a while, Jeanne and her guy hung out, but when one of the agents mentioned a record deal with Virgin, then shook his hand, he left her."

"Okay," I say. "Then what?"

"I felt so bad I went over to Jeanne and swore to her she would be next. She said, 'I bet,' popped two pills from her heart key chain, and walked away."

Blaise swallows hard.

"Sorry," he says, then adds that after a while when the agents weren't moving, he grabbed Jeanne's hands and offered to take her back to me, but Jeanne pulled away and said she wasn't in the mood to grovel.

"Grovel?" I say.

"Yeah," Blaise answers.

"Go ahead."

"Eventually, the agent came over. Jeanne grew tall again and even managed to hide the fact that she was drunk or high or both, except the agent, I didn't know, was coming for me."

Blaise looks cold now and keeps wringing his hands.

I wish the story was over and that we could just go back to Tante Constance and celebrate Christmas.

"I told the guy I wouldn't sign unless he signed us both, and the dude asked if I was joking. Then he said he'd seen Jeanne perform, that she had decent stage presence and a smokin' little body but sang like a hundred other girls.

"When I turned around, Jeanne was gone. I found her coming out of the bathroom, holding the red-heart key chain, eyeliner everywhere. I said to her, 'Don't let anyone tell you who you are. What the fuck does he know?' Jeanne kissed my cheek, then her boyfriend came, and she bolted. I was about to go back to the party when I got a weird feeling and sprinted after her. By the time I rushed out onto the sidewalk, the old Renault was speeding down the street, Jeanne at the wheel. I yelled for her to wait, but when she saw me, she accelerated, then was gone."

I look at Blaise. "Jeanne never drove," I tell him. "I mean we used to joke that if I ever found her behind the wheel, I'd better call the cops because——"

"She was driving, Alix," Blaise says. "I swear, and I'm sorry to be the one breaking it to you. I wish I'd told you a long time ago."

Blaise is pulling at his beanie so hard I think the wool might start to unfurl, and the way he is yanking at it while looking at me with his dark brows knitted makes me realize he is telling the truth.

I say, "Jeanne drove into the guardrail."

Blaise nods.

I see the TV, the fireman on the side of the road, the red-heart key chain in his hands, and I cannot recall the newscaster's words, if he mentioned a single driver, if I blocked the truth the way I once blocked out everything about my mother.

I lean against Jeanne's grave.

"Alix?" Blaise says. "You okay?"

His hand is on my shoulder.

"Do you think she——" But I shut my eyes and say, "Never mind."

When Blaise tries to take my hand in his, then says, "Let's walk back to the apartment. I'll make us some tea," I pull my fingers away.

"I want to stay with her by myself," I murmur.

"Okay," Blaise says, then adds, "At first, I thought you knew. I thought everybody did. I'm really sorry."

When I say nothing, Blaise asks, "Will we be all right?"

I should say yes, of course, we will, but I squeeze my eyes shut. It's all too much. I don't know how to feel about any of it, and how I can possibly love a boy who will always be entangled with Jeanne, and with her last night here on earth. I wait and wait and it's not until Blaise's footsteps recede, then fade into the distance, that the dam breaks and my tears come pouring out.

CHAPTER 31

After the caretaker of the cemetery tells me I should go, that it is far too cold to fret among the dead, especially on Christmas Day, I trudge back to Mille et Une Plume in need of only one thing: the feathers. I insert the brass key in the lock, praying no one will notice; Mademoiselle Salomé does not expect me until they return a week from now.

As soon as I am in the parlor, the silver-and-streaked-blue wings seem to stir, and I breathe a little easier. I greet every single feather. I pull the dusty encyclopedia from its box and touch the red plume on the cover, then I check the costume room and know that as long as I am here surrounded by the wings and the ivory bins, I will survive. At least another day. The boutique is ice cold, but I keep my coat zipped shut, and once I settle in the minty room, the window and door closed, I warm up a little. When my brain lures me back to the cemetery, to Blaise and his story, I decide I need time and space.

From him and from it all.

Besides, I tell myself that I will need to spend every waking moment on these new wings, that they will be stunning, that Mademoiselle Salomé won't believe her eyes when she discovers them. Even Pauline will have to acknowledge their power. For a few days, I am incapable of eating or sleeping. I lose track of time and aimlessly walk around the bins. One afternoon, I feel so untethered that in order to anchor myself, I pretend to be Mademoiselle Salomé. Like Pauline, I borrow one of her capes. As I sit at her desk, my pain feels different, more distant, looming large outside my body. I gather charcoal pencils and clean paper and, surrounded by the plumes, I draw a brand-new pair of wings.

At first, it's a sketch. Barely visible.

Something I'm unsure of.

Rudimentary.

Long bat-like things. More skin than feathers. Edgy contours. Some areas translucent, others opaque with, I imagine, sleek, oily, vulture-like feathers. The more I draw, then pause, and draw, the more the pain hovers like a thick cloud above me. The clock in the parlor ticks. Near midnight, I think I hear a knock on the window. Or it's a bird who flies into the glass. I startle, ignore it, then go back to work. Hours later, shivering from the cold, I hear Jeanne whisper something about the prince of darkness, and suddenly with Mademoiselle Salomé's cape still wrapped around my shoulders and the moon shining a cool crescent into the bay window, I see Jeanne seated behind a figure on a galloping black horse, arms wrapped around his waist, wisteria hair blowing in the wind, a pair of ghastly wings protruding from her shoulder blades.

The wings I am sketching.

I hold my pencil high above the page scared to continue, but the wings in all their glorious darkness come to life. They grow from Jeanne's back at strange angles and like a wedding veil they trail gunmetal gray and dirty, behind her. More burden than aid, more villain than savior, more foe, than hero. They burn in my imagination.

On the last evening before everyone's arrival, the oak's branches blow wildly in the wind. Feeling empty, I stare out into the night. The temperatures drop below zero. A dead branch breaks and collapses in the courtyard. Frost builds around the windows. I am so cold I can't stop shivering. I put on an extra sweater under my coat and pluck griffon vulture feathers from the study's far back corner. I've never seen anyone, not even Salomé, hold these feathers before.

I tilt them in the crook of my elbow and stroke them with my ice-cold fingers as if they were fledglings. They smell of sulfur. I sense their meaning, "souffrance." Like a salty mist over the ocean, their essence starts at the quills and travels through them and escapes from the rachis into the barbs, then veins, out into the air, around me. They are the door to the shadowy part of the underworld. By the time I return them to their bin and climb into bed, exhausted, the cold in my bones spreads into my heart.

CHAPTER 32

The day the shop reopens, I stand outside Mille et Une Plume blowing in my hands as if I, too, was returning from a great trip. I'm anxious everyone will take one look at me and know that in a strange, sleepless haze I pretended to be Mademoiselle Salomé and stayed at the boutique unwelcomed. Another part of me is sad to no longer have the feathers to myself.

At 7:30 a.m., Mademoiselle Salomé turns the corner, waves, then wishes me une bonne et heureuse année, which makes me realize I missed New Year's Eve, and that another year has snuck up on me. The feather artist asks how my holidays were. I study the sidewalk; say, "Fine"; then follow her inside, glancing around to make sure there are no obvious signs of me. Or perhaps of my madness.

An hour later Pauline arrives in a cashmere sweater, her hair in sleek braids, complaining of the cold, then teases me about my ash-like complexion. I notice everyone's tan. By now we have congregated in the costume room. Pauline mentions a spontaneous trip to Spain. Manon says the weather in Bordeaux was unseasonably warm, and Raven's golden skin has turned a deeper shade of brown. I smile a small, tight smile, then excuse myself to get organized for the day. Faiza follows and, looking into my eyes, asks, "Comment ça va, poulette?" I fake another smile, then force myself to exclaim over the new molted feathers—West Indian whistling duck semiplumes, purple-throated Carib bristles, chimney swifts—Raven and his mother brought back.

Before lunch, Mademoiselle Salomé pulls Manon, Pauline, and me into her study and says that except for the fundraiser coming up in April and a few important haute couture projects, our common goal should be to finish the last outstanding three pairs of wings.

"The maleficent wings should be next." Salomé looks each one of us in the eyes, then says, "I can't wait to see how they turn out."

Manon winces.

I stare at the ivory bins pretending I haven't already been dreaming of dark wings, but the feathers sway, and I momentarily wonder if they will call me out, if my journal with my appalling drawings will fall open in front of everyone. But then Pauline laughs, and Mademoiselle says, "I hope the three of you collaborate, partner, and remain open to possibilities."

The feather artist smiles.

"In the end, we are a family. Come find me if you have questions. Faiza will be around, too, but she will mostly tend to our other projects, and Raven, well—" Salomé pauses. "Never mind."

Pauline says, "Don't worry, Salomé. I'll take Alix under my wing." The pre-apprentice winks in my direction.

Manon tucks a wisp of strawberry-blond hair behind her ear and exhales loudly.

I want to say that I am fine on my own or that I would rather work with Manon, but before I can even consider it, Mademoiselle Salomé says, "I don't think you'll need to, Pauline. I'm certain Alix will dazzle us."

That afternoon, I sit at the worktable alongside Manon, and Pauline sits at her ebony desk. Raven has finally returned from God knows where and meanders around, leisurely organizing the new feathers.

I sneak glances at him and remember our time spent beneath the gnarled oak, of how much I have changed since. Raven has returned from vacation more handsome than ever. It's his tan and his grown-out curls and laisser-faire attitude.

He must feel my gaze because while he lightly touches an English ringneck pheasant feather, then a scarlet ibis plume, he turns in my direction and shoots me his sexiest smile.

"Want to feel them?" he says, coming over and bumping my shoulder with his. "You could use them for your new project."

I shake my head, then turn to Manon who is cursing under her breath, struggling with a new sketch, and I offer to help her instead. Pauline draws for a while, then Raven, in passing, gestures to neon-blue dyed ostrich feathers, lying hidden at her feet.

He says, "I'm surprised Mother hasn't already confiscated those."

Pauline pulls out one of the feathers and explains that sometimes she needs colors that real birds can't provide. She also pulls out a few cans of spray paint—one is electric yellow, the other hedge green, another fuchsia.

Before any of us can ask questions, Salomé waltzes out of her study and says, "What can't a bird provide?"

Pauline quickly hides the feather back under her desk, but the cans are in plain view.

Mademoiselle Salomé confiscates each one, drops them in the garbage, the loud clunks making us jump, then she says, "I thought you knew better, Mademoiselle Bellamy."

"These paints cost a fortune, Salomé! And besides, I'm not doing anything," Pauline cries.

The feather artist says never to bring garbage again in her shop, point final.

As soon as Mademoiselle Salomé is gone, Faiza kneels by Pauline and scoops the blue plumes in her arms and carries them away, mumbling something about returning the feathers back to their pure and original state.

Manon leans toward me and softly says, "If Faiza is able to fix them, I'll use them for the next pair of wings."

Later, when everyone is on break and Faiza is looking for extra sewing needles, I say, "What is with Pauline?"

Faiza opens a box of very fine size sixty-five needles for a georgette dress with feather tassels. "Pauline is the great-grandniece of Gabrielle Bonheur Chanel, as in *the* Coco Chanel, and Pauline's father currently runs the flagship boutique." Faiza carefully places the needle inside her sewing machine. "You get my drift?"

"Sort of."

"Okay, poulette. Let me be clearer. Mademoiselle Salomé has done quite a bit of business with Chanel. Part of why Salomé became Paris's main d'or is because of Pauline's father. Monsieur Bellamy helped sell a fall line a few years back that used Salomé's signature capes and feathers along the cuffs of the dresses. Mille et Une Plume tripled in revenue. Salomé's relationship to Pauline is, shall we say, complicated."

That night, as I am wiping the counters and making a grocery list, Raven lingers. He makes light of his mother tossing the paints and tells me Pauline is always pushing boundaries, pushing buttons. He says it's nothing new, and that it's his turn to ask me a question.

He asks, "Where did you stay during the holidays?" He makes a face. "Not with Jeanne's boyfriend?"

"Why do you care?" I say, draping the cloth near the sink.

"Curious. Maybe a little jealous."

Raven tells me he was on the verge of not coming back to the boutique after the holidays, but his mother threatened to cut him off if he didn't do something job-wise, or life-wise, and also because he missed me.

"Perhaps your mother has a point," I say. "Have you thought about that?"

Raven shrugs, then musses my hair. "I like it short."

"Thanks. It was a Christmas gift from a new friend."

As soon as I utter these words, I am taken back to Anne Cazel's salon de coiffure, the train ride, how ridiculously happy I was, but as soon as I remember the moment of my legs wrapped around Blaise's waist, I shake my head and bury the memories into the deepest parts of my body. Because after the phoenix came the cemetery, because, like always, the bad follows the good, and I cannot think about Blaise and his fingers pulling at his beanie, or his hand on my shoulder, or him saying, "I thought you knew," and "Will we be all right?" Because if I do, I might start to unravel, and besides the answer is no.

I stroke the feathers in their bins, then look up into Raven's sky-blue eyes and say, "I missed you, too."

Raven tugs at the waist of my jeans.

The prince of darkness hovers between us. "How dramatic can these villainous wings be, do you think?"

"It's the Dream Show, Pixie. The crazier the better."

When he leans in to kiss me, I pull back and blurt, "But can they be *dark*-dark?"

Raven lifts an eyebrow.

"More nightmare than dream."

Raven grins and slips his fingers through mine. "They can be as terrifying as you want as long as they're incredible."

"Good," I say, but again pull away, pick up my drawing papers, and hand him the prince of darkness wings.

"Holy shit," Raven says, rifling through my sketches. "Mother will freak."

I close my eyes.

"What feathers will you use and how will you create the leathery part?"

"I've been dreaming about the griffon vulture plumes."

Raven plucks one—long, oily, and sleek. He runs his thumb on the gunmetal gray, making the room smell like sulfur.

"Pixie?"

"Yeah."

"Did I tell you Mother talked a lot about you on our trip? She thinks you're brilliant." Raven pulls me closer. "Tiens," he says, then he unhooks the silver coin from his neck and ties it around mine. "I was going to give it to you on our date."

The necklace is warm. The raven in flight imprints itself against my skin. I know I shouldn't love it, but when Raven adds that I'm the one who should be wearing a bird on my chest anyway, that my love for them is palpable, that I speak the language of feathers, and that he thinks I'm brilliant, too, then kisses me, I kiss him back.

CHAPTER 33

The first question Mademoiselle Salomé has when she sees the sketch of my prince of darkness wings is if Manon, Pauline, and Faiza have studied the drawing and if they approve? Disappointed because the feather artist does not freak as Raven suggested, I call the women into the study.

"Oh purée," Pauline whispers, leaning in close to the sketch.

Manon examines it for a long time, then says, stroking her finger on the leathery part, "I think you could use silicone here. But I'd rework the dimensions. I'd try to contain them a little more because a dancer *will* have to wear them."

Salomé agrees.

Faiza shivers. "They're bringing up a lot of emotions. You should use black leather around the spine," she says, pointing, "and I think there should be less translucence. Maybe slender crescents only at the bottom or along the sides."

Pauline is still staring, her eyes like saucers. "Oh purée," she repeats. "I didn't know you had this in you."

I exhale and say, "Thanks everyone for the suggestions." Then on my way out, Salomé calls my name.

I wait for her to tell me she disagrees, that they're all wrong, but the feather artist says, "No one's ever used the griffon vulture feathers before. I think the Moulin Rouge's costume director will love them." Salomé pauses. "I think they'll own the stage. But be careful," she says looking at me again with her dark stare. "They seem untamed."

One evening in mid-January, before closing, the feather artist enters the costume room as I am pulling out the overflowing trash bag from the industrial garbage bin, the part of my job I hate the most. By now the black leather frame of my griffon vulture wings lies next to Manon's newest one—elliptical, bee-like wings made of wire I helped draw. I have the sudden and silly hope Salomé will compliment my frame in front of everyone, but she only runs her palm against Pauline's spoonbill, the feathers fluttering gracefully. Beside them is another Pauline creation—the same spoonbill wings but mini, the size of my hand, hot pink and playful. The feather artist lifts the baby wings up and laughs.

She says, "Pauline, I adore your free spirit."

Then Mademoiselle invites her to attend the Petit Palais fundraiser as her plus-one.

Pauline swoons. "I'd be honored, Mademoiselle Salomé."

Manon rolls her eyes so far back I think she might faint, and Faiza frowns ever so slightly when Mademoiselle Salomé shares that, this year, the premières are not included. I'm disappointed, too, and jealous of Pauline's status and talent, but mostly I want to be alone to finish building my wings. I want to be free of them.

When Manon plops down next to me and murmurs, "I hate Pauline Bellamy more every day," I look at my sketch again, then at the frame of my sharp-edged wings. I ask the hand stitcher if the measurements work and after looking at them for a long time, Manon nods, then says, "Are you sure you want to construct those things, Alix? Because I feel like they might suck the life out of you."

They already have, I don't say.

SPRING

CHAPTER 34

All through February and March, I nest inside Mille et Une Plume, keep Raven's silver coin clasped around my neck, and construct the wings. I make two failed attempts, then finally something gives, and as I close my eyes and see Jeanne and the prince galloping, it dawns on me that these wings should be more pliable. With Manon and Faiza's support, and even Pauline's, I begin to work on their flexible spine and that changes everything.

One Saturday morning, the day after Pauline and Mademoiselle's attendance at the Petit Palais, Pauline causing a city-wide stir in a ravishing gold dress with the mini spoonbill wings pinned to her waist, I answer a phone call from the Four Seasons's hotel manager. He says that la duchesse de Vaugirard showed him my bouquet and that he is thinking he would like about six to eight with a five-thousand euro deposit on the front end, and five thousand more when we deliver them in person at 31 rue George V.

I am so stunned I thank him, then ask if I can call right back. I look out at the gnarled oak, at its branchlets packed with tender green buds, some already exploding into leaves, and squeal, nearly crying. I'm about to get up and grab my journal, scribble the date beside the words *Four Seasons*, when Pauline pokes her head into Mademoiselle's study.

"What are you doing here?" she says. "Pretending to be the boss?"

"Just answering the phone."

I go to the costume room certain I left my notebook underneath loose griffon vulture plumes at the worktable, but my journal with the leather cover, with *everything* in it, is not there. I return to the study and panic.

"Have you seen my journal?" I ask.

Pauline has taken a seat at Salomé's desk.

"We should talk, Alix," she says, propping her thigh-high boots on the table.

My heart, like a caged bird, flaps.

"You are a talented petite main," Pauline says. "It's true. Those dark things you're making. They *are* something."

I look into her midnight-blue eyes and wince.

"Last night at the fundraiser, Salomé told Paul Lugubre and my father that the only wings rivaling mine were yours. Can you believe it?"

Pauline digs through her purse and pulls out my journal.

"Before you get mad, let me explain."

I lunge at her, but Pauline swiftly moves the journal out of the way and adds, "Honestly, I was shocked and needed proof that you were, you know, that talented. I do love the feather bouquets. Their concept." She smirks. "What did you write again? *Feathers are meant to be given not kept.* Awww. That's sweet."

"Pauline," I say.

She holds a finger up. "What a contrast, these bouquets to the wings you are creating. If only those feathers were yours to sell." Pauline gives me her best pout.

"Are you done?"

Pauline shakes her head. "I also took the liberty of confiscating the plumes from upstairs, your bouquet of bliss, I think. As evidence, if anyone asks."

"Those feathers were scraps," I say, exasperated. "And they were in *my* room."

"Your room?" Pauline says. "Not for long."

"What do you mean?"

"Look, Alix," Pauline continues. "I would rather not be the one who tells Salomé about your Oliver Twist tendencies.

Do you know how finicky the feather artist is about the use of her beloved molted plumes? You sold her stuff behind her back. Unforgivable."

Perhaps because Pauline speaks with such assurance, and because my voice has left me, and because what she says is partially true, I nod.

"What if we made a deal?" Pauline says. "I don't tell anyone anything, and right after the final wings are built you leave. I mean you got great experience. And then I speak to my father and see if he can get you a gig somewhere else at another house in the city. Hell, Paul Lugubre might take you, maybe even as his sketcher? Wouldn't that be a win-win?"

"No." I look at her wild eyes, pleading with my own. "I love it here far more than you do."

Pauline flutters her hand in front of her, then says, "Oh, but this place is about to change. Once I become Salomé's apprentice, I'll turn the boutique into a rare dernier cri salon where only the most trendsetting come to dress. Can't you see someone at the Met Gala in a giant pair of spray-painted wings?"

"Salomé will never agree," I say. "And what about Manon? Mademoiselle Salomé might pick her."

Pauline laughs. "Puh-lease. Manon and I go way back, Alix. She is a great hand stitcher, but Manon is not a leader. And," she says, grinning, "if she needed help from a petite main as green as you to sketch her wings, she shouldn't get the job. Should she?"

The idea of Pauline becoming not only apprentice but changing everything inside this precious place makes me shake with anger.

"Besides," Pauline flips her hair and says, "I know how to draw, I'm a leader, and I haven't stolen anything."

That day, then the following and the following, I debate whether or not to tell Mademoiselle Salomé what Pauline's long-term dreams are, but I have been lying to the feather artist for so long about so many things I wonder if I am just as bad as Pauline. Besides, Pauline goes in and out of Mademoiselle's study as if she'd signed the apprentice contract already.

One evening, the fully built skeleton of my prince of darkness wings collides into the worktable. With nearly all the wings finished, we are running out of room. I ask Faiza if I can move my project into the sewing lab, behind the machines. The première acquiesces but, laughing, tells me to never leave her by herself with those monsters.

Through the weekend, alone inside the boutique, I work, sewing flight feathers and semiplumes and down feathers, not just from a griffon vulture but also from the underbelly of a turkey. *La plume de dinde*, I remember, means "wildness"—from beyond the grave, something man cannot control. I use the softer feathers to add thickness and heft, and when I finally pull back and look at what I've done, I gasp. The wings are still terrifying, but they look soft and alive. I run a hand over them, and for a second Jeanne hovers nearby.

I can almost see her crying outside a bathroom at a party, and I wish I could have done more for her. All over again, I hear Blaise's story. That he yelled for Jeanne to slow down, to stop, but Jeanne still drove away and crashed her boyfriend's car into the guardrail—and something new abruptly dawns on me. Jeanne *chose* to be reckless. She drove high and drunk on purpose and left me and a myriad of other people who loved her behind. I wonder if perhaps I shouldn't let her go.

CHAPTER 35

One rainy night, I roll the mannequin inside the sewing lab. Like Mademoiselle Salomé showed me, I kneel, attach the harness to the center of the wings, then yank the prince of darkness wings up, hooking them to the bust. I step back and watch in awe as they pulse to life, three-dimensional, sharp-edged, sleek, and vulturous.

I don't know when Raven comes in, minutes or hours later. Perhaps I don't hear him because of the rain beating on the roof, but when I turn, Raven is near me running a hand through his curls, which are wet from the downpour.

"Jesus, Alix," he says. "Those things are formidable."

Exhausted, I make my way into the costume room and pour myself a glass of water, which I drain in a few gulps.

Raven trails me and asks if I'm okay. I nod. Then, as if everything between us was normal, Raven shakes the water off his clothes, goes to his mother's study, and comes back holding a slender plume, as blue as the sea.

He hands it to me. "This feather comes from the splendid sunbird."

It sparkles in my hand and reminds me of a hummingbird.

Raven says, "You look beyond agitated, Pixie."

The rain claps on the roof. I don't know how much I love my new wings, and I assume Pauline will figure out how to get what she wants, and soon I will be fired regardless of my work. I return the sunbird feather to him, then say, "Pauline wants to turn the boutique into a dernier cri salon when she becomes the next apprentice. She wants to bring on spray paints and synthetic products. Maybe even furs."

Raven laughs. "Told you. She is dramatic."

I say, "If I were lucky enough to ever become your mother's apprentice, I would honor everything she stands for."

The costume room has darkened, and Raven's necklace is a deadweight against my collarbone.

I close my eyes and add, "You know what I think about every minute of every day?"

"What?"

"Who belongs to whom?"

Raven sits down next to me then gently bumps my shoulder. "You can make yourself mad ruminating, Pixie."

Even with the feathers stirring between us and the compliment he gave me about my wings, about them being formidable, I can't pretend anymore. My eyes fill. I unclasp his necklace and return it.

"I should have never taken it," I say. "Wasn't mine to wear."

"I thought you were my girlfriend?"

"Do you love me?"

"Do you?"

"No," I say.

In the semi-dark, I can still make out his damp curls, sky-blue eyes, and the tiny jagged scar on his bottom lip.

Raven exhales. "Damn."

And I know by the way he is looking at me with laser focused intensity, like one of his drawings, that we could keep on dating, kissing, if I laughed, or backtracked, or blew off my comment, but I also know I am just a diversion for Raven, and when I don't say anything, Raven continues to hold my gaze and hooks the silver coin around his neck.

"Is this because of Jeanne's boyfriend?" he asks.

"This has nothing to do with Blaise."

But once Raven leaves, and the door to the boutique clicks shut, I go to the sewing lab, and when I see my dark wings pulsing, everything I have been repressing surfaces back—from my mother disappearing long ago, to the night Jeanne died, to Papa leaving, to Blaise letting me sleep in his apartment, to us kissing, desperate, turning into a phoenix. My heart aches. I see Blaise next to Jeanne's tomb, asking me if I'm okay. I feel his palm on my shoulder, and that's when I recognize my terrible mistake. In my grief for Jeanne, I pushed Blaise away.

CHAPTER 36

The following morning, the rain is gone. I'm worried about showing everyone my finished wings, nervous about what Mademoiselle will say, but when I roll them out of the sewing lab and place them inside the study along with Manon's newest ostrich wings, our snowy owl wings, Pauline's spoonbill wings, and the ones from Bid Day, the women grow quiet. Mademoiselle Salomé circles the griffon vulture feathers. She peers at them from every angle, then asks me, after she touches the spine, if they fold in on themselves.

"Yes."

"Have you named them?" she asks.

"They are my prince of darkness wings."

Mademoiselle strokes the down and semiplumes that lie beneath the flight feathers and smiles something radiant. She says, "Alix's creation commands attention, doesn't it?"

Pauline is wearing a black dress with a gold belt cinched tightly around her waist. She runs her finger on the buckle, then says, "But who on earth will agree to wear them? They look beyond heavy."

"They're not," I say.

Salomé caresses the scallops of my wings, the place where I cut out the crescents of skin, the most fragile parts.

"Mademoiselle Bellamy, have you not done your research on the Dream Show's storyline?" she asks. "The Moulin Rouge's principal performer will wear them. People come from near and far to experience the magic of the show, and they'll see the magic of these wings."

Pauline again fusses with her belt buckle.

Salomé circles my wings, taking photos of them, open and closed. When she's done, she stops at Manon's ostrich wings and notices the tint of blue paint left in them. Manon bites her lower lip and explains that she wanted to show that we believe in molted plumes, and the lengths we will go to repair them. The hand stitcher glances at Pauline when she says this, then points to the ribbons underneath her wires and shows Salomé how her wings will act as sleeves on the dancer. The feather artist smiles, strokes her fingers along the ostrich feathers, and tells Manon she is proud. For a long while, Salomé studies

Pauline's. The wings are nearly as large as mine. They are sensual, sturdy, and full of luminosity, but Mademoiselle Salomé doesn't say anything. She returns to my prince of darkness wings, wraps an arm around me, and says, "Brava, Alix."

On our way out the door, Pauline catches my eye, then smirks, tracing her finger along her throat.

More days pass. Pink cherry blossoms, then lilac burst into bloom. I want to believe that Salomé has come to respect me, and that despite the drama and the politics, I might be the one she chooses as her apprentice. I want to believe that I am the most like her and that Pauline will never be.

As the clock ticks and the Dream Show looms closer, Salomé invites the dancers by appointment to try on the wings and also tells us to please create the final pair, not to wait until the last minute, that by now we should know feathers have their own agenda, that she would like something to contrast the griffon. Glorious, bright, bounteous, and meaningful. But Manon, Pauline, and I only linger by the door of the study, desperately hoping to catch a glance of what each dancer will look like with our wings attached to their back. Faiza is the only one allowed during the fittings.

"Please," Manon and I beg the première when she comes out of the study one afternoon holding a bundle of purple thread.

"Is this dancer trying on my peacock wings?" I say.

"Can we look, only once?" Manon pleads.

But Faiza waves us away.

Manon and I go back to the costume room and argue with Pauline about what the tenth pair of wings should be.

"How about cygnet feathers, preferably spray-painted green, on heart-shaped wings for beauty?" Pauline suggests.

Manon glares at her. "Are cygnet wings even molted?"

Pauline shrugs.

"Whatever," I say, too tired to think.

At night, I write Manon letters explaining everything to her about Raven because she *has* become my dear friend and I want to share things beside plumes with her, but then in the morning I bunch them up and throw them away, thinking Manon might not care about boy stuff anyway.

One May morning, Manon arrives wearing a pastel blue dress. She holds her journal firmly in her hand and a fancy watch in the other. Salomé takes a long look at the watch, then asks Manon to join her in her study. The feather artist and hand stitcher speak behind closed doors for a while, then Manon comes out with a proud air about her and tells Pauline, who has gathered a mound of alabaster cygnet feathers I have never seen before, that swan wings are fine, as long as they are natural, that she can help with the embroidering as the baby plumes might be extra silky.

I frown and say, "But I thought we didn't like those for our final pair?"

"I'm trying to collaborate," Manon whispers.

Later that afternoon, the hand stitcher pulls me aside, tucks her wisp of strawberry-blond hair behind her ear, and shows me a watch with yellow canary feathers embroidered in a tiny sun on its face. Back even straighter than usual, she says, "I've been tinkering with the combination of jewelry *and* feathers."

I tell her I love the concept and what she made, then as we sit at the worktable, I try to focus on the cygnet wings, on cutting the alabaster feathers in long V's as Pauline proposed.

Manon looks around, then quietly says, "One more thing. Raven asked me out on a date, but after thinking about it, I turned him down." She shrugs, grins, then adds, "I don't know about you, Pixie, but I have a lot going on and I don't need a Greek god distracting me, after all."

I could tell her about our fling now, my bunched-up letters addressed to her upstairs, but holding onto the pretty watch she created, Manon comes out of her artistic shell in a brand-new way, and I don't want to upset her. I can't help but love this confident girl. Manon tells me she will also be taking private drawing lessons starting in June.

"Pourquoi pas," she says.

I nod and try to feel the stir of the plumes myself. I try to soak up her enthusiasm, but I feel a little mechanical in the way I approach my work, as if the griffon vulture wings somehow sucked all my joy away. Even at night, in the minty room, I no longer find respite. I sleep in Salomé's study to be as close to the feathers as possible. One dawn, after barely sleeping, I am suddenly not sure I want to ever draw new feathers. Everything feels slippery, out of my control, and at the most inopportune time, I stop believing in myself—or perhaps I never did.

The Dream Show comes barreling down. Most days I do my best to hide my burnout, my blues, but one afternoon, the feather artist enters the costume room and I know by the way she holds herself that something unprecedented is about to happen. We all stop what we are doing, and, as if in slow motion, Salomé makes her way over to Pauline. The feather artist wraps an arm around the girl's waist, the way she once did to me, and says, "After months of agonizing, I have decided to offer Mademoiselle Bellamy the apprentice-ship. There is no reason to hold off the announcement. We are a month away from the show, and I would like to send out invitations with Pauline's name on them." Salomé keeps her eyes fixed on us. "Thank you, everyone, for your efforts. As Pauline and I sit and discuss the contract and long-term goals, we will let you know of upcoming changes, what this will mean for each one of you."

Pauline gives Mademoiselle Salomé a theatrical hug. She tells the feather artist the sky will be the limit. I am still holding the quill of a cygnet feather, unsure if what I heard was a momentary brain glitch when Mademoiselle Salomé asks that I follow her. I slowly stand and brush invisible lint off my jeans. Manon gently prods me and whispers, "Go."

Inside the study, Mademoiselle Salomé points to her leather chaise, then leans against her desk. My heart bangs double-time as I take a seat and I'm slightly hypnotized by her spectacular onyx stone earrings. She seems older, plagued by fatigue. New silver streaks adorn her curls, and when I don't speak, she says, "Is it true you stayed here during the Christmas holiday when the boutique was closed?"

I place a hand on my heart and nod.

"Then is it also true that you've been making secret bouquets and selling them?"

Again, I nod but grow woozy.

The feather artist scans me with her dark eyes and says, "The funny thing is, Alix, had you asked, I'd have been open to the idea. I might have endorsed you. I was stunned by your latest wings, so stunned in fact, it made my decision for the apprenticeship a lot harder. But then Pauline told me she saw you sitting at my desk late one night during the holidays, after she returned from Spain. She said you were wearing one of my capes. At first, I thought Pauline was lying. I told her to stop playing games. But yesterday or maybe the day before, Pauline showed me one of your bouquets."

I can't lift my eyes to hers. I know that trying to defend myself will only make it worse.

"Were you planning on speaking to me about any of it? About using Mille et Une Plume's brand and feathers without my approval? Were you going to tell me about gifting one to la duchesse de Vaugirard no less?"

At Tante Constance's name, I squirm in the chaise.

"Yes," I say. "I was." I twist my fingers. "I just didn't know when or how, and Tante Constance's bouquet was made of feather scraps, paper, and twine."

"Scraps?" Salomé repeats.

"Yes," I say. "Sometimes I plucked feathers from the industrial garbage bin." I swallow hard because I still sound like a thief, then add, "Feathers on their way to the trash."

Salomé crosses her arms, then slowly shakes her head.

I say, "I only *once* sold a bouquet of expensive plumes, and I only *once* gave a friend an eagle albino flight feather for courage because I believed he needed it."

"Isn't that noble?" Mademoiselle says.

Near tears, I say, "I also always wanted to pay you back."

"This isn't about money, Alix," Salomé says. "It's about trust."

I sit with my hands on my lap like the first time I came into this study. I want to tell the feather artist that Pauline stole my journal, that she doesn't respect the feathers, that trusting anyone now besides Manon is a dangerous proposition. I want to tell her that all I desire in this whole wide world is to become half the artist, of the plumassière, she is, to find my light among the feathers, to shine, but my voice is gone or perhaps so full of shame I cannot use it. I close my eyes and wish I could disappear into thin air.

Mademoiselle Salomé sighs and says, "I'm disappointed, Alix."

I stand, take in the gnarled oak through the bay window, the sunshine, flowers, and blue swallows, the drawers along the walls where the dusty encyclopedia sits. *Goodbye*, I tell them. *Goodbye, Mademoiselle Salomé.* I think of Pauline, now the new apprentice, and barely able to breathe, I manage to say, "I didn't mean to lie to you or pretend to be something I'm not. I just got carried away imagining what could have been. I am truly sorry."

I don't hear Manon calling me or Faiza running into Salomé's study. I don't hear Raven, who must have just strolled in, asking everyone what the hell is going on, or the prince of darkness wings pulsing, or all the feathers crying, because I sprint up to the minty room, grab everything I own, shove things in my duffel bag. I run out of the boutique, and on the sunniest day of the year, I walk unsteadily back to rue Jean Cocteau, remembering only later that I've left my garland of ruddy duck feathers behind.

CHAPTER 37

In my old room, I drop my stuff, then take off and wander. I make my way from rue Maubeuge to rue Lafayette, then walk until I'm in front of the Palais Garnier. I look up at the green domes, at the golden statues, the muses, then keep walking along Avenue de l'Opéra. The sun is hot. I grow thirsty and hungry but keep walking and walking. Late afternoon, I pass the front of la Comédie Française, imagine Constance onstage. I think of Blaise, and if my heart could shatter, it would. I walk until evening, until I've made a huge loop and am not far from rue des Trois Frères. For a moment, I think of knocking on his door. I see myself begging for his forgiveness but then imagine him, holding Betty, saying something awkward like thanks for coming, but I'm kind of busy, and I just head back to the 18th and clamber up the stairs into Papa's apartment and collapse onto my bed.

My feet are blistered. I'm sore everywhere and my brain is fuzzy. A few times, I sit up and think I'm in the minty room but grow confused and lie back on my ivory comforter, sadness engulfing me. I'm not sure when but at one point I open my window and perhaps to be closer to Jeanne, I climb onto the ledge. Beneath the stars, I lean forward and look at the sidewalk, and I wonder if final darkness protects us from reaching for and failing to catch the light.

I don't know how long I stay on the ledge, or when it started to rain until I realize I'm soaked. Eventually, I return to bed, grow achy, then toss and turn. I dream. A raven flies. Pauline spray-paints not only feathers but birds. Faiza sits by a fountain and cries. Blaise, Papa, and Jeanne sing at the top of their lungs. When I jolt awake, the sky is dark again. I try to move, but my legs and arms are pinned to the mattress. My forehead is scorching hot. I slowly stand and take a step toward the bathroom but collapse back onto the comforter.

The next morning or perhaps the one after that, I wake again.

My eyelids are crusted shut. Everything is too bright. A lingering soreness in my joints remains. Still, I sit up, my sore throat, headache, and chills gone. I remember the rain. Daybreak streaks silver pink across the sky. I wonder if I dreamed of being sick, but when I press my palm to my chest my T-shirt is damp and I smell like sweat.

Breathe, I tell myself.

Fresh air from the window I must have forgotten to close fills the room, and when I turn my head, I see a humming-bird on the window ledge. *Stopper of time.* Its wings buzz the color of the sky, and its body shines iridescent green. I get up and tiptoe barefoot closer to the window. *Fly*, the hum-mingbird says. The creature hovers, and in that pink-silver morning light, a melody plays from somewhere above the zinc roofs, and the hummingbird and I rise up and up and up until for just a moment, I swear, my toes leave the ground.

CHAPTER 38

I take a shower, then make my way to the bakery. I force myself to eat and drink until I am strong enough to come up with a semblance of a plan. After another day of rest, and after another spent sweeping the apartment until the cobwebs are gone and the kitchen counters cleaned, I head over to the duchess's place.

I know I am taking a chance. Tante Constance might throw me out, especially if Blaise told her I haven't seen him since Christmas, but I know I need to talk to someone, and I can't head back to Mille et Une Plume. When I arrive, the concierge buzzes me through the gate.

"Is the duchesse's grandnephew with her?" I ask, my heart galloping at the thought of Blaise sitting in her kitchen.

"Non, mademoiselle."

As I walk up the paved path, I slow, still afraid my old friend will be in the courtyard next to the chickens, smiling, all dimples, but Tante Constance is the only one sitting outside. She's on her patio chair, dressed in jeans and a mohair sweater, and holding a scepter that glints in the sun. When she sees me, she waves with the hand holding the scepter, and says, "Quelle belle surprise."

At her warmth, I nearly start to cry and let her take my hands in hers.

Tante Constance's snow-white hair is slicked back and bold red lipstick daubs her lips.

"Assied toi," she says, pointing to the chair next to hers, then disappears into her kitchen and brings out two fresh squeezed lemonades in the fanciest crystal goblets I have ever seen.

She sips from hers and says, "Now tell me everything."

I clutch my goblet and tell her about the aimless walking and getting soaked to the bone. I tell her about Jeanne, how I didn't know she was the one driving, how I took the news hard, and I tell her about asking Blaise to leave me at the cemetery when he was looking out for me. I tell her about Raven, about my prince of darkness wings, about Pauline being the new chosen apprentice. I even tell her about the bouquets. How I had only intended to emulate, not sabotage Mademoiselle Salomé.

"Ma pauvre, chérie," Tante Constance says.

For a moment, we are quiet and aside from her tabby cat who purrs and rubs its soft orange fur against my shins, her garden is silent. Even the chickens.

Constance finishes her lemonade, then says, "We all carry a touch of madness. Don't we? After my Louis died there were days where I never left my bed and thought I'd stay there until the end of time. It's okay."

She tells me to stay for lunch and sets the table in the garden. She brings out salads on porcelain plates. As she offers me a piece of baguette and the chickens come clucking, she says, throwing them crumbs, "Once we have talked everything through, and you have rested and feel stronger, I suggest you stroll by the prince's apartment and slip him a new feather."

"Blaise doesn't want to see me."

Tante Constance eats a piece of lettuce, dabs her red lips, and taps me with her scepter.

"I think he does, dear," she says.

I stay in the duchess's garden all afternoon and we talk until I have no words left. Tante Constance says that my mother leaving, and my father traveling but also neglecting me, then Jeanne dying was all too much, that the latter made the floor break from under my feet.

Once in a while, she refills my glass with lemonade, and

then again taking my hands in hers, she says, "The feathers did keep you afloat. You literally built a nest around yourself."

I smile a little, then she adds that she has a few ideas for me, perhaps ways to ground myself, that no matter my standing with Mille et Une Plume, if the goal is to become a feather artist, then that is what I should strive for.

The duchess taps her scepter on the ground, then says, "Don't let one person, however much you revered them, dictate your life. There are many roads that lead to Rome, Alix."

She asks me to visit her often and to a keep a connection to the plumes. For the next several days, I hunt the streets for feathers. I try not to think of the Dream Show, which I will never see. I try to live in the moment. I find feathers from doves, pigeons, wrens, even barn swallows. I bundle them up in newspaper, twine, and ribbons, then write song lyrics on each bouquet. I arrange them in glass jars and ask the nearby baker to place them in her window, priced at twenty-five euros each. The bundles sell out in hours, and I give the baker five euros for each one. The next day, la boulangère places a sign by my bouquets that reads *Pixie Dust, bouquets sur commande.* Every morning, I receive orders.

A few days later, when I visit Tante Constance, she asks me if I have slipped a feather under the prince's door, and I shake my head.

That night, I dream of him. Blaise lies beside me, thick-rimmed glasses crooked on his nose. He laughs, his laugh as real as my sleep is deep, and Betty's sound engulfs us, a pair of phoenix wings deploy behind me, but this time I do not wish to combust or vanish. In my dream, I straddle Blaise and allow the sun-yellow plumes behind me to ignite the room. My heart soars. We kiss and kiss and kiss, until Blaise drops his glasses onto the hardwood floors, and I wake only to realize it is just me under my ivory comforter.

I reach for the molted plumes on my desk and make a new bouquet of fox sparrow flight feathers—soft, small, and shimmery. I bring their rust-orange streaks to my face, trace the tops of them over my hands, my fingers, then run them along the tattoo on my forearm. The plumes warm me the way they once did at Mille et Une Plume.

SUMMER

CHAPTER 39

One Saturday afternoon in early June, as I'm creating un bouquet de vitalité—red robin mixed with dove and song thrush feathers the color of sand, all of which I found inside an abandoned nest while strolling behind the Sacré Coeur—the door to the apartment swings open. Papa walks in. I am so stunned, I drop the feathers.

"Salut, canard," he says, picking up the feathers then returning them to me. "I see you're still into plumes."

As we stare at each other, I notice he has put on a little weight, that his skin is healthier, and that he looks younger. Better.

I say, "It's been a minute."

My father slips his hands in his pockets and chuckles.

After all this time, I don't know if I should kiss him or yell at him or what. I rock back and forth on my heels and say, "Did you get married? Have another kid?"

"No," Fabien replies. "Zanx and I broke up, and after the band guys pulled me aside and told me they thought I needed help, I realized it, too, and I decided to get sober." He shakes his head, then says, "I know my texts were fleeting and didn't explain much. Truth is I hoped to be fully recovered before telling you and it took much longer than expected."

I nod. "Sounds, I don't know, hard."

Papa shrugs. "Wish I'd cleaned up long ago."

I look toward the apartment door, at Papa's bags piled up. I could turn away and hate him forever. I have such a long list of grievances. I could abandon him, too, but perhaps because of all the talking with Tante Constance and because Fabien is my only father, and because, unlike my mother, he has chosen to return, I want to give him another chance. Even if just the sliver of one.

When I take a step forward, he opens his arms, and I realize he isn't carrying his saxophone around his neck.

"Where is your other lover?"

He kisses my cheek. "On the landing. Part of my rehab was learning to put it down and to focus on the people around me. At least part of the time."

I grin and think of second chances, of Blaise and Betty.

"You okay?" Papa says.

"Yeah." And before I can think any of this through, I add, "I have to run an errand but want to make dinner later?"

"See you at seven."

When I arrive on rue des Trois Frères, I grow so nervous I walk up and down the street a few times, then I push open the porte cochère and tell myself that even if Blaise asks me to leave, I will be all right, fine, able to cope with the big feelings. I climb the stairs and have to stop midway to catch my breath. At his door, I suddenly yearn to hear him play the electric guitar so much I have to swallow back tears.

I knock.

No one opens.

After a while, I take one of the red robin feathers and am about to slip it under his door, but I change my mind and pull a dove feather from my back pocket. Cloud white. Its meaning: love. I slide it until the plume is so far in his entryway, I wouldn't be able to get it back if I tried. I jog down the stairs, and for the rest of the afternoon my chest hurts. All I can think about is Blaise and his dimples, how I want to tell him he was right about our kiss, that it was le plus beau baiser du monde. That Jeanne would have never wanted to get between us, that I have been unraveling at the seams ever since last June, or perhaps even before that. That I am beyond sorry.

At seven p.m. sharp, Papa is in the kitchen cooking spaghetti, and I can't believe my eyes. He has made a tomato sauce from scratch and the apartment smells like basil, garlic, and onions. We cheers with Perrier bottles, and I offer to toss the salad. When Papa asks what's been happening, I recount my time at Mille et Une Plume, my great love for the feathers, how I learned to sew and embroider. I tell him about the dusty encyclopedia, the feather magic, what it feels like to see wings become three-dimensional, probably like a song coming to life. I tell him about Pauline becoming the next apprentice, about Manon turning out to be a great friend. I even mention Raven, his mad talent yet utter lack of drive, but then I quickly add how none of it matters anymore because I was fired after too much happened.

"Please don't judge me," I say.

Papa takes a bite of the salad. "Considering my track record, don't worry, I won't."

I ramble more about Blaise and Tante Constance, about my feather bouquets, how last week a clothing store asked me to create bouquets of elegance with a touch of nostalgia for their vitrines, and a parfumerie suggested bouquets of vitalité.

I pause and say, "I was supposed to be part of the Dream Show."

I share little bits of my journal and my eyes fill as I think of the date fast approaching. How I will never see the dancers move with our wings attached to their backs on the Moulin Rouge stage. I wonder if Manon and Pauline finished the cygnet wings.

"You underestimate yourself, Alix. Let's work on that together." Papa smiles. "And besides, I can feel the magic of the feathers right here in this room."

I don't tell him about the hummingbird's visit, speaking to Jeanne's ghost, or thinking about feathers sprouting from my shoulder blades because he will need to give me far more than one compliment and one dinner before I trust him fully again.

After dinner, I tuck away in my room with my sketchbook and pencils, and listen to Papa riffing, stopping, and starting until bursts of notes from his sax turn into something like a new melody. It feels like home. Soon, I think there is a knock on the front door. At first, I'm certain I misheard. I go back to drawing, but the knocking starts again. I walk down the hallway and open the door, the sax still blaring behind me. On the landing, Blaise paces. He's wearing a white T-shirt, no glasses, faded jeans hung low on his hips, and his hair is sticking up. He pinches my delicate dove plume between his calloused fingers, and I have to hold onto the door handle for fear of grabbing him by the shirt and pulling him into my room.

"Really, Alix?" he says.

Blaise hands me the cloud-white plume and turns to, almost certainly, dart back down the stairs, disappear into the stairwell, and never ever talk to me again.

I call out: "It's a dove feather for love."

Blaise stops, hand gripping the railing, and I watch how the muscles in his back tighten beneath his T-shirt.

I keep speaking. "I know you're mad at me, and I know it's maybe a little strange I've talked to Tante Constance more recently than you, but I got fired from Mille et Une Plume, and she was the only one I could think of to talk to, besides you, when everything fell apart." I wrap my arms around myself and wait, eyes focused on Blaise's back.

Blaise sighs.

I want him to turn around so I can look into his eyes when I apologize, but his foot is balanced on the step as if poised for fleeing.

I say, "I still think about the cemetery all the time. I wish I'd gone home with you on Christmas Day, or that I'd banged on your door not just once, but a million times since then to tell you how much I miss our friendship. I'm sorry I hurt you, Blaise."

"When did you bang on my door?"

"I don't know. One day when you were busy rehearsing."

"What about Raven?"

Blaise's voice is low like the rumble of the ocean and for the first time since my mother abandoned me and I boycotted bargaining with the universe, I close my eyes and say, *Dear earth, moon, and sky, please do not take him away, too. I'll settle for friends. I swear.*

"I never loved him." I nearly whisper the words because my throat has collapsed, and a million tears threaten to fall.

For what feels like a century, Blaise keeps on gripping the railing. Then he turns around and looks at me.

"Alix Leclaire."

His gaze is fierce yet earnest. My chest swells and I want to rise up on tiptoes and throw my arms around him, but instead I wipe my cheeks and silently beg for him to take the first step—whatever that is—when someone clears their throat, making both of us startle.

"Bonsoir," Papa says, holding his sax, an amused expression on his face. "I'm Fabien, Alix's dad."

Blaise shakes his hand. "Blaise de Vaugirard."

"You're related to a duchess?"

"Yes," Blaise replies.

I can't help but smile.

Then Blaise says, "Monsieur Leclaire?"

"Please call me Fabien," Papa says.

"Fabien then," Blaise repeats. "Would it be okay if your daughter walked back with me to my apartment, just for a little while?"

My chest feels like it might explode. "Blaise and I have a few things to iron out."

"I see," Papa says.

I'm about to tell him that after being gone for months, he is not about to start parenting me now, but my father adds, "You two be safe." Then he says, "Wait. De Vaugirard. Aren't you the kid who plays at the conservatory and already has a record deal?"

"I was offered one once. Long story."

Papa laughs. "Kid after my own heart." To me, he says, "I thought you were staying away from musicians, canard?"

"I thought so, too," Blaise says.

Again, I turn beet red, and when one of Blaise's dimples makes an appearance, I almost faint.

"Only the wild ones," I answer.

"Well," Papa says to Blaise, "make sure you bring her home before morning, or I'll show you wild, okay?"

"You have my word," Blaise answers.

On the sidewalk, we walk next to each other. I keep tucking my shirt in and out of my jeans. Blaise pretends to play air guitar. Then we start to say something at the same time and laugh. This makes me want to loop my arm through his, but I'm not sure if he would like that, so instead I walk a little closer.

Blaise looks at me and says, "I should be mad at Tante Constance. She never once said you came to visit."

I chuckle. "She is one hell of an aunt."

"Yeah," Blaise says, then with his gaze still on me, he

adds, "I have to be honest, Alix, I didn't think today would go this way."

"Me either," I answer.

And then, at the exact same time, we both say we're glad and laugh all over again.

Inside his apartment, everything I have come to love is the same. Herbs spill from terra-cotta pots, sending waves of rosemary and thyme scents. Betty is as nail-polish red as ever, and cables and amplifiers are piled up in the middle of the living room. His bed is unmade. The kitchen is clean, and a pound cake adorns the table. I'm not sure where to stand or if I should sit. After a moment, I walk over to Blaise's window and look out at the shimmering stars and the zinc roofs that always bring me peace, like live music, or the feeling of home.

It's not until I smell Blaise's fresh laundry scent that I turn and find myself so close to him I have to tip my head back to look into his eyes. The room is filled with shadows, lit only by one lamp next to his bed. I don't know how to start, what to say. Unlike Raven, Blaise does not initiate. There is nothing to smoke, no wine to drink, no gifts or feathers to speak of. Just a tall boy in faded jeans looking at me through his extra-long lashes. I could speak, but instead I place my fingers on his heart and search for the beat. *Thump, thump, thump.* Strong and steady. I slide my hand from his chest to his stomach, tracing the dunes through his T-shirt, until Blaise shudders, then entwines his fingers through mine.

I don't exactly know how we get to his bed, but soon Blaise is above me yanking off his T-shirt, and I am pulling at my jeans, and his mouth is on mine, and it feels like the world has tilted on its axis, not like my dream where I was growing wings exactly, but like our hearts have fused and *we* are the phoenix, one million sun-yellow flames pulsing in the night sky.

When Blaise pulls away and says, "Alix, attends," I sit up and look at him, a question in my eyes.

He grins, all dimples. "I need your yes." He reaches under his bed and grabs a condom.

"Oui, oui, oui," I say. "What about you?"

Blaise laughs, burying his face in my neck, then as he kisses my ear, he whispers, "Yes."

Blaise walks me back to rue Jean Cocteau before sunrise. The streets of Montmartre are peaceful. He has slung an arm around my shoulder and, tucked into his side, I think of Jeanne. I smile and speak to her in my head, tell her how I never want to let go of this boy's hand, how with him my bones not only turn to liquid but to gold or to something even more precious.

"Ça va?" Blaise says.

"Good," I say. "I mean great. I'm just thinking about Jeanne."

Blaise smiles. "She'd give me hell right now, plus The Talk about never hurting your feelings, or else."

We keep strolling. I think of his apartment, of what we did, of losing my virginity, of the replica of Betty I discovered on his shoulder blade, small as a euro coin, and I hear him whisper, "I love you the way I love music, Alix Leclaire."

On the landing, I say, "Will you come get me later?"

Blaise leans his forehead against mine. "Maybe." He grins.

I wait until he is at the bottom of the stairwell, then I open the door and walk into the hallway. I wonder if Papa is gone—habit—if something more important than me pulled him away. His travel bags, usually on the floor for days, are gone. I walk into the living room and when I see his empty mattress behind the partition, my heart sinks, but then I hear him humming and realize his clothes are put away and that his bags are neatly folded under the green sofa.

"I thought you were about to get grounded," he says. "I'm pretty sure it's morning."

When I poke my head into the kitchen, my father is at the table drinking a cup of coffee.

"Nope, it's still dark out," I say.

"God, parenting sober is no joke," he replies.

I laugh.

"So?" he asks.

"So what?" My cheeks turn crimson. I pretend to look inside the cupboards though I am not the least bit hungry.

Papa smiles, then pours me coffee. In silence, we sit cradling our mugs and watch the sunrise, aurora pink, spread across the city.

"I love you, canard," he says. "Blaise is lucky."

CHAPTER 40

When I rouse myself from bed late the next day, the phoenix wings are the only thing on my mind, and at once I know I must return to Mille et Une Plume to create them.

A promise, this time, to myself.

The silver-and-electric-blue wings do not hang in the bay window. Pauline's flamingo-pink spoonbill wings sway behind the glass instead. Next to them are tutus made of ostrich feathers, their color spray-painted to an agonizing green. I try to peer inside hoping to see Mademoiselle Salomé or Faiza bustling about, but the shop looks quiet. I stand frozen, thinking a million thoughts until I cannot take it anymore and push open the door.

"Hello?" I call out.

I walk through the parlor, ready to ask anyone for the opportunity to work here again, but the place feels different. Even the smell is foreign, something like acetone and cigarette smoke. The feathers do not stir.

"Hello?"

I walk through the costume room, and on Pauline's ebony desk I find miniature baby swan wings spray-painted the same awful green as the tutus in the parlor. I run my hand on them and feel sick. Then I open the door to Salomé's study and Pauline sits at the desk, smoking a cigarette with a long holder as bright as the belt she is wearing. Her dress is off the shoulders, tight and silky, and one of Salomé's capes is draped on the back of the chair. But amidst the glitz, Pauline looks stressed. Overwhelmed.

"I tried knocking," I say.

Pauline peers at me through the smoke. She keeps on puffing, then looks at the mounds of feathers on the floor.

"What a disaster," she says, as if I'd never left, as if all this were my fault.

I look out at the gnarled oak and send a silent greeting and ask for guidance. Feathers droop in the ivory bins. A few of them on the ground have been cut at weird angles.

Drawers hang open. Delicate plumes like the blue-and-white extra-long tail feathers of the Lady Amherst's pheasant have spilled out of their bins and are left, forgotten. No one has been sweeping the hardwood floors.

As if Pauline could read my mind, she says, "Okay, fine. I'm freaking out."

"I can see that," I say.

"I thought Salomé would give me freedom and power once I was her apprentice, at least let me build the last pairs of wings my way. I wanted to make everything cooler. You know, du jour, contemporary!"

I nod.

Pauline takes a puff of her cigarette. "I wanted the Moulin Rouge dancers to wear tutus with their wings. But Salomé got so upset. She said this wasn't a ballet and walked out with the dusty encyclopedia."

"Salomé left?"

"Wait. I'm not done," Pauline says. "Then Papa came into the boutique, furious. Not even at Salomé but at *me*. He says everything is a mess. That I'm a silver spoon baby who can't deal with pressure, and to get it together. Can you believe it?"

Pauline points behind the door and I turn to see another tutu, this one made of neon-yellow feathers with a waist band that reads, *Pauline's*.

She runs her fingers through her hair and says, "I got frustrated and just wanted to try other stuff aside from the dumb wings."

I have to admit, her tutu is pretty cool in a punk rock kind of way. Her style is nothing like Salomé's, but I bet Jeanne would have been a fan and somehow that makes me empathize with Pauline just a little bit.

"Where is Salomé now?"

"Who knows?" Pauline replies.

"What about Manon and Faiza?"

Pauline shuts her eyes and takes another drag of her cigarette. "Does it matter? The show is a week away, I never even finished the frame for the final pair of wings, and Raven is, you know, same old, same old."

"Yes, it matters," I say. "Aren't we supposed to be family?"

"Ha," Pauline answers. "I thought Manon would have reached out to you by now. She quit after you left. It seems like she found something in your old room that made her mad at Raven. Faiza," she says, waving her hand, "is moping somewhere around here."

Pauline has gone pale, like she is on the verge of a breakdown.

I think of the letters crumpled in the waste basket upstairs. I'd left them.

I say, "I guess stepping into Mademoiselle Salomé's shoes and being her apprentice is harder than you thought?"

She puts her head onto Salomé's desk and says, "I've been groomed for this my whole life, and now that I have the opportunity to step up, I don't know if I can or even want to."

Because I'm shocked at her honesty, and because I also realize that just like me Pauline is human and struggling, I say, "I can help."

"Even after everything?"

I remember the past weeks and say, "I know this sounds ridiculous, but I've gained some insight." I smile, but then tell her how hard this year really was. How even her pettiness didn't match the pain I've lived through. I add, "I'm sorry you're overwhelmed."

Pauline stares at me, then offers me her cigarette holder.

"You can have it," she says.

I shake my head, then laugh, and tell her she should quit smoking at least inside the boutique for the plumes' sake, and I open the door to the courtyard and the windows. I pick up every single feather and place them back where they belong. I take Pauline's yellow tutu and hang it above the worktable in the costume room where Raven's posters once hung. I tell her I will check on Faiza, and then we will come up with a strategy. Pauline gets up, walks around the desk, then throws herself in my arms, thanking me.

Before I head to the sewing lab where I anticipate Faiza will be, I make my way to the minty room. I want to gaze at the leaf-sea, if only for a moment, ground myself, but to my surprise I find Raven passed out on the apricot quilt, Pauline's suitcases littering the floor around him. I look for my garland, but it's gone.

In the sewing lab, just like I thought, Faiza is sitting with her head bent over the broken snowy owl wings. Behind her are my giant prince of darkness wings. They still command the room, and I shiver at their sight.

"I thought you didn't want to be left alone with them," I say.

Faiza looks like she has aged ten years in a month.

"Oh, poulette," she whispers, pulling me in for a hug. "I'm so glad to see you."

Faiza explains that the day after I left, Pauline's father swooped in to discuss Pauline's apprenticeship. For a while, all seemed well until Pauline began to undo parts of the snowy owl wings, until she asked to create more modern ones, until she started spray-painting feathers and cutting plumes without permission from the feather artist, and one morning after Pauline brandished the mini green cygnet wings, saying she wanted more of that, and less of the boring, old-fashioned archangel stuff, Salomé said that if she couldn't honor birds in the boutique she built from the ground up, she would leave.

"At first, I tried to help and even listened to Pauline's terrible music," Faiza says. "I worked day and night on advancing the swan wings, thinking Pauline would have a change of heart and beg for Salomé to come back but I only got so far, and Pauline started making tutus. I couldn't keep up, and the feathers, I think, went on strike." Faiza clasps her hands and says, "I never thought Mille et Une Plume would end up this way."

When I go back into the study, Pauline is sprawled on the chaise.

I tell her the strategy. Faiza will fix the snowy owl wings. I will ask Raven to find Mademoiselle Salomé, and in the meantime, I will think of a new vision for the final pair of wings.

Pauline puts her arm across her eyes and says, "We don't have the dusty encyclopedia. Raven swears that without it there is no magic, that we will not finish on time."

"Nonsense," I say. "*We* hold the magic." I smile at Pauline, then add, "Though I hate to admit it, I think a cross between your vision and Mademoiselle Salomé's could work. You could work with synthetic plumes for your edgier designs and avoid hurting the molted feathers. You can still honor Salomé's connection to the birds. You could do both."

"You think so?" Pauline says.

"Anything's possible. But now let's get all the wings done and delivered."

Raven sleeps the whole day. Sometime in the evening, he pokes his head into the study, and when he sees me sitting beside Pauline and Faiza, he runs a hand through his curls and says, "What are you doing here?"

I can tell by the way he stands that he is stunned, even a bit uneasy, by my return, but he also seems grateful. I see it in the warmth of his eyes. I ask him to please tell his mother the wings will be delivered for dress rehearsal.

Raven nods, then says, "I'll tell her tonight because I'm off to Guadeloupe in a few days, Pixie."

"Yeah?" I raise my eyebrows.

"After you gave me back my necklace and Manon rejected me, I decided it was time to stop clinging to Mille et Une Plume." He half smiles. "It's time I investigate what *I* want out of life. For better or for worse. I'll be working in a hotel by the sea, drawing for pleasure."

And before I can wish him my best, Raven says, "À la prochaine, beauté," then chucks me under the chin and leaves.

Later, in the sewing lab, inspiration prickles into my fingertips. I close my eyes, see the hummingbird beating its iridescent wings, asking me to fly, and I know what I want to build. But before I start, I look at the empty wingback chair, give Faiza Manon's address, and tell her to go get her, that I am asking for help, except Manon declines my invitation. She says to Faiza she will only consider working for me once I have opened my boutique. I imagine her and me running a feather shop, and goose bumps rise on my arms, but the clock ticks and my new wings wait.

Days go by in a blur.

For my final pair of wings, I imagine combining rhinestones with plumes from the Bali bird-of-paradise. I want the dancer to burn as they wear them. Pauline tells me I could use orange spray paint to make the colors look more like flames, but I tell her these are my wings to construct. No one else's.

"Fine," Pauline says, throwing her hands up.

I pick a combination of bright orange rooster feathers, found in a barn nearby, and Dupioni silk, plus the bird-of-paradise feathers and place them on the floor. I think of Blaise bent over Betty, then over me. When Faiza pokes her head into the costume room, I laugh and tell the première about the phoenix, how I have been riding on the back of music and feathers for months or years now, how the process of making art has saved me.

While Faiza puts her last touches on the snowy owl wings, I make the frame for mine—two moon crescents that will shoot up from a dancer's shoulder blades—then I calculate their dimensions and figure out how to rotate the wings so they will turn and fold. Faiza helps. I mold silicone and meticulously sew strands of dupioni silk to the bright orange rooster plumes.

"Not too much glue, poulette," Faiza scolds. "Only a dot beneath the needle."

I nod and make the change.

My fingers grow sore, and my eyes burn. But then one early morning, as dawn is breaking, I find Faiza asleep beside me, her fingers clutching a dusty orange rooster semiplume. The feathers inside the ivory bins flutter again. They sing. It's a low hum, a gentle vibration, and it soothes me.

After working around the clock on the Wednesday before the show in four days, it is time to lift the last pair of wings from the floor. I kneel, then pull them up, allowing the wings to come to life. My phoenix wings are enormous. Their tips graze the ceiling. They are flexible and can swoop down and close around the dancer. They are also, as Salomé wanted, bright, fierce, and bold. And if someone looks at them closely, they will find small music notes made of wire attached here and there to the plumes.

Faiza cries with joy.

I am so tired I can barely see.

I drop onto Mademoiselle Salomé's chaise, pulling one of her velvet capes over my shoulders. I think of the feather artist, then of Manon, and wish they were here to celebrate. For a long time, I gaze at the wings beating softly in the study.

CHAPTER 41

On the morning of the Dream Show's dress rehearsal, I rummage through the costume room to find the finest Mille et Une Plume outfit and slip on a wrap dress with a colibri roux, also known as the rufous humming-bird, embroidered on the shoulder. It is the smallest of its kind yet also the most territorial. I eat breakfast, wait until Blaise and Papa drive up to the front door in a rented van where they help Faiza and me place the ten pairs of wings into the back, then we drive to the Moulin Rouge.

At the entrance, I sit in the idling van and try to keep my fingers from shaking. A guy with a beard, who calls himself the stage manager, opens the double doors and says, "Mille et Une Plume?"

He peers inside the van and adds, "Rumor had it you didn't have the wings and the dancers were going to have to perform in their practice sets. Good thing it was rumor."

Two guys come and lift one pair of wings after the next until Faiza and I are following the men with a final pair down a long corridor. We make a few sharp turns, then enter a room marked private, the dancers' dressing room. Inside are dancers preparing for the stage, and sitting on a stool is Mademoiselle Salomé. She's next to Pauline. The feather artist is dressed in an ivory pantsuit. Her curls are loose, and she wears a pair of feather earrings I have never seen before. She holds my ruddy duck garland in her lap.

I stand timidly, unsure what Mademoiselle will say about me in this dress, about my fleeing that day, but Salomé reaches her hands out and pulls me to her.

"Je n'en crois pas mes yeux," she says. "I—" Mademoiselle Salomé pauses, squeezes my fingers, then adds, "I should have never left." She smiles an apologetic smile. "I guess we all make mistakes." Then gazing at Pauline, Faiza, me, then at the wings, she says, "I knew you would finish on time. My heart told me so, but I did not anticipate the final wings' exceptional beauty."

Looking at me again, the feather artist takes off her earrings and hooks them on my earlobes. She touches the copper and amethyst feathers that are now brushing my neck, and says, "I made them back in Guadeloupe. When Pauline told me you picked this dress, I wanted you to have them. The copper feathers are from the rufous hummingbird and the amethyst, as you know, from the starling."

She returns my garland.

She says, "Manon found it and, well, I hung onto it."

The dancers crowd us. Faiza, Pauline, and I begin the final leg of work, fitting the wings to the girls' backs. We pin, sew, alter, then harness. The dancers *ooh* and *aah* as they stretch and spin, wings fastened behind them, shimmering. I watch Mademoiselle Salomé make subtle adjustments, mesmerized, and abruptly I remember my mother in this very room, one of the dancers handing me the pink powder puff. My heart fills and I wish the little girl in me could see me now grown and immersed in plumes, just as she wished for.

That night and the following evening, under bright lights, with a crowded audience, the Moulin Rouge dancers perform with the Mille et Une Plume wings at their backs. They pivot, bend, and glide, feathers light and fluid behind them. They are women-birds who seem to be rising from the ashes, and as I sit in the front row between Faiza, Pauline, and Mademoiselle Salomé, I remember the date, June 22.

A year since Jeanne died.

In my head, I tell her I love her, then focus on the stage, on the fair dancer swaying with the black wings streaked with electric blues, on the girl with skin as brown as Salomé's, the girl who spreads her snowy owl wings and playfully grazes the sprightly blonde in Manon's cornflower-blue Tinker Bell wings. It is impossible to name a favorite. I am in love with Faiza's red-shouldered hawk, with Pauline's hot-pink spoonbill, with the redhead who wears the ostrich wings like sleeves, and with the dancer with sleek black hair who struts with my purple peacock wings, but then everyone gasps. A woman with silver hair enters the stage and slowly deploys the prince of darkness wings. The black-and-gunmetal feathers flutter like great big curtains. This maleficent queen seems she might steal the show, but then the final dancer bursts onto the stage with the phoenix wings at her back. She is on fire. It is a duel between lightness and darkness. The audience claps, and when the king chooses light, all ten dancers spin and spin, a thousand and one feathers swirling beautiful, strong, and alive. I want to stand up and yell bravo. I want to jump on the stage and kiss the dancers, but instead I keep my eyes glued to the women-birds and drink them in.

I am not sure how long I stay seated after the performance, but when I look up, the salle de spectacle is empty except for Mademoiselle Salomé. She stands in front of my seat, hands clasped to her chest and curls exploding around her.

"Alix," she starts.

I look the feather artist in the eye and say, "Again, I'm really sorry for—"

But Salomé holds her hand up. "It's all in the past," she says. Then she asks if I would like to come back to Mille et Une Plume. "Only if that's what you want."

I stand there quiet for a moment, thinking of Pixie Dust and of Manon's idea from earlier. For us to work together.

I take a deep breath and say, "I want to be a feather artist like you. But I want to open my shop and make feather bouquets. I want to enrich people's lives in my way."

Mademoiselle Salomé looks at me with that piercing dark gaze I have come to love and trust. I think of voicing my needs. I think of Paris, of Montmartre, of rue d'Orchampt, of Blaise and rue des Trois Frères. I think of Papa. I think of the feathers undulating in their ivory bins.

I add, "I'd love to stay and help until I figure out how to stand on my own. Money matters, but my title does not. Petite main, apprentice, seamstress, hand stitcher, sketcher. Don't we all do everything anyway? It's the people I care about. I want Manon to come and work with me. We'll make a great team."

The feather artist smiles.

"You can start your business from the boutique. If it's helpful. I'll give you a raise of course and we could talk about feathers that interest you, how to partner on goods."

Beaming, I ask, "You would do that for me?"

"Bien entendu."

I nearly jump for joy, then say, "While I was away, my father came back." I blush and add, "I also have a new petit copain, Blaise. He is a musician."

Mademoiselle Salomé pulls me into her arms, her citrusy scent wrapping around me. "I'll need to meet him then, this Blaise. Make sure he is a gentleman."

"He is," I say. "I checked his credentials."

Salomé laughs. "Let's take a trip to Guadeloupe at the end of the summer." She adds, "We'll bond over molted feathers like gardeners bond over seeds and vegetables. What do you say?"

"I'd love that," I answer, then I tell her I think she and Pauline will make a wonderful duo, that over the past few weeks Pauline has learned to truly compromise, and I grow so dizzy from happiness I nearly swoon walking toward the exit signs, and Salomé catches my elbow, helping me stay upright, bringing us closer together.

CHAPTER 42

One warm and sunny evening at the end of June, on my birthday, Blaise and I stroll from rue des Trois Frères to the duchess's place for a small gathering.

"Here are my lovebirds," Tante Constance cries, pulling Blaise and me into her kitchen where Papa is standing a little awkwardly next to a few of the duchess's friends and neighbors. At *lovebirds*, I blush and Blaise kisses his great-aunt on the cheeks.

"Tantine," he says. "Bonsoir, Monsieur Leclaire."

"Fabien, please," Papa replies.

Constance hooks her hand around Blaise's elbow and says to my father, "This boy is a prince. You shall adore him."

Everyone laughs.

In the garden, we toast with fresh lemonade and eat

scallops and smoked salmon. The chickens cluck at our feet and the tabby cat lies beneath my chair. Once in a while, between pauses in the conversation, I gaze at Blaise. Tonight, he wears his neon sneakers, thick-rimmed glasses, and a faded black tee, and when he sees me looking at him, he grins, all dimples, and I have to restrain myself from getting up and attacking him.

The night is young.

Papa plays the sax and people dance. Tante Constance brings out a tarte au framboise with eighteen candles and makes me blow them out and make a wish. This time I keep the wish to myself: *Don't ever let me forget her.* I devour a piece, another, but then grab Blaise by the hand and wave bonsoir to everyone. There is one more place I want to visit. It takes us a while to get to the cemetery because we can't keep our hands off each other, but once we arrive, we find Jeanne's tomb and sit chatting beside her. The moon illuminates us, then the stars come out one by one. We stay and stay, words and stories tumbling from us. And when, near dawn, Blaise finally pulls me up to my feet and we walk away, bleary-eyed, I turn one last time toward Jeanne's grave. Among the purple wisteria I placed in the metal buckets, shining in the first light, is one long turkey feather. New. Bold. Striped with a white fluffy tip.

I think of Emily Dickinson, of "Hope Is the Thing with Feathers," then wave.

"Love you more than our bloodred sunsets," I say.

✦ ✦ ✦

ACKNOWLEDGMENTS

This book is flying on the wings of many.

Thank you, first and foremost, to Krestyna Lypen. You make my prose sparkle. Thank you to Algonquin Young Readers: Stacy Sparrow Lellos, Ashley Mason, Adah Li, Laura Williams, Kerri Resnick, Andrew Wang, Alana Bonfiglio, Chloe Puton, Ivanka Perez, Laura Lutz, Moira Kerrigan, Rebecca Carlisle, and Shaelyn McDaniel for championing Alix and her feathers. Thank you to Elise Howard for taking a chance on me then, and saying yes, not once but twice, to an A. K. Small story. Thank you, Tracey Daniels, for joining the feather team.

Kelly Chong, your cover is magical.

My thanks to Wendi Gu, at Greenburger J. Sanford Associates, for believing in my writing.

Atticus, thank you for the beautiful poem. Your words resonate deeply.

Ann Hood, thank you for being you, for noticing Alix's Oliver Twist tendencies and for shrewdly pointing them out, and for being the one who introduced me to Emily Dickinson's body of work a million years ago.

Laura Chasen and Erin Raets, I loved having you in my corner as I drafted and redrafted the manuscript.

Benjamin Roesch, the quick IG guitar lesson—electric vs acoustic, plugged vs unplugged—was invaluable.

Jess Bruback, your various hues of radiant purple hair were one of the early inspirations for the book. Thank you.

Now, onto my writerly friends who seem to always have my back. I couldn't do this without your enthusiasm and belief in me. Rachael Lippincott, you are my inspiration. Your authenticity, in work and in life, is a gift to all of us. Anna Godbersen, I adore your books and taking your class reminded me that writing is an act of love and discovery. Thank you, Ann Cardinal, for our Sunday chats. Christine Byl, love you always. Deborah Stoll and Sue Henderson, thanks for reading parts of WINGS in the early days.

Anthropologie Columbia, thank you for opening your doors and for showing me what it means to be the new girl inside of a boutique.

Librarians and indie bookstores, especially Park Books and White Whale, I'm beyond grateful for your hard work and support.

To my favorite two plumassières, merci Nelly Saunier and Fabienne Fleury! You have inspired me for years. And to my favorite plumassièr, merci Eric Charles-Donatien. In a different life, I'd have wanted to be your mentee.

To la Maison Dior and Raf Simons, thank you for your beautiful documentary *Dior and I* and for showing us the experts behind the scenes.

Papa and Maman, this story would have never come to life if it weren't for you and the experiences you've offered me.

To my daughters, the three of you are my light.

Paris, je t'aime. Montmartre, you are my birth cradle. Birds, I revere your mystery.

Thank you readers for picking up this book and blowing life into it.

Finally, to Kurt. You rival Raven with your charm, but your love is as powerful and genuine as Blaise's. Every book of mine lives due to you.